D0930041

DANCER'S
DEBT

Also by John Lutz

Nightlines
The Right to Sing the Blues
Ride the Lightning

DANCER'S DEBT

John Lutz

ST. MARTIN'S PRESS

NEW YORK

Library of Congress Cataloging-in-Publication Data

Lutz, John, 1939–
    Dancer's debt / by John Lutz.
      p. cm.
    ISBN 0-312-00028-6 : $16.95
    I. Title.
PS3562.U854D3 1988   87-29937
813'.54—dc19   CIP

"A Thomas Dunne book"

First Edition

10 9 8 7 6 5 4 3 2 1

Wilt thou seal up the avenues of ill?
Pay every debt, as if God wrote the bill.
                    Ralph Waldo Emerson, "Solution"

You purchase pain with all that joy can give,
And die of nothing but a rage to live.
                    Alexander Pope, *Moral Essays*

DANCER'S
DEBT

1

Nudger wished his armpits weren't perspiring so heavily. That was the only thing not right about the situation. He cursed inwardly and regretted he hadn't come up to his office from Danny's Donuts earlier and switched on the window air conditioner, now gurgling away valiantly behind him in an effort to overtake the fierce St. Louis summer heat. He knew the window unit would win, but it would take time.

Other than the heat, and the crescents of dampness beneath Nudger's arms, everything about the scene was on the mark. Five minutes after he'd sat down behind his desk and started to sort through his mail, he'd heard a floorboard creak on the landing outside. Then a knock on the door. He'd called, come in, and in she'd walked, pale and cool as vanilla ice cream. Like something right out of a detective novel.

She said her name was Helen Crane. She was of average height but regally erect. Her taut carriage, and her blond hair swept back and up, made her appear tall. Her skin was unmottled and smooth, her eyes slate gray and calm. Curves refused to be reduced to planes by her tailored blue skirt and blazer.

Nudger noticed that the blazer was frayed at the wrists, the pearls about her neck were obviously synthetic, and her dark blue high heels were probably of some material that had never been on any other animal. She knew how to dress, this one, but she had a budget that required polyester.

None of that mattered when she cast her measured, cool-fire glance about the office. She was something intensely real, yet the

1

sort of women men build dreams around. Royalty with a K-mart wardrobe, and the cream of royalty at that.

"You *are* Mr. Nudger?"

"Constantly."

"I want to hire you," she said.

Ah, perfect! He invited her to sit in the chair in front of the desk, and he apologized for the heat in the office as she settled her graceful frame and crossed slender legs that were exquisite at least to the knees. The bone structure of her face was strong yet refined, wide and precisely symmetrical. Outside, in the sultry summer, an emergency vehicle siren rose plaintive and wavering in the distance, like Circe beckoning. It seemed to go with the face. With the rest of her.

"It doesn't feel all that warm in here," she said.

He said, "Somebody refer you to me, Miss Crane?"

She tilted her head to the side and gave him a look of quiet reappraisal, as if for the first time she'd realized there were larger, obviously more prosperous investigative agencies in the city. "I was told about some good work you did in New Orleans, Mr. Nudger. The person who told me wants to be anonymous."

Nudger felt a little tingle of wariness at the nape of his neck. This was the sort of prospective client who often showed up in private detectives' offices in books and movies, all right, but not in real life. Not in Nudger's life. He hadn't really expected her visit to pan out; any moment she'd start in on her Amway pitch.

"I don't take just any job," he said.

"I wouldn't ask you to do something illegal."

"What about dangerous? I don't like danger."

"Danger's a matter of degree," she said.

"So's body temperature. I try not to let anything happen that'll lower mine below the level that indicates life."

"I don't think there's a great deal of risk involved," she told him, "but I can't guarantee it. On the other hand, this building might collapse and kill us both any minute." She looked around.

"Or any second. What I mean is, risk goes along with living on this planet, doesn't it?"

"All too often," Nudger said. "What kind of trouble are you in?"

She crossed her arms delicately, cupping her elbows in her hands, and settled back in her chair. "It's Jake Dancer who's in trouble."

She said this as if Nudger knew who Jake Dancer was. As if everybody knew. "And he is? . . ."

"My lover."

"Which oughta go far to balance out his bad luck."

She smiled faintly, as if she were used to such compliments, maybe a little bored with them, but still felt obliged to acknowledge them. The responsibility of beauty.

"So what kind of trouble has found otherwise lucky Jake Dancer?" Nudger asked.

"I'm not sure—which is one of the reasons I came to you. Jake's been horrendously upset about something lately. Really frightened, and he doesn't sleep nights. He's drinking more heavily than ever, and I'm sure he's doing drugs."

"You talked to him about it?"

"I've tried, but he won't discuss it. I get the feeling it's because he can't. The very worst things in life are beyond talking about."

"I might not be able to help him, if he doesn't want me to butt in," Nudger said.

"I don't want him to know I hired you," Helen Crane said. "I only want you to follow him, watch him, then tell me what it is that's torturing him. He's had enough trouble; he doesn't need this, whatever it is. He sure as hell doesn't."

"What trouble has he had?" Nudger asked.

"Something happened to him in Vietnam. He never told me what. But it changed him. He came back the friendly, likable Jake who went overseas, but at the same time it's like he was never able to recapture the rhythm in his life. He makes the rounds restlessly, drinks way too much.''

"Vietnam was years ago," Nudger said.

She shrugged. "Time's got a way of slipping cogs for some people.''

"You mentioned drugs.''

"He doesn't have a habit, but he uses them.'' She wriggled on the chair and sat straighter, as if there were a string attached to the top of her head, tugging her up. Charm-school posture, incongruous in the bargain clothes. "I don't want you to get the wrong idea about Jake, Mr. Nudger. He's not one of those sullen vets who blame Vietnam for everything bad that's happened to them. Everybody likes Jake Dancer—everybody. He doesn't complain or ask for pity, but his pain's so evident that people just want to help him. It's like they *need* to help him because of something in themselves. Jake brings that out in people.''

"That why you're trying to help him?''

"No, that's only part of it. I love him. We love each other. But he won't talk about what's causing his agony. And it isn't Vietnam; it's St. Louis. Nothing in all the years since Vietnam ever made him jump with fright when he heard the phone.''

"Would you describe him as at all paranoid?'' Nudger the psychiatrist.

"Oh, just the opposite,'' Helen said. "Jake's too trusting, too naive, in his special way. That's why people tend to want to protect him. And they can sense he'd do anything for them.''

"How long have you known him?'' Nudger asked.

"We dated each other in high school. Well, not dated, exactly. Ran in the same crowd. Then, after school, he was drafted. He came home on leave from Fort Leonard Wood before shipping out to Vietnam, and we became lovers. It's stayed that way.''

"Do you regret it?'' Nudger asked.

"If I did, I wouldn't be here. Gotta expect some choppy water now and then.''

"But it sounds as if you've been through a typhoon and the weather forecast is more of the same."

"Maybe. Could be a calm ocean bores me."

"Hmm. Does Dancer have family here in town?"

"No. There was only his father, but he died three years ago. If there are any other relatives, they're not close enough for Jake to have mentioned. It's me he needs. But for the first time, he won't let me help him."

Nudger swiveled in his chair and stared out the dirt-smeared window at the building across the street. The pigeons that were always perched on the ledge had made a mess there. Nudger hated pigeons. Defacing, lice-carrying vermin with wings. They didn't even sing, like other birds. Instead they cooed insults.

"Will you help me to help Jake?" Helen Crane asked. "Will you, Mr. Nudger?"

Nudger wasn't sure how to answer. He needed the money; office rent was due, and Eileen was closing in on him in her relentless quest for back alimony. But he was uneasy about taking this case. He sensed that a fellow could get hurt following Jake Dancer around town. Nudger's need for money, his fascination with Helen Crane, tugged at his better judgment, causing him to lean toward saying yes, but not with quite enough angle to fall on the side of danger and necessity. He wasn't ready to help Helen Crane.

Not quite.

"Mr. Nudger?"

"Do you like pigeons?" Nudger asked.

"Tell you the truth, no."

That did it.

2

That evening at six-thirty, Nudger sat crammed in his parked Volkswagen on Osage Avenue in South St. Louis. In the outside rearview mirror he could see the entrance of the brick apartment building where Jake Dancer lived with Helen Crane.

It was an old, flat-roofed building with green trim that needed paint. Over the front door was a large stained-glass window that looked as if it belonged in a church. The small front yard had a grassless path worn across it diagonally, and a kid's balloon-tired bike leaned into the shrubs near the entrance so that its handlebars were invisible. Osage was a long street with good and bad blocks. The apartment building wasn't a bad place for this part of town, and Nudger figured the rent wasn't much.

Helen had told Nudger that Dancer would sleep most of the day, then leave in the evening without telling her where he was going. He'd been doing that for the past week, she'd said. She'd tried following him once herself, but he'd seen her and there'd been an argument. Then Dancer had invited her to go drinking with him and she'd refused. Sounded like an up-and-down relationship to Nudger. Yo-yo love. He knew it well.

It was hot in the Volkswagen. He wished, not for the first time, that the little mechanized Beetle had an air conditioner. But not many twelve-year-old Volkswagens came so equipped. There were other things about the car he didn't like. Oh, the dents and the faded red paint didn't bother him. And he liked to think the lack of an adequate heater in the winter had made him hardier. But St. Louis was subject to at least one brutal heat wave every summer, and it was then that Nudger seemed to find himself in the sort of cases that required long hours sitting in the sun-heated, cramped little car and feeling like some sort of casserole.

Then there were the times when the Volkswagen refused to start and merely sputtered at him, as if it were cursing him in German. Nudger didn't like that. Once it had almost cost him his life. *"Götterdämmerung,"* the VW seemed to have said. Nudger suspected it of war crimes.

Danny knew of a woman out in the country who'd bought a new car and was going to sell her nine-year-old Ford Granada. It was a bigger car; it was air-conditioned. Danny said it had enjoyed loving care and was in fine shape for its age. Nobody had ever said that about Nudger. He figured he might drive out and take a look at the Granada.

On the other hand, the car's owner was one of Danny's rare regular customers at the doughnut shop. Would a woman on a steady diet of Danny's Dunker Delites treat her car better than her own anatomy?

Nudger squirmed around on the hard vinyl upholstery, checking the street behind him in the mirror and trying to get more comfortable. He could feel his shirt peeling away from where it was plastered with perspiration to the seat back. If he'd been smart, he would have brought a thermos bottle full of something cold to drink. The inside of his mouth felt as if he'd been snacking on chalk.

He peered up at the top floor, west unit—Helen Crane's apartment—and saw that, though the end window was open, the drapes were still closed, swaying in the faint summer breeze. The windows that probably looked out from the living room were shut, and their venetian blind slats were angled for privacy. An air conditioner jutted from the center window and was still running; Nudger could see condensation dripping steadily from it onto the bricks below. It was probably cool in the front room of the old apartment.

Just as Nudger was about to rationalize the idea of hurriedly put-putting to Grand Avenue and getting a Diet Pepsi from one of the drive-through franchises, then quickly returning, a man fitting Dancer's description emerged from the apartment building.

He sat straighter to improve his angle of vision in the mirror. The man reached the sidewalk, hitched up his pants, flipped away a cigarette, then lowered himself into a rusty blue Datsun—Helen Crane's car.

As soon as he saw the tiny Datsun pull away from the curb, Nudger tried to start the Volkswagen. The miniature engine seemed to chuckle at him, as if it enjoyed keeping him in suspense as to whether it would turn over. The starter ground out messages of Teutonic disdain.

Then the engine rattled to life as if to say it was all a joke, and it clattered enthusiastically as Nudger made a nifty U-turn and dropped into traffic behind the Datsun. Old allies, a German car following a Japanese car driven by a veteran of a later war. The patchwork of history. At least Dancer was driving a car that might not be able to outrun the Volkswagen; they could have a low-speed chase not dangerous enough to require seatbelts.

Dancer drove to Grand Avenue and turned north, then aimed the little Datsun up the ramp to Highway 44 and drove east toward downtown. Nudger stayed well back in the outside lane, keeping the Datsun in sight and enjoying the air rushing through the Volkswagen's rolled-down windows and beating a drumlike rhythm in the closed back of the car.

Dancer got off the highway on Memorial Drive, then took Market west and wound north on side streets until he found a parking space near the Old Post Office.

He climbed out of the Datsun and casually slammed the door behind him as he set off walking along the sidewalk. He was dressed in gray slacks and a blue sport coat, no tie. A nice-looking guy, even from a distance.

Nudger drove past him and glanced over for a closer look. Dancer took long strides and swung his arms loosely, moving as if he'd never known worry. His wavy black hair was especially thick above his collar, giving the impression his head was tilted back so

he could breathe in something sweet, though actually he was looking straight ahead. Nudger couldn't make out Dancer's expression,
but he seemed reasonably alert, not as if he'd been drinking before
leaving home. And he was treading a more or less straight line.

After finding a place to park the Volkswagen, Nudger cut back
to the corner and fell into step about half a block behind Dancer.
They walked at the same casual pace.

There were quite a few people on the downtown streets tonight.
The Cardinals were in town, and a game with the Cubs was due to
start in half an hour in nearby Busch Stadium. When that happened, the streets would be considerably emptier.

After about five minutes, Dancer adjusted his collar, buttoned
his sport coat, and entered the Marriott Hotel. Nudger followed
him into the plush lobby and watched him head for the lounge.
The place was still full of Cubs fans wearing blue caps and jackets
and behaving with jovial hostility as only Cubs fans behaved. One
of them had what appeared to be a stuffed cardinal—the bird—
dangling from a piece of string as if it had been throttled. The guy
was dragging the thing across the floor so it bumped up and down
while his buddies laughed. Sports in America.

Dancer would spend time and money in the teeming lounge,
Nudger was sure. But he didn't see any point in going in himself
and drinking beer he didn't want and listening to baseball argu-
ments no one could win.

He sat in the lobby for a while, watching the blue-adorned fans
from Chicago make fools of themselves, then he wandered back
outside and up the street about half a block where he could stand
and admire the night. To his right glowed the lights of the stadium.
Ahead of him and to the left soared the graceful curve of the Arch,
catching the rising moonlight on one gleaming side and looking
like an ethereal silver ribbon hurled skyward in exuberance.
Beyond the Arch, stars were beginning to glitter over East St.
Louis, as if to cheer that depressed area with a free show of gran-
deur. There were times when Nudger wouldn't trade this city, his

city, for any other. There were other times he'd trade it for Detroit.

The game had begun. A distant rushing sound reached Nudger: the stadium crowd roaring over hometown heroics. Instant reward for a job well done. Baseball was nothing like life.

Voices from the direction of the Marriott broke into Nudger's early-inning musings.

Dancer was standing on the sidewalk flanked by two men. One of the men was tall, the other was about Dancer's height, which looked to be about five feet ten. They were both beefy beneath lightweight gray suits. Neither of them wore ties, but the tall guy had a tight vest buttoned all the way up to where his white shirt was unbuttoned to reveal a gold chain. The Marriott doorman glanced at them, saw that Dancer was drunk and being supported by the other two men, then looked away; he had the familiar situation pegged and it didn't require further attention.

The two men began walking Dancer in Nudger's direction, each of them holding Dancer by an upper arm. Dancer was laughing and talking, but Nudger couldn't make out what he was saying. The other two men laughed now and then, too, but not as if they thought whatever Dancer was ranting about was all that funny, or even slightly amusing. They seemed instead to be laughing at a private, subtle joke of their own. The bigger one had a shrill horse-laugh that cut through the warm night like sharp ice and touched a nerve in Nudger.

He moved ahead of them for about a hundred feet, then crossed the street so he wouldn't attract their suspicion.

As Dancer and his two companions passed a pool of illumination from a streetlight, there was a shadowy flurry of motion, a change in the timbre of their voices.

It took Nudger a few seconds to realize the two men had turned on Dancer and were beating him. Leather soles made scuffling noises on concrete. Bodies jockeyed for leverage, arms rising and dropping with force.

"Hey!" Nudger yelled. He swallowed hard and started across

the street. The curb was higher than he'd thought and he almost twisted an ankle. "Leave him alone!" *And leave me alone!*

A horn blared and it occurred to Nudger he was in the middle of a busy street; the yellow center line was beneath his feet.

He paused to let a huge gleaming shape flash past him, hearing the driver curse. Nudger leaned into the passing vehicle's rush of air, then he looked both ways and ran on toward the struggle on the opposite sidewalk. He was aware of a knot of people outside the Marriott, huddled together silently and staring at what was happening, as if they were actors in this scene but without lines or action. Bystanders only. Couldn't do a thing to help.

As Nudger closed in on the fray, he saw for the first time the glint of metal. The big man in the vest had drawn a knife.

Nudger hesitated, experiencing one of those wrenching moments when he questioned his decision not to carry a gun. Then he swallowed the coppery taste of fear and ran on. He wondered for an instant what he was doing here, why he did what he did for a living. Why wasn't he selling appliances?

"A cop!" somebody down the street finally shouted. "Christ, get a cop!"

The two men stopped beating Dancer when they noticed Nudger's approach. He felt a brief satisfaction. He was galloping to the rescue, spooking the bad guys. Any second they'd turn and run. Bullies were cowards.

The big one stepped forward, raising the knife and holding it delicately out in front of him in the manner of an experienced knife-fighter. "C'mon, fucker!" he yelled. He was up for this, and not running away; he wanted blood. He waggled the long blade. "This is all for you, Mr. Macho. Hoo-eee! C'mon, you Rambo cocksucker!"

Nudger decided that one wasn't spooked; he involuntarily slowed his pace but kept closing distance anyway.

Then the smaller assailant grabbed the big man's arm. Somewhere a woman yelled something about the police.

The big man shifted the knife in his grip so it rested flat against his palm, then whirled with surprising grace and slapped Dancer across the face with it. Dancer, who'd been doubled over between the two men, slumped all the way to the pavement and lay curled on his side.

The smaller man kicked him in the back, then both of Dancer's attackers turned and ran down the street. They were pumping elbows and knees hard, gray coattails flying. As they rounded the corner, two teenage boys pretended they were going to give chase, but they wisely turned back. Maybe they'd glimpsed the knife. Maybe they'd simply gotten smart young.

Nudger helped Dancer to his feet, getting his toes stomped for the effort. That irritated him; sometimes he developed ingrown toenails when his feet were stepped on.

Dancer groaned. "Ah, shit, man, didn't they do a job on me?" Alcohol fumes rose from him. And something else; he'd vomited onto his shirt. Drinker's vomit. Nasty.

"Can you stand by yourself?"

"Oh, sure." But he slumped against Nudger.

"Hurt bad?"

"No," Dancer said. He actually managed a crooked grin. "They were only trying to make an impression on me, you might say." There was a thin cut along his left cheek, where he'd been slapped with the flat of the knife blade, like a shaving cut from a straight razor. Not serious, but it would be painful when Dancer sobered up.

Some impression, Nudger thought. Dancer almost lost his balance, did a precarious little shuffle, said, "Wheee!"

People were starting to gather. Nudger knew the police would be along soon to ask questions, possibly of him. Explanations would be demanded. Facts would be made known. Among them that Nudger was following Dancer, working for Helen Crane. Dancer would find out about the arrangement. A no-no.

"Come on," Nudger said, and began walking Dancer north on Broadway, toward where the Volkswagen was parked. People stared after them, then gradually lost interest.

Dancer had to stop and vomit twice on the way to the car. There was no blood in what he was retching onto the sidewalk; Nudger wasn't sure if Dancer was sick because of the beating or because he'd drunk past his limit.

"Where we goin'?" he asked, as Nudger dumped and shoved him into the passenger seat of the Volkswagen. Dancer seemed to have grown extra arms and legs without joints.

"Someplace where you can sleep off your drunk." Nudger pushed on the door until it latched, as if he were closing an over-stuffed trunk. There—Dancer was in!

Nudger walked around the front of the car and got in behind the steering wheel. He got the balky little engine going and jerked the VW away from the curb abruptly enough to snap his and Dancer's heads back. Minor whiplash.

"Car's little," Dancer remarked. "Reminds me of a coffin."

"Me, too, sometimes," Nudger said.

"Get in an accident, they just weld six handles on it and bury you, huh?"

"I don't like to think about that," Nudger said.

"Can you get the ballgame on the radio? I got a bet on the Cards."

Nudger tuned to the KMOX broadcast of the game. The score was already five to nothing, favor of the Cubs. "Shit!" Dancer said.

"It's not over yet," Nudger told him.

"It's never over till the final out," the play-by-play man said over the radio. "We just gotta keep our heads high and hang in there and wait for a break." Just then one of the Cubs hit a home run. That made it six to nothing. Baseball was like life after all.

"Turn off the radio, will you?" Dancer said.

Nudger did. Then he got his roll of antacid tablets from his shirt pocket and thumbed two of the chalky white disks into his mouth. Dancer was smelling up the car; it'd be a long time before the odor went away, Nudger realized glumly. He chewed rhythmically, letting the bouncing motion of the Volkswagen aid the action.

By the time he turned the car onto the highway, Dancer was asleep, and most of the knots in Nudger's stomach had finally come untied.

"Can't pay . . ." Dancer moaned, as the Volkswagen picked up speed and the wind buffeted his perspiring face. "Ain't no way. . . ." He opened his eyes momentarily and glanced over at Nudger. Headlight beams from cars passing in the opposite direction flashed across his features, as if lending him vitality and animation and then instantly snatching it away. "You got a hit, pal? Or maybe some money to lend me?"

"I got nothing but hope," Nudger told him.

He'd have had less of that if he'd noticed the black Chrysler convertible that followed them from downtown.

3

It was a job getting Dancer upstairs. The steps had never seemed so steep, and Dancer had a way of moving in every direction at once while supporting himself not at all, as if Novocain had been shot into his knees. Nudger finally worked him through the door of the apartment on Sutton and left him leaning against the wall.

The phone was ringing. He ignored it. Eileen again, probably. She'd been hounding him every day at his office about the alimony he owed, leaving snide remarks on his answering machine. As if she actually needed the money. As if he actually had it.

Still breathing hard from his journey up the stairs, he crossed his living room to the sofa that made into a bed and removed the cushions, stacking them on the floor. He leaned forward, gripped the base of the sofa, and tugged. The only thing that gave was his back. He winced and then kicked the sofa, hurting the toe Dancer had stepped on earlier; he could never remember how to unfold the damned thing.

This time he grabbed it low toward the back of the cushionless seat, quickly, as if to catch it off guard, and pulled up and out. The back of the sofa dropped and pinned his arm there, forcing him to his knees. He cursed. The phone kept ringing. Seemed to be getting louder. Across the room, Dancer slid down the wall and sat on the floor, staring at a point on the carpet between his knees.

Nudger managed to struggle out of the clutches of the sofa. He pushed here, prodded there, lifted there, and it suddenly unfolded into three hinged parts and banged him on the shins. But it was now something like a bed, even if it rose in a sharp ridge across the middle.

He dragged Dancer across the room, leaving tracks in the carpet, and wrestled him up onto the sofa bed. The ridge in the middle disappeared under Dancer's weight. Nudger removed Dancer's shoes, unbuttoned his shirt where it was twisted, and considered him down for the night.

Finally.

The phone stopped ringing.

Everything was suddenly quiet, in control. Silence sang. One of life's special moments.

But there were things to do. Nudger walked to the extension phone in the kitchen and called Helen Crane.

"I've got your roving boy here," he said, as soon as she answered. "He was drunk downtown and a couple of his acquaintances tried to beat him up."

"Is he okay?" The concern in her voice burned over the line. Love, for sure.

"He's sleeping it off here in my apartment. He's got a slight cut on his face from a knife, but otherwise he's fine. Even blissful."

"A knife? They tried to kill him?"

"I don't think so," Nudger said. "They could have but didn't. I shouted at them, then somebody mentioned the police, and they took off running."

"You get a look at them?"

"Not much of one. A big guy and his average-size co-sadist, both of them wearing gray suits. The big one was very big, and very ugly, with a gorilla physique. I think he might have been blond, but I'm not sure. It was dark; things were happening fast."

"So Jake's in real danger," Helen said worriedly.

"Of one degree or another. He's also in danger of having his car—your car—towed away. It's parked down on Eighth Street by the Old Post Office."

"I'll take a cab downtown and get it," she said. She said it in a tone that suggested she was used to cleaning up in Dancer's wake. She didn't care, Nudger reminded himself; everybody loved Jake Dancer.

"And don't worry about Dancer for now, Helen. He'll be safe here."

"When he wakes up," Helen said, "talk to him, Mr. Nudger. Try to find out who those men were, what he's got himself involved in. But for God's sake don't tell him I hired you. I don't know if he'd forgive me for that right now, for interfering. Maybe he'll be grateful to you for saving him. He ought to be. Maybe he'll open up to you somewhat, out of gratitude. Try to get him to do that."

"I'll try," Nudger said, "but I can't guarantee he'll remember anything about tonight when he wakes up. He was state-of-the-art drunk."

"Just try! Please!"

"'Course I will."

"Thanks, Mr. Nudger."

"My job."

Dancer smelled the coffee and groaned. Progress. He hadn't responded to the swirling morning light blasting in through the living room windows, or to Nudger shaking him by the limp shoulder.

"The Cards won, seven to six," Nudger told him.

"Huh?" Dancer rolled onto his side, started to get up, then fell back. Old spaghetti limbs.

Nudger held out the sports page of the morning *Post-Dispatch* to prove he was telling the truth about the game. Dancer scanned it with one bleary eye.

"Be damned," he said.

"You won your bet," Nudger told him, tossing the paper onto an end table.

"Yeah. Bartender at the Marriott owes me a free drink." Dancer managed to sit up. The sofa bed formed a ridge beneath him and twanged. "Whas'a time?"

"A little after nine. In the morning."

"Ummrph," Dancer said.

Nudger looked at him closely in the light. He had angular, almost esthetic features beneath a mass of black curls. His build was muscular but on the slim side, and his hands were delicate for a man's, with pale, tapered fingers. There was a vulnerable quality in his large brown eyes. He almost appeared feminine, but there was a lean and wasted masculinity about him that offset his physical beauty. Wiry strength. Even with the knife scar on his face he looked like a debauched choirboy the world had roughed up and left disillusioned and slightly bewildered. Ruined Irish poets had that air about them. He'd probably look that way until he hit sixty. If he lived out the month.

"Where'm I this morning?" he asked.

"In my apartment. My name's Nudger. I helped to keep two of your friends from beating you and doing some creative whittling on you last night."

Dancer drew up his knees and shook his head vaguely. "Sorry. Sure don't remember any of that."

"You remembered the bet on the game."

"Yeah, I did." Dancer shot him a wary look. "My name's Jake Dancer," he said. "Thanks for . . . taking care of me." He turned and sat on the edge of the sofa bed, then started to stand up and

felt pain and realized he'd been hurt by more than too much booze.
He sat back down heavily and used his long fingers to probe gingerly around his ribs.

"Who were the guys who did that to you?" Nudger asked.

"Don't know, told you."

"Listen, I saved your ass. Risked mine. So you at least owe me
an explanation. Would they have killed you?"

"Killed me? I don't think so." Satisfied that none of his ribs
were broken, he struggled to his feet. "Wow! Gonna be sick, I
think."

"Bathroom's that way," Nudger said, pointing, thinking about
the carpet. "Need some help?"

"Naw, I can make it."

Nudger watched him use his hands on the walls and furniture for
balance as he stumbled into the bathroom. Despite his hungover
condition, he moved with coordination, even grace.

After a few minutes Nudger heard retching. Then running water.
The toilet flushed. Flushed again.

When Dancer returned he'd removed his stained shirt and had
wet and slicked back his dark hair. He was wearing a white
sleeveless undershirt, his wrinkled dress slacks, and black socks.
"Christ, I'm sorry about this," he said. "I *am* grateful to you,
er . . ."

"Nudger," Nudger reminded him. "You look better."

"Nudger your first or last name?"

"Only name I use, except on applications."

"Well, thanks for what you did, Nudger." Dancer contorted his
right arm and ground his fist into the small of his back, where the
shorter of the two men had kicked him. He blew out a long sigh,
as if he'd brought relief from his pain. Then he limped toward his
shoes.

"I'll rustle us up some breakfast," Nudger told him, talking like
a grub cook on a cattle drive, as if that might make the idea of
food more appealing."

"Naw. Really. Couldn't eat."

"Coffee, then? Orange juice?" Now he sounded like a waiter. Dancer sat on the edge of the sofa bed and pulled his shoes onto his feet. He looked up and grinned. It was a boyish, crooked grin that revealed even, very white teeth. It was a grin that would melt the hearts of the wariest females and assure mothers that all was well. A grin that would buy time or gain favor or get the loan at the bank. A grin that could get you into trouble on either side of it. "I'll stick around," Dancer said. "The orange juice did it."

Nudger went into the kitchen and noted that Mr. Coffee had done his stuff.

"Black's fine," Dancer called in.

Nudger filled two mugs with the steaming black liquid, then got the bottle of fresh orange juice from the refrigerator and poured almost half of it into a large drinking glass. It was good orange juice; he'd have his after Dancer left.

Five minutes later he was sitting across from Dancer at the kitchen's Formica table, watching him let the rest of the juice trickle from the bottle into his drained glass. Dancer woke up like a longtime confirmed alky, with an internal drought and mad with thirst.

Nudger sipped his coffee, wishing he'd poured some juice for himself. "None of my business," he said, "but how come you drink so heavy? I mean, last night . . . you were pretty soused. Problems?"

"You could say that." The last of the orange juice disappeared; Dancer set down his glass. He started on the coffee, which was hot enough to prevent him from gulping it down as he had the juice.

"You a veteran?"

Dancer's eyebrows rose in surprise. "Huh? Why would you ask that?"

"You got the look."

"You're shittin' me. There is no 'look.'"

"You make me think of my younger brother," only child Nudger lied. "When he came back from Vietnam."

Dancer gazed into his coffee mug, or at the steam that was rising from it. "Yeah, that's where I was, in Nam. Like your brother."

"Figured as much. You're the right age. Have a rough time over there?"

Dancer didn't answer. Then he gave his grin. "I guess I do owe you some explanation, Nudger. You pulled me out of harm's way and I'm sitting here drinking your coffee."

"And juice. All of it."

"Yeah. Well, I did have a tough way to go in Nam—not that I was the only one. I'm still alive, anyway, sort of. But since I came back I drink a lot, and I got onto drugs over there and brought that back with me, too. Not that I have a habit. But I need something once in a while, you know what I mean?"

"Sure."

"So things kind of got out of hand. Seems all I do lately is drink and do drugs. But drink mostly. I admit I can't control it. And I gamble a lot. Too much. I've run up some debts. That's what the tough-guy stuff was all about last night; somebody I owe wants his money. At least that's what I figure. I'm sort of hazy on last night, tell you the truth."

"I can believe it," Nudger said. "Do you know the two solid citizens who worked on you?"

"I don't think so. It's hard to remember a lot of things lately." Dancer's grip tightened on the coffee mug, which had to be searingly hot. Did the guy like pain? "What happened in Nam sort of haunts me from time to time." He glanced up at Nudger and showed him that grin again, very reassuring. "Oh, I'm not violent; none of that phony Vietnam flashback stuff you see in movies or on television. Phony sometimes, anyway. I'm not looking for excuses for my failures, and I'm not playing for understanding or pity. It's just that sometimes I have bad dreams."

"And you owe money."

"Lots of money. To lots of people."

"Got a job?"

"No. I'm on unemployment and partial disability. I carry some shrapnel in my back and right leg. I get by, but right now I can't pay the money I owe.''

"Where you living?''

"With my girlfriend. She's all that keeps me a little bit straight in this life.''

"If you owe all this money and can't pay, there's no way to keep the bone-crushers from coming after you again,'' Nudger said.

"I could borrow more money to pay them.''

"That won't work. Only make things worse.''

"Yeah, you're right, Nudger.'' Dancer lifted his cup, took a long sip of the steaming coffee.

"You'll burn your tongue,'' Nudger said.

"Least of my problems.''

"Your girl's name is Helen.''

Dancer suddenly looked suspicious, frightened. "How'd you know that?''

"Your wallet fell out of your pants pocket last night. I looked in it to see who it was I'd brought home and tucked in bed. I saw her name. And her photograph. Beautiful.''

"She's that,'' Dancer said. Thinking about Helen seemed to relieve the fear and suspicion in him.

Then he said, "I've troubled you enough.'' He stood up and got his wallet out, withdrew a five-dollar bill. Nudger saw that it left the wallet empty. "I feel like I owe you for your trouble, Nudger.''

"Giving me that five would leave you broke.''

"Been broke plenty of times.''

"Not this time.''

Dancer saw that Nudger meant it. He put the bill in his pocket and extended his hand. "Thanks a lot. For the coffee, the juice, for everything.''

"I can drive you where you want to go,'' Nudger said, as he shook Dancer's hand.

"No. I'll take a cab downtown and see if the police ticketed or towed my car.''

"They haven't. I phoned Helen and told her where it was. She got it last night and drove it to her place."

Dancer's naive brown eyes shone level and steady. "You sure take over a fella's life, Nudger. You look at this, look at that, draw a lotta conclusions."

"Sorry if I went too far."

The gentle smile. "No, that's okay. Thanks again."

Jesus, this guy was easy to fool. A victim looking for a victimizer. He needed somebody to look after him, all right. Something about him; he almost begged to be lied to, as if it might protect him from harm.

"I'll put my shirt on and get outta your life and go home," Dancer said. "I got cab fare, anyway."

Without thinking, Nudger took a long swallow of coffee, something he'd warned Dancer against. It burned his tongue.

"Not many people would've gone to so much trouble for a stranger," Dancer told him. He seemed ashamed. "At first I thought . . . well, maybe you were gay or something. Making some sort of play. But that wasn't it at all." His voice took on an admiring quality. "Guess you're just a hell of a good guy and a straight shooter."

Nudger shrugged. "You remind me of my kid brother."

4

After Dancer had left, Nudger drained the very last of the orange juice from the bottle, throwing back his head and letting the few acidic drops roll tantalizingly over his tongue. It only made him thirsty for more. He popped some ice cubes out of a stubborn plastic tray and settled for a glass of cold water. Then he called

Helen and told her Dancer was on his way to her place with a soiled shirt and a hangover.

"I was expecting him," she said. "That's the pattern. He'll hang around here most of the day, almost like he's hiding out. Then this evening he'll go someplace and drink too much, get home late, and start the cycle all over."

"He ever stay out all night before?"

"No. Usually he gets in about two or two-thirty. After the taverns close. You find out anything about what's got him so rattled?"

"He said he owes several people money. His theory is the two guys who beat on him last night were sent by one of his creditors to emphasize that he should pay a gambling debt. How's that sound to you?"

"I don't know," Helen said. "Jake always did gamble too much. He know the guys who beat him up?"

"He says not."

"You believe him?"

"I'm not sure. About anything he said. I do think he's still in danger, and I have a suggestion. A friend of mine has a fishing cabin about an hour's drive from the city. It's vacant now and will be for the next three months. He wouldn't mind if you and Dancer stayed there a while. It's isolated and far enough away that nobody'll know you're there, but it's near enough for you to drive in to work every day—if you don't mind a little back-road and highway driving. You can make up something to tell Dancer. Say the cabin belongs to someone you know."

Helen was silent for a few minutes, thinking about the offer. "All right," she said finally. "If I can talk Jake into it."

"Remind him about the knife," Nudger said. "If he's as scared as you think, he'll like the idea of a temporary sanctuary. And while you're staying at the cabin, I'll be sniffing around here to try to find out what kind of trouble he's in and how deep it is."

"Okay, Mr. Nudger."

"Just Nudger will be fine."

"Don't you have a first name?"

"I like to think not."

He gave her directions to the cabin, finding himself envying Dancer. The thought of staying in the isolated, picturesque cabin with Helen, with nothing to do except fish or sleep or whatever, was something he resolutely shoved to the back of his mind with myriad other unprofessional notions. Private investigators weren't made of wood.

"The cabin's key is hanging on a nail under the eaves of the storage shed in back," he told her. "It's easy to find if you know it's there. The cabin'll need airing out, but it's comfortable and has some modern conveniences."

"Thanks, Nudger. Really."

"Dancer should be at your place soon. Phone me if he doesn't show."

"He'll be here, and I'll take care of him."

"It'd help if you had orange juice," Nudger said.

He hung up the phone, then went into the bathroom and showered, starting with warm water and turning the needle spray bitter cold just before climbing out and toweling dry. Get the old brain cells jumping. Maybe stop the old heart one of these days.

Afterward, shaving before the moisture-hazed mirror, he assessed his appearance. A shade under six feet, somewhat better than average build with a slight stomach paunch, wounded yet ever-hopeful blue eyes. An unremarkable, fortyish guy, not yet going gray—at least not on the outside. Nothing there to interest a woman like Helen Crane.

What the hell am I thinking?

He finished shaving, rinsed off his face, then returned to the phone in the kitchen. He hadn't yet put on a shirt; it felt pleasantly cool to stand near the open window that looked out on the brick wall of the building next door. There was often a breeze down the gangway.

With his left hand he poured another cup of coffee. With his right he pecked out the number of the Third District station house.

He asked for the desk. Sergeant Ellis answered. Nudger asked
him if Lieutenant Hammersmith was in. Ellis said yes, then he
asked Nudger if he wanted to talk to the lieutenant. He said no,
he'd see Hammersmith in person. Ellis asked if Nudger wanted
him to tell Hammersmith he was coming. Nudger said no, let him
think it was serendipity. Ellis snorted and hung up.

Hammersmith was behind his desk in his office at the Third.
Nudger figured Ellis had told him about the impending visit. As he
entered, the lieutenant didn't get up. Nudger was sorry to see one
of Hammersmith's horrendous greenish cigars smoldering in an
ashtray on the desk.

Hammersmith had been handsome in his younger days on the
force, when he and Nudger were partners in a two-man patrol car.
But his dashing quality had metamorphosed to a sleek corpulence.
He sat like an officious, smooth-complexioned Buddha with razor-
groomed white hair and pale gray cop's eyes, thriving on authority
and a sense of irony that kept him sane in the midst of madness.

When he saw Nudger, he picked up the cigar and puffed. The
tiny office seemed to waver in the resultant haze. Hammersmith
said, "Ah, you were in the neighborhood and you thought you'd
duck in to chat about baseball and the weather. Maybe trade a
baseball card or two."

"No," Nudger said. He dropped into the hard wooden chair in
front of Hammersmith's desk. The chair was uncomfortable, to
discourage unwelcome visitors who took up too much of Hammersmith's time, but the air was better lower in the room.

"You owe me money I'd forgotten about," Hammersmith spec-
ulated, "and you're here to pay."

"You wouldn't take the time to chat with me or swap baseball
cards, and you remember everyone who owes you money."

Hammersmith seemed hurt. "You disappoint me, Nudge.
You're here because you want a favor."

Nudger nodded and watched Hammersmith work on the cigar.
Puff! Puff! Wheeze! Wheeze! Another thick pall of smoke devel-

oped and mercifully drifted toward the ceiling. Nudger was sure the office had been painted beige and it was Hammersmith's cigars that had turned the walls green.

"As if I don't already have enough to do," Hammersmith said, "daily, sometimes hourly, hurling my body between honest citizens and crime."

"You don't hurl your body anywhere except to your car and back," Nudger told him. "Ever hear of Jake Dancer?"

"No. And I have a feeling I'll wish I hadn't just now. He's a factor in a case you're involved in?"

"The prime factor."

"This a major case? Or am I helping you to find a missing dog? Or someone's dentures they're sure they left at a motel? Remember that one?" Hammersmith smiled.

"This is big time," Nudger assured him. There was no reason to rehash the missing dentures affair, or to point out that said dentures were used to establish who had been at the motel and when and why.

"Life and death?" Hammersmith asked.

"It seemed like it for a while last night."

"Hmm. Such a lot of trouble you are, Nudge."

"For me, too. I can't help it. It might be genetic."

Hammersmith grunted, picked up the phone, and asked around his fat cigar for Records. Nudger couldn't understand him, but apparently whoever was on the other end of the phone was used to requests that sounded like tapes played at low speed. The lieutenant spoke some more garbled bureaucratese into the phone, then sat back, rolled his cigar from side to side in his thin-lipped mouth, and waited, continuing to foul the air in the office with intermittent puffs.

After a few minutes he put down the cigar in the ashtray as if it interfered with his hearing rather than his speech, and pressed the receiver tighter to his ear. Nudger watched the cigar smolder and teeter on the edge of the glass ashtray, wishing it would roll onto the desk and set something on fire.

When Hammersmith had hung up the phone he said, "Jason Lee Dancer. Thirty-six-year-old male Caucasian, hair black, eyes brown. A DWI conviction last year, another charge last month— license not suspended but on shaky ground. It'd be wise of him not to drink and drive anymore. Those were his only brushes with the law, Nudge."

"I'm not surprised; he's not the violent type, despite getting into a recent tussle. Got an address on him?"

"Forty hundred block of Osage."

Helen's address. "Him, all right," Nudger said.

Hammersmith contemplated the cigar balanced on the ashtray, as if considering leaving it there because of its nastiness. A strand of smoke writhed up from it like a snake looking for something to strike. "You into something actually dangerous?" he asked. There was a hint of concern in his voice.

"Not dangerous so far," Nudger said.

"Who's this Dancer?"

"Somebody who owes gambling debts. A couple of strong-arms tried to convince him last night that he should pay up. I helped scare them away."

"They must have been having an off night."

"I said I helped," Nudger said, "and that's all I did. One of those honest citizens you referred to was yelling for the police. That helped, too."

"I've got a hunch there are things I oughta be told about this case of yours."

"I know the rules," Nudger said.

One of the buttons on Hammersmith's phone began blinking frantically. He picked up the receiver, listened for a while, then, without change of expression, replaced it and said, "You had breakfast, Nudge?"

"Not really."

"Good. Me neither. A woman's body just bobbed to the surface and washed ashore alongside the McDonald's riverfront restaurant.

Isn't that convenient? She's badly decomposed, but the uniforms
on the scene say it looks like a homicide."

Nudger had seen bodies that had been submerged for several
days. "Ripe ones," the cops called them. He could imagine the
reaction of people eating McMuffins on the floating-barge franchise when such a corpse put in an unexpected appearance. His
stomach did some tight and intricate maneuvers.

"I guess you're going to be busy," he said, standing up. He
moved toward the door.

"Don't rush away, Nudge," Hammersmith told him, standing
up himself and getting his revolver and belt holster from a desk
drawer. "I want to hear more about this Dancer character, and
whatever it is you're working on. We can talk about it over Egg
McMuffins." He strapped on his holstered gun and cinched the
broad black belt tight over his protruding stomach.

"I do have errands . . ."

"Aw, come along, Nudge." Hammersmith started for the door.
"It's not far. I'll drive."

"That part of the riverfront's not even in your district."

"I'm dual watch commander today," Hammersmith explained.

Nudger knew he didn't really have a choice. Not if he valued
Hammersmith as a contact in the department Nudger had resigned
from so many years ago. And he *had* just been granted a favor.

He followed Hammersmith's bulky yet oddly graceful form outside to an unmarked Pontiac. The sun felt hot on his face; he wondered what it had done to a dead body given up by the river. He
reached for his roll of antacid tablets as he slid into the warm car.

"Stomach still bothering you?" Hammersmith asked, wedging
his bulk in behind the steering wheel.

"'Fraid so."

"Forgot about that. Breakfast is on me."

Nudger popped two antacid tablets into his mouth and chomped
down on them.

Hammersmith pulled out of the blacktop lot onto Chouteau Avenue, switched on the siren, and had fun with the morning traffic.

5

They were giving refunds at McDonald's. Nudger went with Hammersmith to the river side of the converted barge, excusing himself and stepping on the toes of some of the diners who'd lost their breakfasts and their appetites at the sight of the thing that had bobbed into sight alongside their on-deck tables. The workers behind the long counter were busy, smiling sickly and trading money for half-eaten Egg McMuffins, sausage biscuits, and Danish rolls. A tall man in a white shirt and tie, who might have been the manager, stood near the milkshake machine and looked absolutely distraught. Nudger wondered, if the body had surfaced during lunch, would McDonald's have subtracted the refunds from the total of hamburgers their sign claimed sold?

Hammersmith was leaning over the white metal railing and peering down at the muddy, sliding brown water of the Mississippi. Suddenly he leaned farther out, gripping the rail, his elbows cocked back as if to counterweight his plump body.

"Humph," he said, and straightened.

Nudger looked to his left, in the direction Hammersmith had peered, and saw the recovery team just moving the body around the stern of the floating franchise toward the shore. The gentle sound of the river lapping at the restaurant's hull rose in the warm air. Nudger began to sweat.

By the time he'd followed Hammersmith back through the crowded restaurant and across the gangplank to shore, the body was laid out on the large, rough bricks of the levee near one of the overgrown chains used to keep the restaurant moored. In the knot of men surrounding it, the only face that didn't wear an expression

of illness was that of Dyett, an assistant ME Nudger had seen
before at violent death scenes. The sweet stench of decay was
cloying, but the wiry, redhaired, and red-faced Dyett had apparently developed inner calluses that desensitized him to the by-
products of death.

Nudger joined the silent group of men, looked down, and saw
why so many breakfasts had been spoiled. His own stomach
lurched.

The woman's nude body had been in the river for days, and the
water had done its work. She was decomposing, and swollen with
trapped gases. Her face was puffed to a blanched, almost fea-
tureless mass. The eyes were gone, and Nudger thought of the
huge catfish that fed along the bottom of the river. Her hair, which
might once have been blond, was wild and seemed ridiculously
short atop the enlarged face, as if she were wearing a tiny wig for
laughs. The woman's breasts were swollen wide, the nipples
shriveled and dark.

One of the recovery team divers, in a glistening black wet suit,
spat off to the side. "Good Christ!" He unconsciously brushed his
gloved hands on his hips; he'd touched death.

Nudger felt a rage and a pity at what he saw. And something
else; the reduction of a human being to this tossed-up pale flot-
sam scared him. We are transient creatures, and some variation of
what lay on the levee's red bricks awaits us all. Every man there
felt that dark certainty, at least to some degree. Even Dyett must
have felt it. The sensation was part of every murder scene and
victim.

Hammersmith bent down beside Dyett and studied the woman.
Water, and maybe something else, ran from beneath her to puddle
and then inch around Hammersmith's regulation black shoes.
"How'd she go?" he asked.

Dyett tugged a transparent rubber surgical glove onto his right
hand and snapped it tight. He felt here and probed there. He might
have been a butcher assessing a piece of meat. Nudger flinched
each time the body was touched.

The assistant ME, still in his squatting position, shrugged and said, "Can't tell you the cause of death for sure right now. I'd estimate she's been swimming for about a week, but it'll take some work at the morgue to say how long she's been dead." Hammersmith grunted and stood up, looked for a moment at the bright sky. His expression suggested he'd seen nothing there that would provide answers. "Who first saw the body surface?"

"Couple vacationing from Detroit," a blue uniform said. "Mr. and Mrs. Thomas Quinn. I got their statement. They were eating breakfast on the upper deck when the wife noticed something paler than driftwood floating in the water. At first she thought it was a huge fish, she said, then, when she got her husband's attention, they both realized what they were looking at. The missus screamed and pointed, and everybody on the restaurant rushed to take a look." The cop smiled and glanced over at a McDonald's employee hosing down the decks. "Most of them wished they hadn't."

"Where are the Quinns?" Hammersmith asked the uniform.

"Sick. They went back to their hotel, the Clarion. They'll be in town through next weekend for the ratcheters' convention."

"The what?"

"The husband works for a company that manufactures reversible ratchet wrenches, sir. There's hundreds of them here in town."

"Thousands, I would imagine," Hammersmith said.

"I mean ratcheters, sir, not wrenches."

"Uh-huh."

The uniformed cop backed away, trying for invisibility.

Hammersmith looked down again at the body, wrinkled his nose, and fired up a cigar. "What about her neck?" he asked Dyett, who was now kneeling next to the dead woman instead of squatting. Taking strain off middle-aged legs.

"I was just looking at that." Dyett gingerly poked white flesh with his gloved fingers, then squinted up at Hammersmith and grinned. "One for you," he said. "There's a wire imbedded deep in her neck. It wasn't apparent right away because of the gaseous balloonation."

"The what?"

"Her neck's swollen around the wire," Dyett explained, "so that you can barely see it imbedded in her flesh."

"Then she was strangled to death."

"Probably," Dyett said, "but that's hypothesis at this point, Lieutenant." He stood up and adjusted the waistband of his pants, still with the glove on. For now, he was done with the corpse. "I'd like to get her out of this sun." He said it as if the woman were alive and he was afraid she might burn rather than tan and be in discomfort.

Hammersmith nodded and the paramedics standing nearby moved in. Something popped and hissed in the woman's body, giving under the pressure of gases expanding in the heat.

Nudger swallowed the bitterness of bile and turned away. For a second he thought he might vomit, but he willed his stomach to be calm. He watched a tugboat churning its way upstream, making gradual progress against the inexorable current.

"Want some breakfast, Nudge?" Hammersmith asked. "On me, remember."

Nudger wasn't impressed; Hammersmith frequently offered to buy meals when he knew the potential recipient would eat sparsely or not at all.

"Not hungry."

"Just coffee, then," Hammersmith said. "C'mon, Nudge." He began walking toward the canopy-shaped gangplank to the restaurant.

Nudger followed. Behind him the riverfront land rose so that only the tops of the downtown buildings were visible, and from that rise of ground soared the Arch, glistening silver in the morning light and dwarfing every other visible object. In front of Nudger, beyond the floating restaurant, was the wide, ponderously rolling river, with East St. Louis industry sprawling gray and squalid on its opposite bank. A thin, dark haze hovered over the east side, like an impotent imitation storm cloud.

Hammersmith put out his offensive cigar per the city ordinance, taking care of pollution on their side of the river, then ordered for both of them and carried the tray to an upper-deck table overlooking the water. The floor was still wet from being hosed down, and smelled like ammonia.

Nudger saw that Hammersmith had gotten more than coffee for himself. There was an Egg McMuffin, orange juice, a Danish roll, and a potato patty on the tray, along with the two coffees.

Hammersmith sat down opposite Nudger and placed the tray on the table between them. Nudger pried the lid from his coffee cup and added cream. He was hoping the hot liquid would settle his stomach and erase the bitterness that lay at the base of his tongue. He couldn't stop thinking about the dead woman on the levee.

"A messy one, huh?" Hammersmith said, biting into his Egg McMuffin. Egg spurted and butter ran down his fingers. Nudger almost retched. "Drink your coffee, Nudge; make you feel better."

Nudger thought that was sound advice. He sipped the hot coffee and swallowed carefully. He did feel steadier.

"This Dancer case you're working on," Hammersmith said, "we got anything about it on file?"

"That's what I'm trying to keep from happening," Nudger said. The breeze off the river was cool on his perspiring forehead. He and Hammersmith were the only ones on the upper deck.

"Is Dancer in some kinda trouble that might make him one of our fair city's statistics?" Hammersmith asked.

"Depends on who he owes. The two goons who beat him up last night weren't actually trying to kill him. But they made it clear he was prominent in their employer's thoughts."

"I can ask around the gambling scene and try to find out who he might owe," Hammersmith said. "No promises, now. As you can

see, my own crime-fighting takes up a lot of my time. And the
local gambling fraternity's understandably closemouthed."

"Thanks, Jack."

"We'll keep each other informed about this, right?" Hammersmith said.

"Sure," Nudger told him.

Hammersmith chewed another bite of Egg McMuffin and gazed
out at the wide river. He seemed uneasy, hesitant. Not like him.
Nudger was beginning to wonder if Hammersmith had some reason, other than companionship and the perverse desire to disturb
Nudger's delicate stomach, for suggesting they share breakfast.
Their conversation about Dancer could just as easily have been
initiated on the drive back to the station house.

"How are you and Claudia getting along, Nudge?" Hammersmith asked.

Ah, that was it. Hammersmith must have heard about Nudger's
and Claudia's new arrangement, wherein they could each go out
with others. It was part of Claudia's quest for her inner self, according to her and to her analyst, Dr. Oliver. She still loved
Nudger, they both assured Nudger. Nudger thought they had a
funny way of getting across their point. He loved Claudia and
didn't like this new openness in their relationship. And he hadn't
been with another woman since they'd started this idiocy. Not that
the thought hadn't strutted high-heeled across his mind; he was a
monogamous guy, but there were limits.

"Nudge?"

"She's seeing other men," Nudger said.

"You two have some trouble?"

"Not me. Claudia. She says she needs to be with somebody else
occasionally. Oliver says it has to do with her self-actualization."

"Sounds like a bunch of crap," Hammersmith said.

Nudger nodded. "It's just that." He swished his coffee around
in its cup and met Hammersmith's eyes. "You see her with someone else, Jack?"

Hammersmith took a large bite of potato patty and nodded.
"Chesty guy who looks like he lifts weights. All-American type.

They were at a play out in Webster Groves; they seemed more than
friendly, Nudge.''

"Biff Archway," Nudger said. He felt a thrust of jealousy.
"She told me she wasn't going to see him anymore. Said he was
involved with the girls' field hockey coach.''

"Huh?''

"He teaches out at Stowe High School with Claudia.''

"What's he teach?''

"Sex education.''

"Ah," Hammersmith said, as if much had been explained.

Nudger was developing heartburn, even though he hadn't eaten
anything today. He pushed the coffee away and chewed on some
antacid tablets.

"You let me know if I can help," Hammersmith said. He'd
always liked Claudia and said she was too much quality for
Nudger. He was right about her, Nudger knew.

He'd known that within a few weeks after he'd talked her out of
suicide and they began seeing each other steadily. They'd both
been lonely until then; now Claudia wanted to bring back that
loneliness—for Nudger. He could see other women, sure. But
there were no women he wanted other than Claudia. No women he
wanted in addition to Claudia. Obsession: one of his character
flaws.

Yet a picture of Helen Crane flashed onto his mind's screen,
faded, and then remained, obscure but identifiable. None of that!
he cautioned himself. Helen Crane was his client and Dancer's
woman.

"Didn't *you* get quiet?" Hammersmith said, interrupting
Nudger's morose contemplation.

"Sorry," Nudger said. "Thinking.''

"Source of all your trouble." Hammersmith wolfed down the
last of his breakfast and leaned away from the table. "I better get
back and see what the evildoers have cooked up for me. You can
finish your coffee in the car.''

Nudger placed the half-empty cup on the tray with the debris
from Hammersmith's meal. "I'm done with it," he said.

On the walk up the levee he thought about Helen Crane and Claudia and the woman from the river. All three of them, love and fear, longing and death, beauty and horror, mixed together in his mind. It was eerie, as if they were connected in some way, but he didn't know how or why.

He didn't want to know.

6

"There's a woman upstairs in your office, Nudge," Danny told Nudger when he walked into Danny's Donuts to check with ersatz receptionist/secretary Danny about the morning's investigation business. Or lack of same.

"She leave a name?" Nudger asked, looking around the empty doughnut shop. The office workers from across the street who frequented Danny's on weekday mornings were long gone and thinking about lunch.

"Nope. She's a kinda pert blonde. Dressed nice. A classy woman, Nudge. If she was a doughnut, she'd be a Dunker Delite."

Nudger decided not to argue against that inappropriate analogy; somber, sad-eyed Danny was supersensitive about the doughnut shop's specialty. Nudger could remember Danny's basset-hound eyes actually misting when a customer told him what a Dunker Delite was really like.

"She's been up there about twenty minutes," Danny said. He began straightening a stack of white, folded to-go boxes. They were still pure, flat surfaces unprofaned by grease stains. "I told her I didn't know when you'd show up, could be a while. She insisted on waiting for you."

"I know who she is," Nudger said. He moved to the counter and gazed into the showcase to see what Danny had left: a few glazed, some of the shapeless, ominous Dunker Delites, lots of cream horns. The cream horns might be half-price tomorrow; the filling oozing from their ends was beginning to stiffen.

"Where you been all morning?" Danny asked.

His eyes still focused on the doughnuts on their greasy paper napkins, Nudger recalled the woman from the river and his stomach rolled. He looked away from the doughnuts. "Downtown on the riverfront," he said. "Watching people fish."

Danny took a swipe at the counter with his grayish towel, leaning so he could leave the other end of the towel tucked in his belt. "I do some river fishing now and then. Down south of the city."

Nudger was surprised; Danny had never mentioned that he liked to fish. And the polluted, turgid Mississippi wasn't a favorite of fishermen. Not those who liked to eat what they caught. "What you fish for?"

"Oh, mostly buffalofish," Danny said.

Buffalofish were large, lackadaisical creatures that probably put up about as much fight as a swamped radial tire. They were edible, though, and cheap, and a favorite in St. Louis's poor neighborhoods. Nudger had read in the paper recently that Mississippi buffalofish were tainted with mercury. Or had it been dioxin?

"Never have caught one, though," Danny admitted.

"What do you use for bait?"

"Day-old doughballs. Make 'em out of unsold Dunker Delites."

Nudger said nothing. Even buffalofish had disdain for Dunker Delites. Maybe word spread underwater, and avoiding certain baits was taught in fish schools.

"Wanna take some coffee and doughnuts up to the office for you and the lady?" Danny asked.

"Sure," Nudger said, keeping up the pretense that he relished Danny's fare. He never forgot there were times when, out of eco-

nomic necessity, most of his meals were eaten here in the doughnut shop. Something buffalofish never had to consider.

A few minutes later, carrying two foam cups of coffee and two
napkin-wrapped Dunker Delites, Nudger trudged up the narrow
stairwell to his office and pushed open the door.

The woman standing by the window was pert and blond, all
right, but not Helen Crane. She was Beverly Brassil, an antique
dealer who, along with other dealers, had recently hired Nudger to
find out who was flooding the St. Louis antique market with imitation Depression glass and selling it as the real thing. A man in a
red sport shirt was standing near her. He needed a shave. Possibly
he was her husband.

Nudger had traced the imitation Depression glass to an auction
house on the south side. The auctioneer had agreed not to sell any
more of the glassware, which he'd trucked up from Arkansas, if
charges wouldn't be pressed. The antique dealers had agreed, and
then had a fine time breaking cases of the phony antique glass.

Beverly smiled at Nudger. It was a nice smile; she was an attractive woman. The man with her was glowering, holding in his
right hand some sort of antique, rusty-looking device with a crank
handle.

"I came on behalf of the dealers, Mr. Nudger," Beverly said.
"I'm sorry, but we won't be able to pay your fee until next
month."

Nudger's disappointment must have shown.

"Here's something on account," Beverly said, and handed him
an envelope containing what appeared to be about three hundred
dollars in small bills. "We'll get the rest to you soon as possible.
But business is slow these days in the antique game."

"I understand about slow business," Nudger said. What was he
going to do, sue these people? He grinned at Beverly; he was sure
she sort of liked him. Didn't want to sue her, anyway. "Want a
receipt?" he asked.

"Not necessary; we trust you. I told them you'd wait for the
money," she said. "You're too nice a man to be greedy with a

bunch of struggling independent business people.'' She waved a
shapely arm. ''And you know, the antique business'll pick up
sooner or later.''

''Speaking of antiques,'' Nudger said, ''what's that thing?'' He
pointed to the contraption in the man's hand. Maybe this fella was
just a friend.

''It's a mechanical apple peeler,'' the grizzly guy said. He held
out the rusty gizmo so Nudger could see it better, smiling wickedly
as if he were demonstrating a medieval torture device. Not just a
friend. ''You stab this thing into the core of the apple, turn this
crank, and it peels the skin off neat as you please.''

''Yeow,'' Nudger said, ''an apple peeler. That's something.''

''Ain't it?'' the man said, glancing at Beverly.

Beverly seemed uneasy. ''Guess we'll go, Mr. Nudger. I'll be
in touch with you soon, I promise.''

''You can turn the crank fast or slow,'' the man said, as they
went out the door.

Nudger went into the half-bath and washed his hands, then
splashed cold water over his face. He felt refreshed, and he had
enough money to stave off Eileen for a while and pay his most
threatening creditors. The world looked better.

When he walked back into the office, Helen Crane was seated in
the black vinyl padded Danish chair near the file cabinet. She was
wearing pale blue again, a well-cut dress this time rather than a
skirt and blazer, and had her long legs crossed. A large, dark blue
straw purse rested against a chair leg on the floor, near a blue high-
heeled shoe that did an admirable job of accenting a neatly turned
ankle. Blue was Helen's color, all right. The office was cooler
now; the window unit behind Nudger's desk was humming away
on high.

''Didn't hear you come in,'' Nudger said. The blondes in his
life moved quietly.

''I took the liberty of turning on the air conditioner,'' Helen told
him. ''I hope you don't mind.''

''I appreciate it.'' He shoved the door closed with a practiced,

backward sweep of his heel, and walked to the desk. The doughnuts and coffee he'd brought up from Danny's were sitting on the
desk corner where he'd put them after walking in and finding Beverly and the apple peeler. "Lunch, if you haven't had it," he explained. "Breakfast, if you haven't had that. Compliments of
Danny downstairs."

"Nice of Danny, but I'm not hungry."

"That's wise," Nudger said. He sat down, ignored the Dunker
Delites, and removed the lid from one of the coffee cups. Hot
liquid sloshed over his thumb.

"How's the coffee?" Helen asked.

"Better than the doughnuts."

She got up, moved to the chair nearest the desk, and slid the
other foam cup over to where she could handle it. "I drove in this
morning from the cabin," she said. "Jake and I like it. It's a nice
enough place, not as crude as it looks from the outside. I told Jake
it belongs to a friend I met through work, and he believed me."

"Think he'll stay there as agreed?"

"I'm not sure. There's no whiskey in the place other than one
bottle." She sniffed at the coffee and pushed it away.

"Your idea?"

"His. The one bottle is Born Again bourbon, and Jake's sworn
not to open it until he's out of debt and our troubles are behind
us."

Nudger was unfamiliar with the brand. "Born Again?"

Helen smiled. "Jake started drinking it years ago because it was
cheap, and because he liked the name. It's made by some southern
distillery whose owner is poking fun at religious zealotry. That's
what Jake thinks, anyway. He also tells me that's how the whiskey
makes him feel sometimes: born again. And my opinion is that's
all the distillery had in mind when they came up with the brand
name, how what was in the bottle made their customers feel."

Nudger was aware of how some alcoholics trying to stay dry
kept a symbolic unopened bottle around. A constant foil for their
willpower, and a reminder that they were winning the battle

against compulsion, that they and not the whiskey had control. It was something else Helen had said that made him curious. "Why would Dancer be drawn to a brand name that mocked religion?" he asked.

"Jake used to be the religious sort. Very much so. When we were younger he even talked a lot about becoming a missionary. He was awfully idealistic. Vietnam changed all that. Jake said he couldn't believe in God anymore after what he saw. I guess I lost most of my faith, too, when he was over there. Or maybe we both got older, is all, and less gullible and more realistic. Do you believe in God, Nudger?"

"When I'm scared."

"Is that often?"

"Yes."

"It's that way with me, too."

She stood up and smoothed her blue dress over her thighs. The light streaming in above the air conditioner got tangled in her blond hair and cavorted there, as if it had found an errant part of itself and was overjoyed. "I just wanted to stop by and thank you," she said, "and let you know where Jake is."

"Fine," Nudger said. He stood up, too. "Going back to the cabin?"

"Later."

"If Dancer leaves," he said, "phone me here or at my other number." He jotted his home number on the back of one of his business cards and handed it to her. He'd been handing out his number a lot lately. "Also, since I'd better not call the cabin, check in with me every day in case I've learned something you oughta know. If you don't have a chance to phone from the cabin, make an excuse to drive to the highway and call me from the pay phone in the truck stop. Or leave a message on my answering machine letting me know where and when I can reach you here in the city."

"I often work evenings. Sometimes late."

"Can I contact you at work?"

"No," she said, too quickly. "My hours are unpredictable. Better let me try to get in touch with you."

She slipped the card into her oversized purse and told him she'd phone regularly. For the first time he noticed her perfume, a faint lilac scent. It was probably inexpensive, and smelled sweeter on her than in the bottle.

She treated him to her oddly restful smile. "I feel better about the situation already, Nudger. You represent money well spent."

Nudger watched her leave the office. There was a special emptiness in rooms she left. A lilac-scented loneliness closed in on him.

He was troubled by the way the elements of this case were assembling: gambling debts, professional leg-breakers, a beautiful woman, and an engaging young war hero who'd lost his faith and found the bottle.

He listened to the descending tap, tap, tap of Helen's high heels on the creaking wooden stairs.

Dancer was safely ensconced at the cabin. This was a good opportunity for Nudger to find out more about Helen Crane.

When he heard the street door open and clatter closed, he got up and left the office to follow her.

7

The Volkswagen started right up this time; it liked following beautiful women. Helen drove east on Manchester to Kingshighway, then took Highway 44 toward downtown. Nudger stayed well back of her blue Datsun, and watched it squeeze like a persistent insect between two tractor-trailers and exit on Memorial Drive.

He cut in behind one of the trucks, breathed in some diesel

exhaust, and took the ramp to Memorial, behind Helen. To his left the downtown commercial section towered and angled against the sky beyond the Old Courthouse, where the Dred Scott trial had taken place. On Nudger's right the Arch soared above the river, where stern-wheelers still churned muddy waters. The amalgam of old and new that was St. Louis.

He saw the Datsun a few blocks ahead, one of a line of cars shimmering in the sun in the left-turn lane at Pine Street.

It was easy staying close but undetected behind Helen in the heavy downtown traffic. Nudger had both windows rolled down in the Volkswagen. He sucked in hot, humid air that was tainted with more exhaust fumes and the dust of construction in progress. There was always construction or demolition in progress in downtown St. Louis. It was a restless city. When there was nothing to build, someone always thought of something to tear down.

Helen made a right turn and cut over to Washington, where she scooted the little Datsun around a belching, rumbling bus and made a sharp left that drew angry honks. She was some driver. She tooled west on Washington for a few blocks, weaving in and out of traffic as if looking for something to dent.

Nudger was relieved to see her park the Datsun on Washington, poke some coins into a meter, and enter an office building.

He found a parking space on a side street, then hurried to follow Helen into the lobby. At the door, he paused, catching a glimpse of her blue dress as the jaws of elevator doors smoothly met to devour her. She hadn't seen him.

The lobby was empty except for an executive type in a dark suit standing slouched near a potted plant and balancing an open attaché case that he was rooting through frenziedly. "Shit!" he said, and snapped the case shut and strode away as Nudger walked over and stood near the elevators. Must have forgotten something at the office.

Nudger craned his neck and watched the floor indicator for the elevator Helen had taken. Up, up, up. He was reasonably sure she was the only passenger. The building was old, and the indicator was an ornate brass arrow that jerked from numeral to numeral, rather than one of the newer digital indicators. So far, the arrow hadn't stopped at any number.

It didn't stop until it had fought its way tremulously to the numeral ten, where it wavered, paused, and stuck. Nudger watched it for a few minutes, making sure the elevator wasn't going higher. The fancy brass arrow stayed firmly on the ten, finally still, as if resting on a precipice.

Nudger walked over to the building directory near the potted plant. There were cigarette butts and dark smudges on the marble floor; people had stood to study the directory, then put out their smokes before crossing the lobby to the elevators. The tenth-floor column showed only a janitor service and something called Partners Unlimited. Nudger didn't know what Partners Unlimited was, but he'd bet against Helen working as a janitor.

A glance at the brass arrow told him the elevator was making its unsteady way back down toward the lobby. He couldn't be sure it was Helen descending, but most of the office space in the building was unoccupied and there wasn't that much traffic. The tenth-floor halls wouldn't be bustling corridors of commerce. He decided to embrace caution and get out of sight.

He left the lobby and crossed the street, standing near the show window of a jewelry store. The diamond rings were displayed in front of a long mirror to make them glint. Nudger pretended to be studying the glittering display in the window while he was actually watching the mirror's reflection of the other side of the street.

Helen emerged from the building and walked toward her car. Nudger waited until she'd lowered herself into the blue Datsun with a flash of long, pale-nyloned calf, then he hurried toward the Volkswagen.

He didn't follow her far this time, only a few blocks north, where she parked in a lot across the street from the Radisson Hotel. The Radisson was a newer hotel that catered mainly to business trade. It was modern, plush, and efficient, all the things peo-

ple traveling at taxpayer expense expected. When Helen had
entered the lobby, Nudger walked in after her.

She was nowhere in sight.

Nudger wandered over and checked to make sure she hadn't
gone into the restaurant off the lobby, then he settled into one of
the chairs farthest from the desk, where he wouldn't be noticed by
anyone entering or leaving the hotel.

There were plenty of people milling around the lobby. The
Radisson was directly across the street from the Cervantes Convention Center, and apparently the plush hotel was a temporary
home for a lot of conventioneers. Nudger wondered if any of them
were ratcheters.

He sat there for about fifteen minutes, noticing several men and
women wearing business suits walk past. On their lapels they wore
large plastic name tags lettered BLAINE CHEMICAL CORP, and they
all seemed to be drifting in the direction of the exit and the convention center. Nudger gathered from snatches of conversation that
they were on their way to attend a banquet.

His lower back was beginning to ache. He was about to struggle
up from his soft chair when he saw Helen crossing the lobby.

She wasn't alone. A short, paunchy man with pomaded white
hair and wide shoulders beneath an expensive gray suit was leading her by the elbow as if she might be blind and stupid and re-
calcitrant. He looked like the sort who'd command a board
meeting. Who'd never be seated near Nudger and the restrooms in
a fancy restaurant. Headwaiters, even gas station attendants, would
bow and scrape for this guy. Helen was smiling and so was he.
They were both sporting plastic name tags that read BLAINE CHEM-
ICAL CORP.

Nudger watched them leave the hotel, then he strolled over and
looked out through the glass door.

They hadn't walked toward a car or hailed a cab. They were
crossing the street to the convention center. A soft breeze worked
under Helen's blue skirt, and after a brief but spectacular leg dis-

play she held down the material with a spread hand to the back of
her thigh, walking in that slightly bent-over yet graceful way of
women dealing with flirtatious weather.

Nudger hurried to the Volkswagen and drove to an office supply
store a few blocks away on Locust. He bought a box of plastic
name tags, printed BLAINE CHEMICAL CORP on one with a black
felt-tip pen, then returned to park near the Radisson. The whole
thing hadn't taken ten minutes.

He got a wrinkled tie from the Volkswagen's glove compartment, slipped it on and knotted it neatly enough on the first at-
tempt, then printed "Richie Nixon" in the space for his name on
the plastic tag. Well, there could be two of them. And coincidence
added plausibility; who this side of sanity would choose Nixon as a
pseudonym? Must have happened at birth, right? With the name
tag pinned on the left lapel of his threadbare brown sport coat, he
walked briskly into the convention center.

Signs pointed the way to the Chemical Foundation luncheon.
Nudger fell in behind some other late arrivals, but he stopped and
stood still near the door to a large room as they paused to hand
their luncheon tickets to a waiter.

The room was filled with white-clothed tables, and around each
table sat men in suits, along with well-dressed women. Silver
clinked with polite muted volume; crystal glittered in bright overhead lighting. The diners were being served fruit cups by an army
of black-vested waiters who coasted adroitly among the tables,
maneuvering trays above their heads so they wouldn't bump the
conventioneers who weren't yet seated. The fruit cups looked delicious and goaded Nudger's sleeping appetite awake, despite his
stomach's nervous tightness.

"Ticket, sir?" the man guarding the door asked. He was a
somber, middle-aged man with military posture. His vest was red
and had silver braid crossing it diagonally, no doubt indicating
some sort of authority that he liked more than was healthy.

Nudger thought of pretending he'd forgotten his ticket, but he
knew the next step would be for the doorman to ask for someone

to vouch for the forgetful diner. Richie Nixon knew no one in the chemical business.

"I'm not attending the luncheon," Nudger said firmly. "Got an emergency meeting. Something happening in India. I'm supposed to meet Gallaway here. You know Gallaway?"

"No, sir. I work for the hotel."

Nudger smiled. "I know. I thought Gallaway might have left a message here for me."

"Nobody's left a message, Mr. . . . Nixon."

Nudger nodded. Very businesslike. "Okay. I'll hang around here for a while and wait for him."

Ten minutes later, the ticket-taker closed the wide doors to the room, nodding to Nudger before he disappeared. Nudger knew the man would be standing just inside the double doors. Nobody was getting in there to nab one of those fruit cups.

After another fifteen minutes, Nudger took a chance, opened one of the tall doors slightly, slowly, and poked his head inside.

The white-haired man he'd seen leave the Radisson with Helen was at a lectern, speaking. Helen was seated at a table near the front, facing three-quarters away from Nudger, listening to what the man had to say. By the angle of her head he guessed she was staring up at him in intense concentration—or pretending very convincingly.

". . . half the amount of the precontamination market value of their houses!" the speaker loudly proclaimed. The audience applauded enthusiastically.

A man nearby said, "Hear, hear! Hear, hear!" Nudger hadn't thought anyone actually ever said that except in old David Niven movies.

There was a tap on his right shoulder. He turned to find himself staring into the placid face of the door guard with the general's vest.

"Sir?" the man said softly. "Can I help you?"

"You know who that is up there speaking?" Nudger asked.

"No, I don't."

"Gallaway," Nudger confided.

"Thataway," the man said, motioning with his head for Nudger to leave. The guy was wise. Must have been the jacket. Or the hand-printed name tag. "The speaker's name happens to be Morrison."

"You lied to me."

"Yes."

Nudger felt better knowing it hadn't been the jacket.

Morrison was saying, "'Clean' is a much misused word by many in our society! We mustn't be intimidated by that word! 'Clean' is a relative term!"

The man who'd said, "Hear, hear!" said, "Bravo! Bravo!"

Nudger smoothly backed out of the room. With great dignity. The door closed, and he was sure he heard the snick of a lock.

He left the convention center and walked back to the Volkswagen, listening to his heels hit the pavement, mulling things over.

It was obvious that Partners Unlimited was an escort service, and that Helen was a hired escort. Nudger knew there were two kinds of escort services: those that exclusively provided escorts to accompany people to official functions better not attended alone, and those that also provided prostitution. He knew there were more of the latter than the former, but Helen didn't seem the type to be a high-priced prostitute. And though she dressed stylishly, she didn't have the clothes, car, or apartment that suggested she made the kind of money a woman with her looks could command in that kind of market.

He sat in his hot little car, knowing he might be able to make an afternoon and evening's work of this. Find out if Helen Crane stayed with Morrison, went out to dinner with him and his chemical comrades, returned with him to the hotel. She'd said she frequently worked nights, hadn't she?

Nudger decided that if Helen was going to spend the night with Morrison, he, Nudger, didn't want to know about it. It was, in fact, none of his business; Helen was his client, not the object of his investigation. He'd only wanted to learn something about her for his own security, to understand best how to deal with Dancer's dilemma.

He felt unreasonably disillusioned. Almost betrayed. Ridiculous! After all, he'd known nothing about Helen Crane. Who was he to have such high expectations for her?

But that was the thing about Helen; she was the type of woman who was up on a pedestal five minutes after men met her. And Nudger knew there were plenty of men who'd relish dragging her down. Who'd pay dearly for the opportunity.

As he drove slowly along the baking streets to his office, he told himself that Partners Unlimited might be one of the straight escort services in the city, and that Helen might be a paid escort and nothing more. Someone who merely provided a few hours' ornamentation in public for people like Morrison.

He wasn't sure he could believe that. He wondered if Dancer believed it. And if he didn't, what did he think of Helen's line of work?

'Clean' was a relative term.

8

Hammersmith didn't believe Partners Unlimited was strictly a legitmate escort service. The morning after seeing Helen Crane at the Radisson Hotel, Nudger had asked him to check with the Vice Squad and then call back. Hammersmith was on the phone before noon.

"Vice tells me Partners Unlimited is sometimes straight, and sometimes provides prostitution," Hammersmith said around his cigar. Nudger was glad he was miles away from the Third District station house and was hearing Hammersmith's slurping and puffing without the accompanying greenish pall. "The service had a soliciting-for-prostitution conviction five years ago, Nudge. That was when a guy named Brad Marlyk bought control. Since then, Partners Unlimited leaves the actual soliciting up to its employees on their own time, except for occasional exceptions that don't seem to bother anyone here on Vice."

"Why aren't they bothered?"

"Because the city prosecutor can't find a way to hang a conviction on Marlyk. So why arrest and charge the guy? Nobody likes to waste their time trying to close legal loopholes wide enough for elephants. Almost nobody, anyway."

"You don't sound convinced," Nudger said, rocking back in his squealing swivel chair.

"I'm not," Hammersmith said. "Cynical me, Nudge. It's hard to believe that if his professional escorts are lying down for his clients, this Marlyk isn't getting some of the profits."

"Maybe he considers his employees' after-hours social activities their own business."

"Life doesn't work that way, even if court does."

"So true. Still, the operation doesn't seem that tight. You think Marlyk is paying somebody on Vice to keep hands off his service?"

"Possibly. It's not called the Vice Squad for nothing. This escort outfit involved in whatever you're working on, Nudge? What we were talking about the other day?"

"My client's one of Marlyk's employees. But she doesn't seem the prostitute type."

"Jesus, Nudge." Slurp, slurp, puff, puff. "The ones that don't seem the type make the most money."

Also true, Nudger had to admit. The richest prostitute he knew had the face and body of a fourteen-year-old until she was well into her thirties. She fulfilled the unrealized cheerleader fantasies of men's youths. Pom-poms and all. Still, there was a special quality about Helen Crane that went beyond her physical beauty. She

simply *couldn't* be selling her sexual favors. Not Helen. Or was
Nudger idealizing her? Being the male chauvinist pig that Eileen
had once called him because he'd idealized *her*. Hmm . . .

"Is there any way I can find out if my client's one of Marlyk's
prostitutes?" Nudger asked.

"How come you need to know? What do you care how she gets
her money?"

"I care because what she does for money might have some bear-
ing on her boyfriend, and he's the one I'm trying to help."

"Maybe you oughta ask her, Nudge. Her answer might be a
lulu."

"I will ask her, but I want her answer corroborated."

"'Corroborated' is a word I hear a lot in police work," Hammersmith said. "It usually means somebody else is telling the
same lie. I'd ignore the word completely if it didn't sound so good
in court."

"Does that mean you won't help?" Nudger asked, knowing better. Hammersmith felt he had to make people work for his cooper-
ation; he didn't want to be taken cheaply. That attitude had in a
strange way helped him to advance in the department. That and the
fact that he was a good cop who played politics with gusto and
shrewdness. And sometimes surprising subtlety.

Hammersmith sighed loudly. It was probably a manufactured
sigh. The lieutenant was fond of telephone dramatics. "What's
your client's name, Nudge?"

"Helen Crane."

"Sounds classy. She's probably Marlyk's long-white-glove spe-
cialist."

Nudger felt anger kick to life in his stomach. He knew it
shouldn't be there; his relationship with Helen Crane was professional—his profession. He tried not to let his emotional involvement edge into his voice. "Thanks for your help, Jack. I owe."

"You owe and owe and owe. Pay me back just a little bit by
sharing if you learn anything I oughta know."

"That's a promise."

"Means nothing over the phone, Nudge. Everything but your balls is probably crossed."

Hammersmith hung up quickly. He had an obsession about getting in the last word in a phone conversation. The guy was a jumble of idiosyncrasies.

Nudger replaced the receiver and swiveled to catch the cool flow of air from the window unit. If Helen Crane was a pro and hadn't told Dancer, that could explain what was bothering the tortured vet. Maybe Dancer had found out about her occupation, only she wasn't aware of it. Another kick in the psyche for Jake Dancer. His longtime lover was selling ass to chemical moguls and ratcheters. He might love Helen too much to leave her, and hate what she was doing too much to stay with her. So at night he ached. He roamed. He poked sharp sticks in himself.

Nudger told himself to slow down and stay on course. It was misleading to speculate without enough facts. And, as usual, he was short on hard evidence.

But large men who beat on people were involved in this. And knives were involved. Guns might be next. Damn it, Nudger had a right to know as much as possible! Fear should be granted some privileges.

He picked up a pencil and used its sharp point to tap out a series of random black dots on his desk. He studied the dots. They were in a pattern that resembled the state of Idaho and revealed nothing.

A large gray and white pigeon flapped to perch on the ledge outside the window that didn't hold the air conditioner. It glared in hostilely at Nudger through the glass. Nudger shouted "Scat!" and the pigeon cocked its head at him and didn't move.

He wadded up an old electric bill and threw it at the window and the pigeon flapped away. It had defecated on the ledge.

This wasn't getting him anywhere, Nudger decided. This wasn't detective work.

The phone rang and he lifted the receiver and silently held it to his ear, waiting for the person on the other end of the line to speak first. If it was someone Nudger didn't want to talk to, he'd pretend to be a recorded message on his answering machine. He could do that very well; he'd practiced plenty with Eileen.

Ah, it was Helen Crane. Nudger thought about Morrison and the Radisson Hotel, about his conversation with Hammersmith, about what he knew but didn't want to know. What was he going to do about it? What?

Helen said, "Nudger? You there?"

He said, "I just chased away a pigeon."

She said, "Good."

He said, "How about lunch?"

9

Lunch with Helen was an improvement over breakfast with Hammersmith. They ate at a restaurant up the street from Nudger's office, the B&L Diner. It was a small, clean place that featured a long counter with high stools, lots of white-enameled metal, a window with a view of traffic on Manchester, and good food. Nudger's kind of eatery. There were no clowns, cutesy decor, or kiddie rides at the B&L. The place was real. So was the ground beef.

Helen sat next to Nudger at the end of the counter. They'd ordered hamburgers and milkshakes. There were only two other customers in the diner: an old man at the counter who sipped water and occasionally mumbled to himself, and a young woman with stringy hair who was earnestly sorting through a jumble of coupons. A dime saved here, a dime there; it could add up and save you the dollar you were overcharged at the supermarket. It was that kind of neighborhood.

"Don't you have to watch your figure?" Nudger asked, as

Helen took in a generous amount of chocolate shake through two thick straws. The effort made her lips pucker. Sexy.

"Never had to."

Well, Nudger would watch it. He remembered her walk as she'd crossed the street to the downtown convention center. So graceful next to the aggressive, choppy strides of Morrison the good-time executive.

A house-size bus passed by slowly outside, braking noisily and then accelerating ponderously away from the traffic signal at Sutton, fouling the air with dark diesel exhaust. A hint of its fumes somehow found its way into the diner. Nudger waited for the bus's throat-clearing and hissing to fade before he spoke to Helen.

He said, "I followed you yesterday. I needed to find out more about you."

"Why?" Calm gray eyes. Inquisitive but not surprised or overly concerned. Helen Crane was a woman who analyzed before reacting.

"I was getting scared," Nudger told her. "Gambling debts, Vietnam ghosts, big guys with knives . . . there's a nasty kind of chemistry here."

"Private detectives aren't supposed to get scared." She stated that as if it were a natural law and he must be mistaken about his own emotions. He felt like a robot who'd declared it had a heart. Maybe that was exactly the way she saw him.

"We're also supposed to know as much about our clients and their problems as possible. Especially if we deem it might be a key to our survival."

There was no arguing about something as basic as remaining alive. She took a bite of her hamburger, then chewed and swallowed it slowly, as if she thoroughly enjoyed its taste and texture. Best hamburger she'd ever eaten. "And what did you find out about me, Nudger?"

"Oh, Morrison of Blaine Chemical. Partners Unlimited escort service."

"I see." For the first time she seemed slightly angry and defensive. "My way of making a living bother you?"

"No," Nudger told her, "but I have to wonder if it bothers Jake Dancer. He know you work for Brad Marlyk?"

"Yes. He doesn't seem to mind my escort work."

"Would he mind if it went beyond merely being a paid escort?"

"He would. But my job doesn't include being a whore. Only about half the girls who work for Partners Unlimited also engage in prostitution. Of their own accord. Brad Marlyk doesn't coerce them."

"But he takes a percentage of their wealth."

"Sure. But he also lines up clients for them who are reliable, clean, and pay very well. It's a fair trade, considering."

"Is it possible Dancer suspects you're one of the escorts who sell sex, and that's what's causing him so much agony?"

"No. I think he'd say something to me if that was it. In fact, I know he would. That'd be a simple thing to deal with, compared to what's going on."

"Would he stay with you?"

"You mean if I was hustling and refused to stop?"

"Yeah."

"I think so," Helen said, "but I'm not positive." She wrapped her lips around the twin straws again, then removed them without drawing any milkshake. There were faint lipstick stains on the tips of the straws.

She said, "Something I oughta let you know, I guess. I've told Brad Marlyk to set me up with some of his clients who expect more than just an attractive woman to sit beside them at official functions."

"Meaning?" He was imagining her as a products demonstrator, or maybe a company hostess or model. Showing how easily the controls worked on an industrial vacuum cleaner. Standing and smiling next to a glossy new Buick.

"I'm going to work as a prostitute."

Nudger was surprised. He bit hard into his own plastic straw and put a dent in it, upsetting the hydraulics that allowed him to suck up the thick liquid. "Why?" he asked.

"To pay off Jake's debts. It's the only way we can raise the money in a hurry and get whoever's after him off his trail. I'm leveling with you, Nudger, because I figure you'd find out anyway, and because I want your word that you won't tell Jake what I'm doing."

"You have my word. But you're making a hell of a sacrifice for Dancer."

"It's Jake who's in hell. And as soon as I earn enough money to clear what he owes, I'll quit. There are worse things than prostitution, Nudger. And there are all *kinds* of prostitution. What I'm about to do is at least direct and candid even if it's illegal."

"Are you going to give me the wife-who-doesn't-love-her-rich-husband analogy?"

"Don't need to; you thought of it."

He had at that.

Nudger didn't know just how to react to this development. He felt disappointment and rage. He could understand why Helen thought she had to do this for Dancer. But wasn't there another way?

"Don't you know word processing or something?" he asked.

"Word processing doesn't pay like prostitution. Few jobs do. And Brad Marlyk will be fair to me as long as I'm honest with him." She stared hard at him across her milkshake. Those gray eyes. "You've got to understand, Nudger, there's no other way I can make enough money fast."

"How much does Dancer owe?"

"I'm not sure of the exact amount. But it's thousands. I'll never reach it toiling at minimum wage."

"Christ!" he said. "What if you get beat up? Or catch some disease?"

She smiled. "That's one advantage of working for Partners Unlimited; there are regular medical checkups for the employees."

"Protecting the merchandise," Nudger said. "Like any other business."

"High-priced hustling *is* exactly like any other business, as long as you can turn off a certain part of yourself."

"And can someday turn it back on," Nudger said.

"Don't think I haven't considered that. I'll know when to quit."

"But will Marlyk let you quit?"

She shook her head at his naiveté. "Of course. This isn't a made-for-TV special, Nudger. Brad Marlyk doesn't wear a wide-brim hat and drive a black Lincoln. He's a family man with three kids. They all live in Ladue in a house with a pool and go on vacations together."

"Sure. Flawlessly respectable."

"Don't moralize. I didn't ask you to follow me and dig into my business. I hired you to help Jake."

"It's part of the same package, I'm afraid."

"I agree, to some extent. That's why I'm talking this way to you. I can't trust you unless I'm sure you trust me. We need to be honest with each other."

"All right," Nudger said. "I'm going to see Brad Marlyk."

"Why?"

"He and Jake know each other?"

"Not well, but they've met."

"Maybe they're closer than you think."

"Maybe. I guess that's the kind of thing I hired you to find out."

"How's life at the cabin?" Nudger asked.

"Jake seems reasonably content there for now. I can drive back and forth to work every day; it's a long commute, but I don't mind."

"And the bottle of Born Again?"

"Still sitting sealed on the mantel. Jake looks hard at it now and then, but he never touches it." There was pride in her voice.

"Want another hamburger?"

"No," she said, "I probably better start watching my diet more closely."

"Guess so," Nudger said.

He paid the check and left the diner with Helen, thinking of Jake Dancer in a sanctuary of relative calm surrounded by thick woods. The cabin was a tranquil place; a person could fish nearby, or hike, or simply sit on the screened-in porch and enjoy the breeze and the solitude. Nudger figured he'd done something right for Dancer and Helen and was glad.

He watched Helen drive away in the Datsun, then he walked east on Manchester toward his office. The sun was high and merciless, sending shimmering heat waves off the sidewalk. Nudger could feel the hot pavement through his softened soles. Sunlight glaring off the windshields of passing cars hurt his eyes.

A very large man was suddenly uncomfortably close beside him. Nudger's ear was tickled by warm breath and he smelled the kind of antiseptic, wintergreen mouthwash dentists use. It made him think of gagging and shrill, hot drills. Nauseating.

"Don't look at me, Nudger. Cross the street or you'll become part of the sidewalk."

Persuasive talk. Nudger's stomach drew tight and he stared straight ahead. "Should I use the crosswalk?"

"'Course. We don't wanna jaywalk and commit a misdemeanor."

Nudger thought of telling him his breath should be a misdemeanor, then he decided this wasn't the time. He hoped the guy hadn't just come from root-canal treatment that had put him in an ugly mood.

On the other side of Manchester, the big man directed Nudger to the entrance of K-mart's spacious lower-level garage. They walked to a shadowed corner where few cars were parked. Their footsteps echoed. It was cool in there, and damp. Nudger felt as if he were in a cavern. Or a tomb.

He couldn't help sneaking a peek at the big man. Though he couldn't be sure in the dimness, he thought it might be the larger

of the two men who'd beaten Dancer downtown and been scared
away. The one who'd so skillfully wielded the knife. Great!

"You know where Jake Dancer is," the man said softly. "Now
I want to know."

Oh, boy! Client protection time. This was the shit part of
Nudger's job, and this was the moment he'd dreaded. Sell out or
check out.

He swallowed and said, "Nobody knows where Dancer is.
Probably not even Dancer a lotta the time."

A jumbo fist slammed into Nudger's ribs and he slumped against
a concrete pillar. The world tilted, whirled, then became stable
again but with a slight list.

"Question number two, Nudger: Where's Jake Dancer?"

Sounded like question number one to Nudger, but he said,
"This for the brand-new car?"

"For new teeth. Then we get into double jeopardy."

"Listen, I wish I could answer—"

Breath and spittle shot from Nudger as the fist caught him in the
stomach. Nudger hadn't had a chance to avoid it. The big guy had
the lightning moves of a bantamweight, but he hit like Marciano in
his prime.

"Your friend sick?" a voice asked.

Nudger squinted through his pain and saw a scrawny teenage
boy on a bicycle circling one of the posts in the garage. He was
pedaling slowly and the bike wobbled, but he had control.

"He sure is," the big man said. He bent close to Nudger. "Find
some other occupation, asshole," he whispered. "Sooner than immediately."

Nudger tried to tell him he didn't need vocational guidance from
goons, but he expelled something that sounded like "Aarghsh."

"You stay here with him while I run get a doctor," the big man
said to the boy on the bike. "It ain't serious; he does this every
once in a while, poor guy. From the war."

"Okay, mister, but it looks like you better hurry."

Nudger, braver now, struggled to remind the bone-crusher that he hadn't made good on the new-teeth threat, but instead he lost his B&L lunch on the concrete floor. Damn! He couldn't even taunt when he had the chance.

The big man jogged into the shadows, and Nudger worked hard at getting up but slumped back down to lean with his back against the pillar. He thought he might never be able to move.

His stomach was queasy again and his rib was pulsing with pain. He prayed that nothing was broken.

The kid on the bike wheeled over, dismounted, and bent down next to him. He looked like Michael J. Fox, only ugly. His narrow, pocked face was set in concern and fear. And something else.

He gingerly slid Nudger's wallet from his hip pocket, removed what little money was inside, and tossed the wallet in Nudger's lap as if it were something he'd rendered lifeless and worthless.

"Hope you get well soon," he said, and got back on the bike and rode away fast, his lean body whipping from side to side as he stood high on the pedals. The bike's tires made squishing sounds on the concrete almost until the kid was out of sight.

Nudger pressed his spine firmly against the pillar. He slipped his wallet back into his pocket and worked his way inch by inch to his feet. Then he stood still and breathed evenly, summoning enough strength to walk. A few cars came and went in the vast garage, but at the far, well-lighted area nearer the main entrance. Another galaxy.

After about ten minutes, he felt well enough to stumble out onto Manchester and make his way toward his office. It was only a couple of blocks, and the people who stared at him immediately looked away, probably assuming he was a drunk who'd started early. Worst kind.

Nudger didn't care what they thought. He was enraged. He envisioned himself bending over the limp, terrified boy who'd robbed him, squeezing the kid's skinny neck and demanding his money back. He'd make the little junior desperado pay, all right, then drag him home to his parents. Oh, how he wanted to meet that thieving kid again. No two ways about it.

But he wasn't so sure about the giant with the wintergreen breath.

10

Danny said, "There she is, Nudge!"

Nudger breathed in shallowly, so pain wouldn't flare in his bruised rib, and looked at "her." The owner of the Ford Granada had loaned the car to Danny so he could drive it into the city and show it to Nudger. Let the car sell itself. It was parked now in front of the doughnut shop, deep red and waxed to a high gloss wherever it wasn't rusty. It was rusty almost everywhere.

"Take her for a test drive, Nudge," Danny said. He sounded enthusiastic, as if he were working on commission.

"I don't know," Nudger told him. "I'm not up on my tetanus shots."

Danny's basset-hound eyes registered injury. "You ain't exactly used to a Mercedes," he said rather haughtily.

Nudger told himself to be more tactful. He walked around the Granada. The tires were okay; lots of squiggley little lines on them, anyway. He looked beneath the hood. He was no mechanic, so that told him nothing. A peek inside revealed the upholstery to be red and unripped. The brief inspection covered the extent of Nudger's automotive knowledge.

"Mrs. Fudge says for you to drive it a few days if you want," Danny said.

"Mrs. Fudge?"

"The elderly lady out in Kirkwood who owns the car."

"I do have someplace to go now," Nudger said.

Danny smiled and waved his arms like a used-car salesman making a pitch on late-night television. "So go, Nudge. Enjoy. The air conditioner feels like the North Pole in this baby."

That was mighty persuasive. Could be Danny should be selling cars instead of doughnuts. He and Nudger were probably both in the wrong business.

Nudger said good-bye to Danny, got in the Granada, and drove toward Partners Unlimited.

He was surprised by how well the Granada ran. The engine was smooth, the air conditioner practically spit ice, and the pickup pressed him back in the seat. The car wanted to be friends.

The main office of Brad Marlyk's escort service wasn't downtown where Nudger had followed Helen, but in a strip shopping center out on North Lindbergh, near the airport. It was an area of countless franchise restaurants and motels. Free enterprise run amok.

Nudger recalled that this shopping center had housed several massage parlors a few years ago, before changes in the law had forced them out of business or across the river to the east side. He wondered if Brad Marlyk had gotten his start in massage parlors. Marlyk had to have learned his business somewhere to be so successful; semirespectability was a fragile art.

When Nudger had parked the Granada and entered the surprisingly cool and plush reception area of Partners Unlimited, he was confronted by a thirtyish, garish woman behind a curved desk. She was forty pounds overweight, had long black hair, eyes made up like a raccoon's, and flaunted a very red mouth that twisted itself into a smile when she saw Nudger. The shade of her wet-look lipstick was almost exactly that of the Granada. She was dressed in white, but she was wearing too much makeup and jewelry to resemble a nurse.

Her smile didn't look very genuine. She said, "Help you?"

"Hope so."

The brass nameplate on her desk proclaimed her to be Muffy B. Blue.

"Is that your real name?" Nudger asked, pointing to the plaque.

"Sure. What's yours?"

"A. Nudger."

"What's the A stand for?"

"What's the B stand for?"

The darkly mascaraed eyes narrowed. "There someone you wish to see?"

"You mean like in 'A, B, C'?"

"What the hell is this? You a Groucho Marx fan or something?" Muffy B. Blue looked angry.

A short man with incredibly broad shoulders and a wasp-lean waist was poised in the doorway of an inner office, peering out at Nudger. He was wearing a neat gray suit, had razor-cut blond hair, and was handsome in a coarse-featured way, though his skin was pitted with scars from long-ago acne. If he'd been a big man his features would have appeared horsy, but his diminutive size and the suit lent him a kind of dapper air. A muscular jockey dressed for a night on the town. He said, "What's going on here, Muff?"

"Your receptionist just accused me of being a Marxist," Nudger said.

The man looked puzzled for a moment, then grinned with oversized, perfect teeth, taking on even more of an equine look. "Muff's not interested in anybody's politics," he said. "She doesn't even vote. I mean that."

Muffy said, "I dunno what he wants, Mr. Marlyk."

"I need to talk with you," Nudger said to Marlyk.

"Selling something?"

"Morning-after pills."

"Jesus, you're cute!"

"Actually," Nudger said, "I'm a private detective and I need to talk to you about a client."

"You're so ingratiating, how can I refuse?"

Nudger knew Marlyk would also prefer that the police not be brought into whatever Nudger wanted to talk about. If that was possible. Maybe a little money in Nudger's palm would preclude paying even more to someone on Vice. With offices in the county and city, Marlyk must have a lot of graft spread thin.

He led Nudger into a large office featuring a massive cherrywood desk. Marlyk walked lightly, with an athlete's grace and control. He was probably close to fifty, Nudger estimated, but in excellent condition. The kind of quick little man who'd wear you to a nub at handball and not get winded.

At Marlyk's invitation, Nudger sat in a comfortable gray velvet chair near the desk. He waited until Marlyk had sat down before saying, "Do you know a man named Jake Dancer?"

"Sure," Marlyk said. "He's a close friend of one of my employees."

"How well do you know him?"

Marlyk shrugged inside the elegant suit. "On a scale of what to what? I mean, he's been in here to pick up Helen—that's his friend—and Helen's brought him to a couple of company social functions."

"What kind of functions?"

"Cocktail parties, the company picnic . . ."

"You have a company picnic?"

"Sure. We're a tight group." Marlyk leaned back, picked up a gold ballpoint pen from the desk and rolled it between his fingers. "This is an honest, useful business, Mr. Nudger. I mean that. A traveling executive comes to St. Louis, finds it's to his advantage if he's accompanied by a beautiful woman to some business function or other, and we supply her. That's a power symbol to some executives. And you'd be surprised by the identities of many of our regular clients. They're important and influential people."

"A friend on the city Vice Squad tells me you also occasionally supply prostitutes."

Marlyk gave a neighing kind of chuckle and flipped his head to the side; he really did resemble a miniature stallion. "Your friend's wrong. This kinda business, you always hear loose talk." He dropped the pen onto the desk and sat forward. "So who's your client? Jake Dancer?"

"No."

"You gonna tell me who?"

"No."

"What, then? Dancer done something wrong?"

"Somebody tried to beat him up a few nights ago."

Marlyk pursed his lips over his long teeth. A jet airliner landing or taking off at Lambert International Airport flew low overhead, its thunder shaking the gilt-framed wall hangings. "Guy like Dancer, that's bound to happen. He seems a fine young man, and I mean that, but he's got his problems."

"Problems?" Nudger asked.

"With booze, maybe with drugs. And with gambling. Somebody beat on Dancer, it probably had to do with a gambling debt. The only luck the poor dumb bastard has is in love. Helen Crane's good for him. I mean that. She'd be good for anyone."

Apparently Marlyk meant everything he said. Or maybe just everything he said he meant. "You know any of the gamblers Dancer owes?" Nudger asked.

Marlyk shook his head. "I couldn't help you there. I don't bet on anything unless it's rigged in my favor. And that's not gambling."

"Has Dancer ever mentioned any names you recognized?"

"Not that have to do with gambling. He knows half the bartenders in town, though, some of them running handbooks, so it wouldn't be hard for him to get a bet down." Marlyk hunched his body over the gold pen, and with the forefinger of his right hand rolled it across the desk and up against a glass ashtray. Like a small boy playing with a toy. He was probing around in his mind for words. "Dancer's a likable fella, Nudger, and I'd like to help him with whatever kinda trouble he's in. I mean that. The guy's friendly as an overgrown puppy that's known pain. He makes you want to help him. It's a shame to see a kid like that get sucked into the bottle."

"Has Helen Crane ever mentioned anything that might hint at why Dancer's taken to drink?"

"No. But I don't see Helen all that often. Most of our work's done by phone. The clients call, and we contact our employees and supply them with lists of appointments. And who knows why anybody like Dancer goes lush? Even the psychiatrists and social workers can't answer that one."

The intercom buzzed and Muffy's voice told Marlyk he had an urgent phone call on line four. Nudger suspected the message was prearranged, the loyal secretary helping to rid the office of a pest. The business world being devious.

Marlyk shrugged apologetically. Private call and all that. End of conversation.

Nudger stood up. "You've been a help, Mr. Marlyk."

"Hey, I hope so," Marlyk said. "I really mean that."

He didn't get up as Nudger left.

As he passed through the anteroom, Nudger wriggled his eyebrows and pretended to flick ashes from a cigar, but Muffy B. Blue ignored him except to glance up and murmur "Asshole."

She didn't have to tell him she meant it.

When Nudger got back to his office there was a message on his answering machine asking him to call Helen Crane if it was before two o'clock. After two, Helen's softly modulated voice appealed, would Nudger meet her at the zoo, where she'd be in or around the elephant house until about four?

Nudger looked at his watch. It read 11:05 and it had stopped. Hours ago.

He picked up the phone and used a pencil to peck out the number for time and temperature. After a cool feminine voice assured him his old age would be glorious if only he opened an IRA account at the leading downtown bank, he was informed that it was 3:29 and the temperature was ninety degrees at the airport.

Nudger hung up the phone and headed for the zoo, where it was probably hotter than the airport. The elephant house, huh? If he remembered correctly, that was sort of air-conditioned, but still too warm on most summer days. Not an elephant alive used deodorant.

As he pushed open the door to the street, a bead of sweat dripped off his chin onto the back of his arm. Grateful he didn't have fur, he wondered what the polar bears did in this kind of weather.

Too many creatures in this world were forced to adapt to hostile environments.

11

The bears at the zoo had the kind of setup where they could be inside or out. They were provided with a miniature lake and some phony rock formations outside, but inside it was cool. The kids and the sweat-stained tourists with their cameras slung around their necks saw the neatly printed signs that indicated the bears' Latin names and habitat, but no bears. *Ursus gonnus.*

It was far too hot to be walking around the zoo, anyway. Nudger figured the bears were smarter than the people who kept craning their necks to catch a glimpse of them; somewhere along the line Darwin had gotten it wrong.

Nudger trudged up the asphalt hill to the elephant house, amazed at how crowded the zoo was for a weekday. Several kids trailing spilled popcorn, zoo balloons on strings, and screams ran past him at a flat-out pace that defied the heat. An overweight, florid woman who looked about to keel over with a stroke chased after them, calling "Sparky! Sparky, damn it!" A guy who looked like a weightlifter ambled by with his preschooler son on his shoulders; both of them wore sleeveless T-shirts and blue Cubs baseball caps. Probably down from Chicago for the series with the Cardinals. Nudger elbowed his way toward the concrete steps and wondered how many people at the zoo were from Chicago. Maybe the bears were only smarter than Chicago baseball fans.

The elephant house smelled like the inside of a spare tire. It wasn't as crowded in there. Elephant sounds rose over the murmur of zoo-goers: a snort and sigh, a ponderous shuffling of tree-trunk legs, the low rasp of rough, rough hide scraping concrete, the clank of heavy chains. Everything but an outright loud trumpeting of the sort heard in Tarzan movies.

Helen was standing near the other end of the long building, looking above some kids' heads into one of the oversized stalls. She was dressed in a cool-looking white dress with a red belt, and red shoes with medium heels that allowed her to walk in reasonable comfort. Even from a distance Nudger noticed that her legs were better than the elephants'. She looked too dressed up for the zoo, but then all kinds of people wore all kinds of clothes here, adapting according to metabolism to the changeable St. Louis climate.

She saw Nudger approaching, smiled her placid, restful smile, and said, "Thanks for showing up."

"I'd never forget an appointment at the elephant house."

She glanced back toward the stall and Nudger looked in the same direction. Three large elephants were standing facing the crowd, their front legs chained together animal to animal. Now and then the heavy chains would clink in a kind of rhythm, and the trained mammoths would go into a subdued sort of dance and swing their trunks and sway massive bodies in synchronization, reacting to their training for the daily elephant shows where they performed to music at the command of a trainer. It was hypnotic to watch.

"People react that way sometimes," Helen said, "feel the rhythm and go into their number, not even realizing it." Nudger knew she was thinking of Jake Dancer.

"Why are you here?" Nudger asked.

"It's cool. And I like elephants."

"I mean, why here at the zoo in the first place? It's cool in air-conditioned bars and restaurants, too, and it doesn't smell like pachyderm."

Helen looked away from the elephants and her eyes met Nudger's. There was a kind of low-voltage electricity in those gray eyes. Low-voltage but high-amperage, able to jolt. "I'm here to meet a client," she said. "He always meets his dates at the zoo. Has this thing about animals. Watching them gets him in the mood, he says."

"Sounds dangerous as well as kinky," Nudger said. He wondered what exactly went on after the dates at the zoo.

"He isn't dangerous. All the regular clients are screened by Mr. Marlyk. It'll be the zoo, then the Omni Hotel, then back home to his wife and kids in Chicago."

Hmm, Chicago again.

Nudger had to ask. "What kind of animals does this guy like to watch?"

"Chimps. I'm supposed to meet him in half an hour in the primate house."

Nudger wondered how a man could be excited by watching chimpanzees, but then he'd never really studied them closely.

"Cats," Helen said. "The big cats turn me on. The way they pace and stare at people, and all that power ripples under their smooth coats. I like lions, tigers, but not as much as panthers. Panthers are definitely sexy." Nudger thought she might be putting him on, but he wasn't sure. She gave him a feline glance of her own. "You like to watch cats?"

He nodded. "Tabbies, sometimes. With yarn."

"You're a dog person, I suspect."

"That's me." He hoped she wasn't being personal.

One of the elephants swung its trunk and knocked a metal pail clanking down into the moat that separated humans from the other animals. The kids in front of Nudger and Helen hooted and laughed. The elephant rolled a giant eye at them, unperturbed by the joke. Actually sort of bored. It had seen it all before, dented other buckets. Hell, it probably tossed buckets into the moat for fun when nobody was around.

Helen said, "I've been thinking. I'm worried about Jake."

"That's why you hired me."

"I mean, more worried than I was this morning. He'll get jumpy out there in the cabin."

"His drinking?"

"No. The bottle of Born Again is still sealed. Or was when I left him this morning."

"Is there anything in particular that might put him on edge?"

She shook her head; her blond hair was pinned up off her neck today, a beautiful honey color against the drab gray of the elephant house. "This'll sound daffy," she said, "but I think maybe it's his being in the woods. Jake's a city dweller and has been all his life except for his stretch in Vietnam. Maybe, in this kind of weather, with all the heat and humidity, being in the middle of the woods will remind him of the jungle, of his experience in the service."

Nudger considered that. It was possible. It was more likely that Dancer had drinker's jitters and needed action and alcohol. It wasn't easy for a guy like Dancer to stay on the shelf when the world was spinning by outside and he wanted things and wasn't sure what they were. When he was scared and there was no one, *no one*, he thought he should include in his troubles.

"I talked to a girlfriend," Helen said, "and she's going out of town for a week and says Jake can use her apartment. It's way down in Mehlville, where Jake doesn't hang out and shouldn't run into anybody he knows. I mean, he might be able to get out now and then, or at least look out the window and see some traffic and people. I think he's more likely to stay put there."

Mehlville was a southern suburb of St. Louis, twenty minutes from downtown; Nudger wasn't sure it was far enough away to ensure Dancer's safety. Helen was talking as if it were New Delhi. "Who's this girlfriend? The one with the apartment."

"Marge? She works at Partners Unlimited, but she's got a job for a week down in Florida on a boat."

"What kind of job?"

"Being Marge, is all."

"Oh. Have you known her long? I mean, do you think it's safe to confide in her?"

"Well, we never shared girlhood secrets, but we're friends. I thought it over before asking her about the apartment. And I didn't mention where Jake is now. She's one of the few people I trust, Nudger, and she'll be out of the state for a week or so anyway."

Nudger scratched his head and watched an elephant watch him. The elephant coiled back its trunk and scratched behind an ear.

"All right," Nudger said. "It'd be better than having him get cabin fever and disappear on us." But he wondered if maybe it would be safer for everyone if Dancer did drop completely out of sight for a while.

Helen smiled. "There's only one hitch, Nudger. Marge isn't leaving town until possibly day after tomorrow, so somebody needs to stay with Jake while I'm in the city, to keep him out of the bottle."

"A private detective you hired?"

She touched his arm. "The same. All you'd have to do is drive out in the morning, then back into town in the evening. Or you could just stay the night out at the cabin, sleep on the rollaway bed. It'd only be one night, maybe two."

"Guess it's okay," he told her, but he didn't like the idea. What he did like was the opportunity to study Dancer some more, to try to figure out what kind of clockwork made him tick so dangerously, like a bomb set to self-destruct no matter who tried to disarm it.

"Thanks, Nudger," Helen told him. She squeezed his arm this time. She really was grateful for his help. Really loved Dancer. There was a basic directness and pluck to her that was enduring, that would be there until she died no matter what other parts of her were destroyed by time or experience. Calmly, she leveled with herself and everybody else, and the hell with where it took her. Maybe that was what some people called character.

"I'll pack some things and drive out to the cabin in an hour," he told her.

She drew a long breath that made her breasts rise softly beneath the white dress. Nudger realized he'd drawn in his own breath and was holding it.

"I better get over to the primate house," she said.

God! Nudger thought.

She started to walk away and he grabbed her arm, stopping her, hoping he wasn't smudging the pure white material of the dress sleeve. It felt crinkly-clean in his grasp, something delicate and easily debased. "You sure this guy won't hurt you?" he asked.

"Positive. Some other girls gave me the story on him. He's a family man. And Mr. Marlyk knows his business and weeds out the dangerous kooks."

"There's still risk, Helen."

"Like in everything else."

Nudger released her arm and watched her walk away. The elegant sway of her hips beneath the white dress turned male heads and attention away from the elephants.

"Those are African elephants," an old man with watery blue eyes and very few teeth said beside Nudger. "You can tell by their ears. Indian elephants, they got them little ears like cabbage leaves."

"Didn't know that," Nudger said. He wanted to get out of there, now that Helen was gone. He felt a compulsion to walk over to the primate house and sneak a look at the monkey fan she was meeting, but the thought made him feel remotely ashamed, as if he were contemplating an invasion of privacy. And maybe he was.

The old guy next to him was encouraged by Nudger's response. Nice to run into someone who didn't know what you knew. "There ain't no tigers in Africa," the old man blurted out, spraying brownish saliva on Nudger. "Only India. You see 'em in all them safari movies, but they ain't a tiger in Africa except at zoos."

"I'll be damned." Old rascal knew about Africa and India, all right. Nudger turned and started out of the elephant house.

"Tiger's actually a friendly cat," the old fella said behind him. Nudger didn't believe that.

As he strode through the simmering zoo toward an exit, he thought about what he'd promised Helen. Remembered her calm gray eyes. Nudger saw himself as a gatherer of information. Sometimes he had to turn over a rock to find what he needed, and that could be dangerous; something he didn't expect might rear up and bite him. That was an occupational hazard. But he always refused bodyguard jobs, which was what this Dancer thing was turning into. Nudger was afraid of the people who scared people who needed bodyguards. He was afraid of whoever was threatening Jake Dancer.

But here he was, about to climb into his (maybe his) Granada and drive out to an isolated cabin to stay with an unstable man somebody thought of as a target. Insane. Would he have even considered it if the request hadn't come from beautiful Helen?

As he walked from the zoo he heard a seal yelp. From the direction of the aviary some sort of exotic bird let out three frantic screeches. Another beast, possibly a big cat, snarled lackadaisically.

Like the jungle, Nudger thought, closing his eyes for a moment and feeling the searing weight of the sun. An animal some distance behind him emitted a drawn-out, barking laugh. There was an unmistakable dark, primal humor in it that drilled to the bone.

Had to be a laughing hyena.

Had to be laughing at Nudger.

12

The Granada rode smoothly and kept Nudger cool on the way to the cabin. He had to admit he was growing fond of the car. After the balky little Volkswagen, it seemed particularly amiable and large as a Lincoln, and it had an impressive extension of shiny hood topped with a chrome ornament that gave the impression of prestige despite all the rust and the many miles on the odometer. Everything about the car felt right; machine befriends man.

He turned the air conditioner down a notch as he passed the roadside Burger Palace, then slowed the Granada. The franchise hamburger eat-and-run was his signal that he was near the turnoff. There was the staked wooden sign: MUDDY RIVER ROAD. Nudger made a right turn and the Granada's tires whined and ticked on the narrow, two-lane blacktop that was sticky from the heat. He followed Muddy River Road for a few miles, then turned sharply onto an even narrower dirt road.

Lush green woods pressed in around the car, and the ground began falling away as he neared the river. Stones bounced off the insides of the fenders, and deep ruts made for a rocking, rough ride, causing Nudger's stomach to feel hollow and queasy. He popped an antacid tablet, chewed absently, and studied the cabins he infrequently passed. Only their roofs were visible through the trees, a shingled peak here, a crooked stone chimney there. People in this area had a thing for privacy.

Then he spotted the familiar dark cedar-shake roof. He slowed the car to walking speed until he saw the dusty dirt driveway almost obscured by foliage, and made a right turn.

He was on more of a private road than a driveway, and more of an obstacle course than a private road. A good test for the Granada's suspension. For the suspension of a military tank.

There was a lot of creaking and clunking from the car's undercarriage, but it plowed on, jostling Nudger so violently he had to concentrate to keep his grip on the steering wheel. One of the windows began a loud rattling in its metal frame.

Finally the Granada rocked around a dipping bend, and the cabin was in front of Nudger.

He parked the car near the plank front porch, waited for the haze of dust to settle, then climbed out into the sun-dappled, late-afternoon heat. There was a rustling sound off to his left. A small brown rabbit bounded away, trapped in the coiled constriction of its hop, and disappeared into the woods.

The cabin was an A-frame with a steeply sloping roof and windows only in front and back. Nudger clomped up onto the porch and called, "Dancer? Jake?"

No answer. A huge black crow squawked at him from a tree behind the cabin; that was the only sound.

It was possible Dancer had heard the car approaching and was staying out of sight. Though Helen had told him Nudger was coming, he'd have no way of knowing who was driving the Granada.

"Dancer? Me, Nudger!"

Nudger pounded on the door.

After almost a minute had passed, he tried the knob, found the door unlocked, and pushed inside. The hinges creaked as if they belonged on a haunted mansion rather than a modern little A-frame hideaway.

The place was hot, the air unmoving and stale. Where Nudger stood he could see the entire single room of the cabin, black vinyl sofa and chair, braided area rug with an Indian design, rough-hewn coffee table, parchment-shaded lamp, stone fireplace with a large half-log for the mantel. The log was cut evenly down the center and sanded to form a flat surface on top. Toward the back of the cabin were a small sink and stove and an oak table. Nudger couldn't see all of the sleeping loft, only the front portion and the corner of the bed.

"Dancer?"

He crossed the room and slowly climbed the thick wooden steps to the loft. If Dancer was up there, he was baking, because the temperature had to be over a hundred near the peak of the cabin's high roof.

Nudger half expected to find Dancer sprawled on the bed, and was listening for the sound of breathing as he climbed.

He heard breathing, but only his own, tense and raspy with effort.

The loft was empty. The bed, with its quilted coverlet and brass headboard, didn't appear to have been slept in. The tiny, slope-ceilinged room was heavy with heat and silence and the sharp scent of cedar. A brown spider crossed the floor and eased into a crack between the planks. A wasp droned steadily, high in the angle of the roof; it liked the heat.

Nudger looked at the bed, thought about Helen, and went back down the stairs to where it was cooler.

But not much cooler. He went over to the window unit on the north side of the cabin and switched it on high. Then he stood in the cool breeze for a while, staring at the door and waiting for Dancer to come out of hiding and walk in. "Sorry," Dancer would say, "but I gotta play it careful, Nudger." Or maybe he'd tell Nudger it was his, Nudger's, turn to hide while people searched for him. Some childhood games didn't change much; they only got more serious.

Five minutes passed and no one came through the door.

Ten minutes.

Nudger noticed the bottle of Born Again bourbon on the log mantel and walked over to it.

Still sealed, as Helen had said. So Dancer had probably left the cabin sober. But maybe in search of a drink. He might sneak a drink someplace rather than let Helen see that he'd opened the bottle on the mantel, the one that was supposed to be drunk from only after his debts and all their troubles were cleared away. The bottle of cheap booze gleamed with an odd beauty, catching the brilliant light streaming through the front window. An amber promise of a future without fear.

When an hour had gone by, Nudger locked the cabin behind him, climbed in the Granada, and drove back to Muddy River Road. Dancer was on foot, so someone surely would have seen him if he'd left the area of the cabin. Maybe he was still walking, on the highway with his thumb out for a ride, only minutes from the cabin turnoff.

At a tiny liquor store and service station, Nudger described Dancer and asked the hard-faced, mustached old woman behind the counter if she'd seen him that day. She said no and went back to watching a country-western variety show on a portable TV with a screen about the size of a matchbook. Johnny Cash was singing "Orange Blossom Special," but his voice from the tinny little speaker sounded like Dolly Parton's.

Nudger drove down the highway to Burger Palace, glad to get away from the country music. He was a blues man, but still he couldn't shake Cash's somber voice from his mind. The guy wasn't so big in the business for nothing.

Burger Palace was clean and cool, all shiny steel and orange plastic. Nobody was at the counter, but about half a dozen teenagers lounged in a corner booth, while a sad-looking man in overalls and a greasy white T-shirt ignored them and munched a hamburger a few tables away.

"Help ya?" a pimply teenager behind the counter asked. He had slicked-back blond hair, a nose like a pig's, and the name Fred sewn onto his gray and orange Burger Palace uniform. There was at least one of him at every burger joint.

"Has a guy been in here recently, average height, dark hair, nice-looking? He'd be sweating from walking a long way, maybe just wanna use the phone."

"Not as I can remember," Fred said. His little blue eyes

gleamed with sudden interest and suspicion. "How come you're looking for him?"

"He's my brother," Nudger said. "He was in an accident about three years ago, and every now and then he forgets where he is."

"Jeez! Want I should call the highway patrol?"

"No, no," Nudger said. "We like to keep this in the family, not raise a ruckus."

Fred nodded, understanding. Nobody liked a ruckus. "Let's ask Norb," he said, and swiveled his head toward an open door behind the counter. "Norbert!"

Norbert was the manager, and had been trained where all fast-food-franchise managers were indoctrinated. He had the polyester slacks, the short-sleeved white shirt, and the gaze of perpetual irritation above a pasted-on smile. And he wore the tie, the askew red tie that was never totally unknotted, only loosened enough to be slipped over the manager's head each night and slipped back on each morning and tightened so that the narrow end hung longest. Norbert went with Fred; they were a set.

Nudger repeated Dancer's description to Norbert, who listened attentively, as if there might be hidden meaning between Nudger's words, then shook his head. "Never seen the man," he said firmly. A decisive guy. Managers' training again.

"I seen that mother," the teenage black cook behind the serving counter yelled out. Burger Palace had it all.

"Corky," Norbert the manager said officiously, "take time out from them fries and talk to the man. He's looking for his brother."

Corky walked out from behind both counters and approached Nudger. He was about six foot three and weighed around ninety pounds. "Dude didn't look like he'd be your brother," he said to Nudger.

"Half brother, actually," Nudger said.

Corky smiled. He had a gold eyetooth. He didn't believe Nudger was telling the truth but didn't care. "Man come in here about two hours ago," he said. "Got a large cola to go, said make it with plenty of ice."

"Yeah," Fred said, "I remember now!"

Corky glanced at him and flashed that eyetooth.

"He use the phone?" Nudger asked.

"Naw," Corky said, "he stood there by the door for a while, sippin' soda through his straw, then went on out to the highway. I seen him trying to thumb a ride while he was walkin' backward, then he went on outa sight." He looked over at Norbert. "That's all I seen, 'cause I was whippin' up some specials for the supper business."

Nudger saw the specials lined up under the heat lamp in a sickly glare that made their wrappers look yellow. "You don't know if he got a ride?"

"No way to know, man, I be busy."

"Which direction was he walking?"

"That way," Corky said, pointing in the direction of the city.

"You sure?"

"You bet."

So there it is, Nudger thought. A nifty bit of detective work, only too late. Not much satisfaction in that.

"Okay," Norbert said. "Couple of cars at the drive-up window." Norbert was being decisive again.

When Corky and Fred had bustled back to work, he told Nudger he was glad he could help him, though he hadn't helped at all. Norbert would go far in the burger biz, Nudger decided.

He thanked all concerned and went back out into the heat, relieved to be away from the mingled smells of pine disinfectant and cooking grease.

On the drive back to the city, Nudger watched for Dancer but didn't see him. He knew he should have driven to the cabin directly from the zoo and not stopped by his apartment. Probably shouldn't have left Dancer alone in the cabin at all. The people stalking Dancer weren't amateurs. Some bodyguard. Helen would be crazy about this. She should have hired the guy who liked monkeys.

13

"Where've you been all day?" Claudia Bettencourt asked Nudger, as he let himself into her apartment with his key. She was dressed up and he thought she was getting ready to go out, but as she kicked off her high-heeled shoes and worked the clasp on her gold necklace, he realized she'd just returned home. He hoped she'd had a bad time on a date with Biff Archway.

"Where have *you* been?" he asked.

She didn't answer. Instead she crossed the living room, unzipping her dress as she walked; she was lean and graceful and the play of her hips beneath the loosened material caused a distinct tightening in Nudger's groin. Her slender bare back was a rich brown; had she been going to one of those tanning salons? Flirting with skin cancer? Nudger would have to ask her about that, but not now. She might have spent the weekend on a beach somewhere with Archway, and Nudger didn't want to know about that.

He and Claudia, at her insistence and that of her analyst, were trying to get used to the arrangement whereby she could go out with other men, and Nudger, if he so desired, could keep company with other women. Claudia claimed she needed her new freedom to recover fully from her disastrous marriage to the despicable Ralph Ferris.

Nudger hated Ralph Ferris even more than he hated Biff Archway, but not by much. So he'd finally agreed to continue their romance under Claudia's conditions, but he wasn't sure how long he could live with the arrangement.

Archway, the all-American type who taught at the girls' high school where Claudia taught English, also coached the basketball

team. Unnaturally healthy and handsome, he was a martial arts
master, a spiffy dresser, and had about him the air of the college
football all-star who'd kept himself in peak condition into middle
age.

A fella too good to be true.

So Nudger had quietly checked into Archway's background.
He'd been an all-star receiver at Kansas State, and voted best-
dressed athlete on the team. He was in peak condition. Chesty, jut-
jawed kind of guy for whom women automatically developed
round heels. The world was a comfortable place for Biff Archway.
The bastard.

Like a late-blooming sixties flower child, Claudia had proclaimed that she needed to "find herself." Archway had become
her "other men" and was part of that process. Meanwhile, Nudger
often woke up at night wondering just what Biff Archway was
doing at that precise moment.

Well, whatever Claudia was doing these days, or nights, she
wasn't attempting suicide.

He walked into the kitchen, opened the old round-cornered refrigerator, and got out a cold can of Busch beer. Claudia had the
air conditioner on in the living room but not in the kitchen, and it
was warm in there. Nudger popped the tab on the can, feeling cold
beer fizz out and trickle between his thumb and forefinger, then he
hurried back into the living room.

He sat on the long sofa and sipped his beer, glancing around the
apartment. It was an old and spacious high-ceilinged place on
Wilmington in South St. Louis, with steam radiators, patched plas-
ter, and stained-glass windows flanking a bricked-up fireplace.
Tonight it was neat and clean except for a few magazines tossed
onto one of the chairs by the front window; their four-color pages
were spread and kinked, and they vaguely resembled bright birds
that had crashed. The floor lamp near the cluttered chair was on,
throwing soft light through its yellowed, fluted shade. It was the
lamp Claudia left on when she was away from the apartment at
night. The air smelled of lemon-scented furniture wax. There were

no damp rings on the coffee table, the cushions on the furniture were squarely arranged, and the ashtrays were clean. No sign of Biff Archway.

Claudia returned to the living room. Though it was only a few minutes past ten, she was wearing a knee-length tan robe and was barefoot. She padded over and sat next to Nudger on the sofa. He wondered if she expected him to spend the night, maybe trump Biff Archway for a change.

Biff Archway. Jesus, he had to stop thinking about Biff Archway! The guy would probably soon die of a strong heart anyway. Or maybe too powerful an immune system or softening of the arteries. "Excessive health," the death certificate would read. Too much wheat germ could kill.

Nudger looked over at Claudia's lean profile: dark hair, firm mouth and chin, nose too long but very straight. There was a quiet nobility about her, as if she'd stepped down from a medieval painting in a museum and into the real world. She turned to him and focused warm dark eyes on him; an old master would have had a tough time capturing the strange combination of whimsy and sadness in those eyes. It was as if she'd just been told a good joke and a bad piece of news. "Still don't want to talk about your day?" she asked.

Nudger took a long pull of beer. It stung his throat, made his voice slightly husky. "I've spent most of it in bars," he said. "Not drinking."

He told her everything then. About Helen Crane and Jake Dancer and the big man with the powerful punch and equally powerful breath. About how Dancer had disappeared from the cabin and Nudger had spent most of the evening going from place to place asking about him. No one had seen Dancer but they all wished him well and hoped whatever troubles he had would fade away. He was such a great guy, likable and good-hearted. Could charm the skin off and then back on a snake, Dancer.

"So who'd want to kill this saint?" Nudger asked.

Claudia said, "I don't know. Maybe it's what you think; he

owes someone money and can't pay, and that someone wants to make an example out of him in case other debtors might get the idea they don't have to pay either.''

"That's possible," Nudger said. "I suppose even likely. It's been the plot of a lot of late-night movies.''

"Life imitating art," Claudia said. "It happens.'' She crossed her slender legs beneath the tan robe, causing the material to part for a moment and reveal smooth thigh. Nudger's eyes sent a signal to his groin. Groin said thanks. "You think this Helen Crane is a sexy number?'' Claudia asked.

"I think she's in love with Dancer," Nudger said, but he was also thinking it wouldn't hurt anything if Claudia got a little jealous. Let *her* suffer; let *her* wake up at night and wonder. That element of justice might cause her to reconsider her position on this matter of mutual freedom. Possibly she already had regrets. Too bad for her.

"If you're attracted to her," Claudia said, "maybe you should act on it.''

Nudger leaned away from her, dumbfounded. "Are you kidding? This is a professional relationship. And I told you she's crazy about the guy I'm trying to find.''

"You also said she was a high-class prostitute; why not extend your professional relationship? You and she could be each other's clients.''

Nudger laughed. He didn't know if she was serious. Maybe she didn't know. How did he get into such a confused affair? How had the world come to this?

She smiled and said, "Let's go to bed.''

So she'd been joking. He guessed. He resented what she'd said anyway. "Where were you tonight?'' he asked.

"Went to a spaghetti dinner at the school. After the PTA meeting.''

"See Archway?''

"Yeah. But he left early with Myra the field hockey coach.''

Nudger recalled meeting coach Myra. "The woman with the big hips and muscular forearms?"

"That's the one."

"They seem suited."

Claudia leaned sideways and kissed Nudger on the cheek. Nudger felt like a substitute put into the game for Biff Archway. She raised her body and probed his ear with her tongue. Her robe parted again. More leg. Suddenly he felt first-string.

She got up and walked into the bedroom. He followed as if on a leash. Pathetic.

Claudia had switched on the window unit and the bedroom was cool. She was nude beneath the robe, and already lying on top of the covers when Nudger finished undressing and lay down beside her.

He stroked her smooth thighs and stomach, her teacup-size breasts with their ripe brown nipples. Sometimes he imagined those breasts swollen and nurturing his child. Strange turn of mind for a fortyish veteran of a bad marriage. What might it mean?

Claudia rolled halfway onto him, tight against his side, and began licking his chest, rubbing her cheek against the dark hair that grew thick up near his throat. Nudger encircled her with his right arm and caressed the curve of her firm buttocks and the small of her back. She bit him playfully on the chest. He heard her soft, throaty moan, and the silk rustle of their flesh as she snaked a leg up along his. The bedsprings creaked. His blood was pulsing in his ears. The phone was ringing.

Phone?

She rolled away from him and pulled the receiver from its cradle with a clatter, then managed a breathless hello.

"Yes," she said firmly after a moment. "Fine. Yes, he's right here. I'll, er, call him." She handed the receiver to Nudger.

"Hammersmith," she whispered.

Nudger held the receiver to the side of his head, not quite touching his ear. He glanced down at his flagging manhood and thought about hanging up the phone. Or having Claudia tell Hammersmith that he'd left the apartment without her realizing. He vowed not to let Hammersmith break the mood, spoil what was going on here.

Hammersmith must have heard him breathing into the receiver. "Nudge?"

"Yeah?"

"Wanna see a dead woman?"

14

The part of the morgue they were in was cool. Nudger figured this was one time he'd just as soon be somewhere else and too warm. He flinched. Looked.

The dead woman was about the size of the one pulled from the Mississippi near McDonald's. She lay on a steel gurney with gleaming wire wheels. Gas that had built up in her tissues had been released beneath the overhead hood that some cops referred to as "the fart extractor," and there was little swelling. Still, the woman looked barely human; the river, and the things that lived in the river, had gotten to her.

"The ME estimates she was in the water at least a week," Hammersmith said. He fondled a cigar sticking out of his shirt pocket, as if he longed to light it and dispel some of the antiseptic odor of the morgue. For once Nudger would have been glad to see Hammersmith fire up one of the terrible greenish cigars. Toxic they might be, but they didn't smell of death.

Nudger stared at the woman's pale, ruined face and felt his stomach coil in on itself. He swallowed; it must have been loud enough for Hammersmith to hear.

"What about that, Nudge?" Hammersmith said, nodding toward the woman's flaccid, wrinkled breasts.

Nudger looked and at first didn't believe what he saw. There
was what appeared to be a large loop earring piercing the woman's
darkened and shriveled right nipple. At first he thought crazily that
it must be something the ME had put there for identification;
maybe a tag would be affixed to the ring.

Then Nudger saw that after penetrating the flesh of the nipple
the ring had been crudely clamped together so it was impossible to
remove without tools. An amateur job, nothing a doctor would do.
Not a sane doctor.

"Check out her back and sides, Nudge. That's not damage from
being a floater. It happened before death. She's been whipped.
Tortured."

"The ring through the nipple . . ." Nudger said.

"It's there so a dog leash can be clipped onto it," Hammersmith
said calmly. "Standard procedure among some of the very sick
who are into bondage; I've seen books that give instructions. The
ME says it was heated up before going in, so the wound was cau-
terized and didn't bleed. Sometimes Novocain's used. Sometimes
ice is held to the nipple beforehand to numb it, so there's actually
not much feeling. At first. Could be this is the next logical step
after pierced ears."

"Holy Christ!" Nudger's stomach twitched against his belt. He
felt not only revulsion but rage, and pity for the dead woman. No
human being, no matter how evil or misspent her life, deserved
what had been done to this woman; someone's daughter, sister,
wife, lover. What the hell was wrong with people, that made them
become monsters? "You think she was conscious while all that
was happening?"

"Let's hope not. Let's assume she was drugged up. But there's
no way to know yet. Maybe ever." Hammersmith came within a
quarter-inch of touching the dead woman's pale right wrist with his
pudgy pink forefinger. "See those marks, Nudge? She was bound,
possibly with wire. Gagged, too, I'd imagine, for the, er, operation."

"My God, who'd do something like that?"

"Oh, there are plenty of folks walking around out there capable of that kind of sadism. Look normal as you and me, they do. Well, me, anyway. I did my time on the Vice Squad, Nudge; I know."

"You hear about this kind of thing," Nudger said. "But you don't often see it. If you're lucky, you never see it."

"I've seen it, Nudge. Remember Lars Kovar?"

Nudger nodded. Kovar was a Vice Squad cop who'd been fired from the department a few years ago for allegedly torturing a teenage prostitute. There hadn't been enough evidence to prosecute, but there'd been enough for the Board of Police Commissioners to suspend Kovar indefinitely. He hadn't fought the decision.

"What he did to that teenager was just as bad as this," Hammersmith said. "She lived, but she's drawn into too much of a shell ever to testify against Kovar. Then there was that guy over in East St. Louis who tied his wife to a chair in the basement and set fire to her. And there was this S and M club out in Chesterfield that got out of hand. Way out of hand. That one was hushed up because the people involved had money and high-priced lawyers. Hell, a few of them *were* high-priced lawyers."

"How old was this woman?" Nudger asked. He didn't feel like listening to a litany of sex crimes. His stomach didn't need that.

"'Bout thirty." Hammersmith looked down dispassionately at the corpse. He'd become hardened to this kind of sight over the years, at least on the surface. He could disconnect a vulnerable part of his mind and not feel what Nudger was feeling. "She bobbed up like the other one, down on the riverfront. Near the Robert E. Lee restaurant, actually. Though not where anybody might spot her through a window and lose their expensive steak or lobster. Considerate of her. A guy on a passing tug noticed her, and the boat radioed her location."

"Two bodies surfacing at about the same spot," Nudger said. "Kind of odd."

"Suggests they might have been put in at about the same spot upstream," Hammersmith said.

He nodded to the bored-looking morgue attendant standing

nearby. The attendant, a thin, fiftyish, gray-haired man, himself
with a disturbingly cadaverous look, shuffled forward. Hammersmith said, "Thanks much, Larry," and started toward the
door.

Nudger gratefully followed Hammersmith. He'd been ready to
bolt from the place five minutes ago. He heard the wheels of the
gurney on the polished tile floor behind him; one of them had a flat
spot, or maybe gum on it, and bumped slightly as it rolled.

"You marking the two deaths down as homicides by the same
perpetrator?" Nudger asked.

"Not quite yet," Hammersmith said, "but I don't doubt it'll
come to that after the autopsy reports are compared."

They made their way outside into the thick, humid night.

Though it was past eleven o'clock, it was still oppressively
warm, probably around eighty degrees. The concrete downtown
held each day's heat and added it to the next day. Elderly people in
the old brick houses in the poorer sections of the city, most of
them without air-conditioning or even fans, and unwilling to open
their windows at night for fear of break-ins, found themselves living—and sometimes dying—in merciless brick ovens as the heat
built day after day.

But the air was better out on the street than in the morgue.
Hammersmith touched a lighter flame to the cigar now, sucking
and slurping noisily. The smoke drifted away slowly on the slug-
gish night atmosphere, as if some sort of magnetism were drawing
it toward the bright haze of vapor light at the intersection.

"Why did you want me to see this?" Nudger asked.

"You were there when we fished out the first body," Hammersmith said. "I thought you might as well see the second.
Maybe some case you're working on will pertain to this; maybe
you'll hear something useful as you stumble around town making a
nuisance of yourself."

Nudger didn't believe Hammersmith. The lieutenant liked to
subject Nudger to the gory side of police work, knowing about the

nervous stomach that had made it necessary for him to get off the force. Some friend.

"I think you're a sadist yourself," Nudger said.

Hammersmith surprised him. "Maybe. To some small extent. A cop can be affected by this kind of thing over the years. Like Kovar. A matter of degree, I guess. Opposite side of the coin and all that. But I'll tell you something, Nudge, I think it's a good idea you should stay tuned in on this end of detective work. I don't like seeing you take the danger of your job too lightly. Which you do sometimes, despite the fact you're no hero."

"Not this time," Nudger said. "I'm being plenty cautious. And what I'm working on has nothing to do with dead women in the river."

Hammersmith threw back his head, exhaled a huge cloud of smoke, and stared up at the few stars visible above the glare of the city. "Oh, you never know, Nudge. Einstein had a theory about how some time and place all parallel lines eventually meet."

"Neither of us'll live long enough to be in on that," Nudger said. "And I'm not likely to hear anything that'll help you with these two homicides."

A car passed traveling too fast, its tires humming on the still-warm pavement. Hammersmith turned his attention away from the mysteries of the universe and back to those more earthly and pressing. "But you'll keep the dead women in mind?"

"You've seen to it I won't be able to get them out of my mind," Nudger said. "Maybe ever."

Hammersmith smiled as if to say his methods might sometimes seem mad, but they worked. He was a man who understood parallel lines. Maybe, in his way, better than Einstein.

Nudger brushed aside a tiny white moth that kept trying to flit up his nose, said good night, and trudged through the heat toward the parked Granada. He was glad for the twentieth time since he'd been driving the car that it had air-conditioning, and he decided he'd see what he could do about being able to afford to buy it. He knew a guy who rebuilt old Volkswagens who might be interested in a quick cash deal for his old car.

He lowered himself into the Granada, started the engine, and sat back with the air conditioner blower on full-blast.

He stayed that way without moving for a few minutes before slowly pulling away from the curb.

Instead of driving back to Claudia's, he'd go to his own apartment. He'd lie alone perspiring in his own bed. He wouldn't touch the body of the woman he loved. Not tonight. He didn't want to touch flesh, after what he'd just seen. He'd sleep instead.

If he could.

15

"You don't mind my saying so," the bartender said, "you look like you could use some coffee this morning."

"Didn't sleep much last night," Nudger told him, scooting up onto a bar stool. Edgy's was the name of the place, in South St. Louis on Grand Avenue. It was long and narrow, with potted artificial ferns blocking the view out, and in, the front window. The bar itself was old, mahogany, and almost as long as the room. There was a line of red-upholstered booths along the opposite wall, a few small tables where space permitted, and red vinyl-covered stools along the bar. On one of the dark-paneled walls a dusty blue marlin was mounted on a plaque. It was big enough to have put up a hell of a fight, but a long time ago. The wall behind the bar was mirrored, reflecting shelves of various kinds of liquor; the morning sun found its way in between the bogus ferns and glinted off the mirror and bourbons and scotches and sent breathtaking tinted light in a rectangle over the floor and bar near the window. Stained glass in cathedrals cast that kind of magic illumination. The light picked up tiny fragments of broken glass on the scuffed tile floor.

"New in the area?" the bartender asked as he set a cup of black coffee on the bar in front of Nudger. The cup was white and chipped at the rim and wasn't on a saucer; it rested on a thin cork coaster with EDGY's lettered in fancy red script across it. There was a tiny nude girl perched on top of the s, swinging her legs. LOVE TO PARTY was printed above her head inside a comic-strip balloon.

"Not from the area at all," Nudger said. "I was by here last night but you were closed."

"Oh? Sorry. We had some trouble. Cream? Sugar?"

"Black's fine. What trouble?"

The bartender, a white-haired, wiry little guy in a red vest and candy-stripe shirt, gave a seamed, worldly smile and said, "You wouldn't be a cop, would you?"

"I would, but I'm not. Private investigator."

"You're kidding?"

"Seems that way sometimes."

The wiry little man wiped a hand on a towel behind the bar and extended it to shake. When Nudger gripped the hand, the bartender said, "My name's Billy Edgemore. Call me Billy. I own this place. I never met a private eye before. That I know of, anyways."

"We keep low profiles. I keep one of the lowest. My name's Nudger. The broken glass on the floor have anything to do with last night's trouble?"

Billy glanced in the direction of the glitter and his clear blue eyes narrowed. "Thought I'd swept it all up."

"You did a pretty fair job; sunlight's catching it or I wouldn't have noticed."

"Some glasses and bottles got broke in here about ten o'clock," Billy said. "No major deal. A few customers had an argument, is all."

Nudger sipped his coffee, burned his tongue; would he ever

learn? He'd talked to a bartender in a hotel lounge who'd said Jake
Dancer sometimes drank in Edgy's; Nudger had gotten here just
before midnight and found the door locked and a CLOSED sign
hanging crooked in the window.

"I'm trying to find Jake Dancer," he said. "You know him?"
Billy walked down the bar a few steps, came back, and nodded.
He had on a black bow tie and his hair was parted as if he'd used a
ruler; kind of guy who'd been dealing with the public a long time
and looking dapper was a habit. He seemed to decide he might as
well trust Nudger. Nudger knew why.

"You didn't call the police about your trouble," Nudger said.

"Saw no need," Billy told him. "Still see no need. Too much
trouble in a place like this, the neighbors and the merchants around
here'll raise hell, try to close me down. They can do it, too. The
law don't afford much protection for the tavern business. People in
a neighborhood get up a petition, and that can be all it takes. All of
a sudden I'm selling encyclopedias."

"The police have got better ways to spend their time than ha-
rassing you," Nudger said. "Probably."

Billy leaned with an elbow on the bar. "Jake Dancer was in the
middle of last night's trouble," he said.

Nudger put his steaming cup down on its coaster. "Did he cause
the trouble?"

Billy shook his head, then brushed back a lock of white hair
with a well-groomed but wrinkled hand; he was older than he appeared. "Naw. Jake was sitting at a table, sipping bourbon and
bothering nobody, when it started. Tell you the truth, I think he
was pretty well soused when he wandered in here about nine-
thirty. He sobered up in a hurry, though, when the two guys came
in and started rousting him."

"What two guys?"

"I never saw them before. Both of them were big, but one was
so big he damn near'd qualify as a horse. They sat next to Dancer
for a few minutes, talked, then Jake started to get up and the giant
guy tried to stop him by grabbing his shoulder. Jake swung a beer

bottle from the next table—full bottle, too—and broke it over the
guy's head. Big bastard blinked and grinned. Then the other guy
makes a grab at Dancer and all three are on their feet, along with
half a dozen of the regulars that like nothing so much as to brawl.
Fists and bottles commenced to fly. All this lasted less than a minute, but when it was over Dancer and the two big men was gone.
Somebody said Dancer ran out and the two that started all the
fighting chased after him." Billy shrugged and adjusted his bow
tie. "I closed the place then and spent some time cleaning up the
mess. Came in here at six this morning to finish. That's why I'm
open so early; figure maybe I'll make up for business lost last
night."

"So far you've sold a cup of coffee," Nudger said.

"Naw. That one's on me."

Nudger nodded his thanks and raised his cup in a mild toast.
"How well do you know Jake Dancer?"

"Well enough. Tell you the truth, I got a sort of soft spot for
Jake. He reminds me of my cousin Arnie who got killed in Vietnam. Jake was in Vietnam, you know."

Nudger nodded.

"So I got to know Jake," Billy said, "even lent him some
money now and then. He liked to talk to me, tell me his gripes.
Horses he'd picked wrong at the track, straights he'd thrown away
at poker. That sorta thing. Not his real problems."

"Real problems?"

"Sure. You know Jake for just a little while and you can tell
something's gnawing on his soul. I seen it before. Maybe it's his
wartime experiences spooking him, maybe something else. That's
something he never talked to me about. Guess he keeps it all to
himself, so he can watch it kill him from the inside. Like a rabbit
watching a snake close in and not being able to move away from
the fascination."

"You like him and seem to understand him. Ever tell him he
oughta get help?"

Billy shook his head and smiled sadly. "Naw. If I thought he'd listen, I'd tell him. But guys like Jake, they're on rails that carry them wherever they lead, and there's no use trying to talk them into jumping the track.''

Nudger tried another sip of coffee. Cooler. Strong. Good. But his tongue still hurt where he'd burned it. ''You're a fatalist, Billy.''

''Yeah, I guess. About people like Jake, anyways. Seen too many of them, is all. And it's a shame about Jake, 'cause he's one hell of a guy. Wouldn't hurt a rabid dog came after him. Kind of fella you want to help any way you can. The way I can help him is to let him run a bar tab he'll probably never pay, lend him a little cash now and again.''

''Tell him not to drink so much? Take life slower?''

Billy laughed softly without humor. ''You're wasting time telling somebody like Jake to slow down and cut back on the booze. That I know for fact. One reason we get along and he confides in me is I don't preach at him.''

''He ever mention who he owed money?'' Nudger asked.

''Hell, he owes it to lots of people. Bookies, loan sharks, his girl Helen. Plenty of people probably owe him money, too.''

''You know Helen?''

''Seen her a few times. Jake had her in here some months ago and introduced us. All woman. Maybe I shouldn't say it, but maybe too classy for Jake.''

''She's good for him,'' Nudger said.

''Oh, that I don't doubt. But is Jake good for *her*? I mean, it's like she's on board a sinking ship. He even mentioned he'd borrowed money from her employer. How's that gonna set when Jake can't pay him back?''

''Dancer borrowed money from Brad Marlyk?''

''If that's Helen's employer.''

A white van pulled up outside and a burly man in a sleeveless green T-shirt and stained white jeans swaggered in carrying a long, battered toolbox. He grinned and said, ''Heatin' up out there, Billy.''

"Beer's on me when you're finished," Billy said. He turned to Nudger. "One of my rambunctious customers tore up the plumbing in the restroom last night; Ernie here's gonna fix it."

"For the third time this month," Ernie said, still grinning. He had bad teeth, widely spaced, making him look like a sly jack-o'-lantern.

Billy went with Ernie to the scene of the crime, then returned a few minutes later to stand behind the bar again. From the back of the place came the sound of a toilet flushing several times, then the hiss of water running under pressure.

Nudger finished his coffee and thanked Billy for taking the time to talk to him. He slid down off the bar stool.

"I don't know what kinda trouble Jake's in now, what with a private cop asking for him, but I got to be a sorta father figure to him, and in a way I feel responsible for what he does. I think of him almost like he's a wayward son. A doomed one. If there's anything I can do to help him, you let me know."

"Sure."

"Or to help that girl Helen."

"Why do you feel responsible for her?" Nudger asked. "You hardly know her."

"Oh, I shouldn't even feel responsible for Jake," Billy said, "but fact is I do." He shot his sad, worldly smile over the bar. "Even feel a little responsible for what happens to you now, Mr. Nudger. For anyone tangled up in Jake's life. There's some people carry turmoil around with 'em like a suitcase. They get to where they're going, the suitcase springs open, and out flies turmoil like a horde of mosquitoes that agitates everyone. You know what I mean? That's how Dancer is. It's all his fault and yet it ain't. A damaged guy like Jake, when he goes, he doesn't sink alone. Best you should carry that thought."

"I'll carry it," Nudger said, and walked toward the brilliant sunlight beyond the potted too-green ferns.

Behind him the toilet flushed again.

16

Nudger was running cold water over his wrists in the half-bath off his office in Maplewood. Danny had told him there was a client waiting upstairs; Danny had sized her up, left the doughnut shop, and let her in, as he did most of Nudger's callers. Why not? What was she going to steal, his secondhand IBM typewriter? If there was something really valuable Nudger needed to take care of, he usually took it home with him to his apartment, or put it in his safety deposit box at Citizens' Bank. Better to have Danny let potential clients in off the street, or get them out of the doughnut shop, than to have them walk away. Better to lose a few paper clips than lose clients. Eileen had told him that once; sound advice from an enemy could be the best kind.

But this visitor was already a client.

Helen said, loud enough for Nudger to hear over the running water, "He phoned me last night, late. About one in the morning, actually."

Nudger turned off the water and dried his wrists and hands on a towel that said SHERATON. He felt cooler. Helen wasn't perspiring; Danny had switched on the air conditioner when he let her into the office. Gentleman Danny. Most of the doughnut shop smell was filtered from the office by now, but not enough to make it unnoticeable.

"What did he say?" Nudger asked, walking back into the office. He sat down behind his desk, causing his swivel chair to squeal. Helen winced slightly, caught off guard again. She looked cool, all right, sitting there with her smooth blond hair pinned up and her creamy arms showing beneath pink short sleeves. She was

wearing white cottony-looking slacks today. They were cut high
above her shapely ankles and were tied around the waist with a
thick, woven rope for a belt. She looked like a model ready to
pose on a sailboat in an expensive scotch ad. But here she was,
hooked on a guy who guzzled Born Again bourbon.

"He wouldn't tell me where he was calling from," she said.

Nudger swiveled this way and that. *Eeek! Eeek!* "Why'd he
leave the cabin?"

"He said he felt like it was getting smaller, about to close in on
him. Jake's not the type who can stay alone for long periods of
time anyplace, Nudger."

"Did he sound as if he'd been drinking?" Nudger asked.

"Yeah, he did. But he wasn't drunk when he phoned. I'm
positive of that. He knew what he was saying."

"Which wasn't much."

"Because he knew; he didn't have to keep explaining himself
like somebody who'd drunk a snootful."

"Why'd he call, then? What did he tell you?"

Her face softened; Nudger felt a pang of jealousy and wished he
hadn't asked. Sometimes talking to Helen was like talking to
Claudia. Pale Helen, dark Claudia. They were opposites, yet
strangely alike in ways that ran deep. "He said he just wanted to
let me know he was all right, and that he loved me."

"You think he's all right?"

"No. He sounded scared. Scared in a way that makes you want
to give up and let whatever you're afraid of go ahead and happen.
Get it over with."

Nudger thought about what Billy Edgemore had said earlier that
morning, about the rabbit and the snake. About that kind of deadly
fascination. Swiveling wider in the chair, he looked out the window at the sky beyond the buildings across Manchester. There
wasn't a trace of cloud against the blue. Not a wisp. There was
nothing in the sky but heat. St. Louis, the sultry city. And, like a
sultry woman, she had her seasons, and after the heat she could

wither you with a glance in winter. City of extremes. Could be the
weather made people do crazy things here sometimes.

Nudger swiveled back to face Helen squarely. "Ever hear of a
place called Edgy's in South St. Louis? A bartender name of Billy?"
Helen toyed with the rope ends dangling beneath her pink
blouse. Nautical erotic. "I was there a few times with Jake. I met
Billy. He seemed like a nice man."

"I think he is a nice man. And he sees himself as a sort of father
figure to Jake."

"I'm not surprised; sometimes I see myself as a mother figure.
Jake brings that out in people."

Nudger wondered why that was true. Maybe the human race
lived under the influence of the herd instinct and naturally felt pro-
tective of weak strays. A straggler like Dancer, there wasn't much
doubt he was in danger of falling prey to the lions trailing the herd.
Nobody—except for the lions—wanted that to happen, because
there was something of Jake Dancer in all of us. We could identify, and it made us uncomfortable. Dancer had lost the knack; he
could no longer pretend the world was the way he wanted to see it
and call it reality. That threatened everyone's reality, so they
longed to shelter Dancer, draw him back into the common delusion
and protection of the herd.

Nudger rocked forward in his chair and told himself to stop phi-
losophizing; it had gotten him into trouble a few times and he
didn't want it to happen again. "Anyway," he said, "this Billy
says Dancer borrowed money from Brad Marlyk."

Helen looked surprised, and Nudger was sure the expression in
her gray eyes was genuine. Surprised and a little angry. "Jake
never told me that."

"Oh?"

"I didn't think he knew Brad Marlyk well enough to approach
him for a loan. They only met a few times."

"That you know of."

"Apparently."

Nudger looked out the window again. Same blue void. Then a

pigeon flapped past. It dipped and soared up out of sight onto the roof directly across the street. Nasty. Rat of the air.

"Maybe Dancer owes more than we suspect," Nudger said.

"Maybe this, maybe that. The world's gotten kinda confusing these last few months."

"That's why you came to me in the first place," Nudger said, smiling, "to help make things clear." *Not to muck them up.*

"I guess they'd be even less clear now if I hadn't hired you."

Another maybe, Nudger thought. A big one.

"I'll ask Brad Marlyk about the loan," Helen said.

"It might be better if I ask him."

She thought about that for a moment, then said, "Okay."

Nudger said, "A couple of guys came into Edgy's last night and had a few words with Dancer. There was a brawl, and he ran from the place. They ran out after him. They sounded like the same two men I saw beating him downtown outside the Marriott."

Her eyes widened for a moment. In alarm and indignation. "Was he hurt?"

"No, not last night. He must have got away; he called you after it happened."

Helen bowed her head. Nudger thought she might begin to cry, but she only stared at the clean white rope end twisted around her fingers, as if she were contemplating tying a knot and didn't quite remember which end went through which loop. "Damn!" she said. "What's happening?"

"I don't know," Nudger said. "But I'll find out. I'll keep looking for Dancer. He can answer your question; he knows what's happening."

She looked bewildered, worried. "Does he?"

The phone on the desk jangled. Nudger tilted forward in his chair, picked up the receiver, and identified himself.

"Nudge," Hammersmith's voice said, "we got a problem."

Nudger felt his stomach threaten. It didn't like the tone of Hammersmith's voice. Not at all. "What kind of problem?"

"Claudia."

Nudger immediately thought of the dead women from the river. Had Claudia attempted suicide again? Had she succeeded? *Oh, Christ!* He tried to keep his voice level. "What happened?"

"She's in Room Two Fifty-two at Incarnate Word Hospital, Nudge. She'll be okay, but somebody handled her a little rough and scared her. That was the idea, to frighten her. They managed. She's been asking for you. I think you better drive down here soon as possible. I'll stay with her till you get here."

Nudger thanked Hammersmith, replaced the receiver, and stood up. His hands were sweating. His throat was constricted.

Helen saw the anguish on his face. "Something wrong?"

"Nothing to do with Dancer," he assured her. "Friend of mine got hurt."

"I'm sorry. Hurt seriously?"

"No, I don't think so." He wanted, very badly, to see Claudia as soon as he could.

Helen stood up from the chair in front of the desk, hoisting a gray straw purse by its long strap. She slung the strap over her shoulder with casual grace and precision, in the way of women with purses, lending the common maneuver style. "I hope your friend's okay."

"It'll work out," Nudger said, wondering if it really would. Feeling helpless.

They left the office together, detective and client, confused and scared about people they loved who were pursued by demons inside and out.

17

The room was pale green halfway up, even paler green the rest of the way to the square white ceiling. Claudia lay on her back in a bed next to a nightstand with a stainless steel top. There were a phone, a plastic pitcher and drinking glass on a tray, and a box of

Kleenex on the nightstand with one white tissue bunched on top of it like an elegant flower. The air smelled faintly of mint. Only partially concealed behind a beige cloth folding screen was the room's other occupant, a woman whose footboard chart identified her in large black letters as Rose Allstein.

As Nudger and Hammersmith approached Claudia, Rose peeked around the edge of the screen like a curious animal peering from concealment. "Hi," she said timidly, a friendly, round-faced woman with the starch taken out of her.

"Hi," Nudger said, and Rose leaned back out of sight.

Claudia opened her eyes when she heard him.

"Hi to you," she said.

"Hi," he told her.

Nudger saw Hammersmith part his lips to say "Hi," then catch himself. Enough was enough. Hammersmith got a cigar out of his pocket, stared at it, and put it back.

The lieutenant had met Nudger outside the hospital and assured him that Claudia wasn't badly hurt. He'd talked to the doctor since phoning Nudger; Claudia had been in shock not so much from her injuries as from her fright, and she wasn't as seriously injured as was first feared.

"I'm going home tonight," she said. She still looked scared, dark eyes haunted, as if fear had settled in to live in her forever.

Nudger saw no abrasions or bruises on her. He knew that might mean nothing, not if she'd been worked on by professionals. Internal injuries were the specialty of people like that. What had they done to her? Hammersmith hadn't said precisely. Nudger decided he wouldn't ask Claudia; he'd ask the doctor.

He leaned forward and kissed her forehead. It was cooler than the cool room. "How do you feel?"

She winked. "Feel me and find out."

Nudger smiled. He didn't figure she'd been molested sexually, joking that way. She'd meant to reassure him and she had. "How did this happen?" he asked.

She closed her eyes before speaking, as if that might help her to remember. "They knocked on the door—two men. I left the chain on and opened it partway. One of them said 'We're here to fix your plumbing,' and grinned, then the other one shoved in on the door, and the next thing I knew I was on the floor and they were beating me."

"With what?" Hammersmith asked.

"Their fists, that's all. Stooped over me. And they were so . . . methodical. The big one hit me in the stomach so I couldn't breathe, couldn't make a sound. Then they started hitting me in the sides and back, taking their time. Every once in a while one of them hit me in the stomach or chest again so I couldn't catch my breath." A tear worked its way out from under her tightly clenched eyelid, broke free, and tracked down her cheek. More tears followed, as if a barrier had been breached.

Claudia was silent.

"They didn't hit her hard," Hammersmith said, "according to the doctor. Just hard enough. Nothing broken, Nudge."

"Then they burned me," Claudia said.

Nudger tried to fight down his anger, his own fear, his burgeoning compulsion for revenge. A part of his mind knew that kind of provocation might be the object of what had been done to Claudia. Somebody sending him a message through her, trying to prompt a reaction of rage and then fear. "Burned you where?"

She kept her eyes closed and nodded her head to indicate her chest. "There. On the left breast. With a cigarette. They just lifted my blouse, yanked my bra so the strap broke, and held a lit cigarette there."

"Goddamn them! How many times?" Nudger was aware of Hammersmith gripping his upper arm, squeezing. Somebody walked past in the hall, soft-soled shoes making squishing, squeaking sounds on the waxed floor.

"Only once," Claudia said. "Then they heard a noise down in the vestibule and got out of there. Lem Akers came home. That's what they heard and what scared them away, or they'd have done more to me, I'm sure." Lem Akers was the seventy-nine-year-old retired ironworker who lived alone in the apartment adjoining Claudia's. "The big one was laughing when he held the cigarette ember on me," Claudia said, "watching me intently like I was something he was using for an experiment. Enjoying the results." She swallowed, opened her eyes, and Nudger saw raw terror like pinpoints of black light deep in the pupils. He felt as if he were seeing to the back of her skull. "I couldn't even cry out! . . ."

He kissed her again, on the lips, tasting the salt of tears, and stepped back from the bed. He waited a moment before speaking again, not trusting his voice to be steady. "Bastards! What else did they say to you?"

"Nothing. Only when they broke the chain lock off the door frame, that 'plumbing' wisecrack. Made me think they were going to rape me, and they might have. After that all I heard was their breathing, and the big one laughing. It was a high, phlegmy kind of laugh. Ugly." She shuddered.

"Ever seen either of them before?" Hammersmith asked.

"I don't think so. No, I'm sure I haven't."

Nudger felt a choking burden of guilt. He'd been responsible for this somehow, he was sure. Getting Claudia involved secondhand in one of his cases past or present. His half-ass way of making a living; dangerous for him and everybody he knew. Somebody was trying to get even with him, or warn him away. Maybe they'd even thought he was in the apartment with Claudia. Or they might have followed him there sometime when he went to see her, when he'd spent the night, and thought it was *his* apartment. *Stupid scumballs!*

"I got a man assigned to sit outside the door to this room," Hammersmith said. "Nobody's gonna hurt you here. When they release you tonight, you and Nudge come by the Third District and go over some mug books to see if you can identify either of those guys. I don't like to ask you, but it's a good idea to do it while this is still at the top of your memory."

"I'll go with you now if you want," Claudia said.

Hammersmith smiled. "Tonight's soon enough."

"I'll stay with you tonight, afterward," Nudger told her.

She reached out slowly and brushed the back of his hand with her fingertips. "Trying to take advantage of the situation?"

"That's me," Nudger told her.

"Doctor said for you to rest," Hammersmith said. "You'll be sore for a couple of days, but you'll be okay."

"That's what he told me," Claudia said. "Then the nurse gave me something. I don't feel much pain now except for the burn, and that's tolerable. At first it wasn't."

"I'll phone here this afternoon," Nudger said, "and find out what time to come get you tonight. In the meantime I'll look around your apartment and see if there's any clue as to who your gentleman callers were."

"Okay."

Nudger touched her gently on the cheek, kissed her again on the lips.

"Bye, lover," she whispered. Then louder, to Hammersmith: "Bye, Jack. And thanks."

Hammersmith said, "Bye."

Nudger and Hammersmith started for the door.

"Nudger," Claudia said, stopping him. "I've been trying to get in touch with Biff Archway to tell him not to come over today as we planned. If he shows up while you're at the apartment, no trouble, all right?"

"Promise," Nudger said tightly. *Jesus!* he thought. He followed Hammersmith to the door.

"Bye," Rose said. Somber. She'd heard part of the conversation. Nudger said, "Bye."

Hammersmith said nothing.

In the emergency waiting room a Dr. Martino—short, swarthy, no-nonsense—found time to tell Nudger that none of Claudia's injuries was serious or even remotely life-threatening. Bruises around the ribs, some in the pelvic area. And of course the burn, not on her nipple but near the areola. Martino adjusted his gold-framed glasses and shook his head when he described that, as if to say, "The things people do to one another." He saw a lot of those

kinds of injuries here, where battered wives found their way in
after confrontations, and where the police sometimes brought victims of violent rape.

He wanted to examine Claudia one more time, he said, but he
was sure she'd be able to go home this evening around eight. Her
ribs would be wrapped and she'd need to see her own doctor in a
few days, to be sure she was progressing as she should. And the
burn mustn't get infected.

Nudger shook hands with Dr. Martino and gave him a business
card with his home phone number scrawled on the back. "Call me
if there's anything she needs, any change," he said. "I mean call
me for the slightest reason." He didn't like or trust the smug bu-
reaucratic undercurrent of hospitals—all hospitals. People got mis-
placed and misdiagnosed; the wrong limbs got amputated. Not
often, but sometimes. Sometimes was frequently enough. He
wanted to let them know here that somebody cared about Claudia,
cared about her a lot.

Dr. Martino said he'd call if necessary and slipped the white
business card into a pocket. Chimes sounded softly four times and
he raised his head as if they were some sort of signal that beck-
oned. He said good-bye to Nudger and Hammersmith, then bustled
down the hall and through wide swinging doors that opened and
closed soundlessly.

"He seems okay," Hammersmith said.

"Yeah."

Hammersmith said, "Hospitals suck. Let's get the hell out of
here, Nudge. Order some flowers to be delivered to Claudia this
afternoon."

Nudger thought those were both good ideas. He chomped on a
couple of antacid tablets. He'd eaten two more by the time he was
out of the hospital.

His heart was whamming away against his ribs, telling him to
find whoever had done this to Claudia and give them back more
pain than they'd inflicted on her.

His stomach, wiser through experience, knew it might not work
out that way.

18

Muffy B. Blue was wearing ruffles today. Lots of them. She still sported the bright red, wet-look lipstick, and too much rouge on her puffy cheeks. Plenty of dark mascara, too. The makeup and the ruffly white blouse made her look vaguely like a clown parodying a sexpot. When Nudger walked into the offices of Partners Unlimited, she glanced up from reading something on her desk and said, "You again. I'm not surprised."

"You shouldn't be," Nudger said, "I've got an appointment to see Brad Marlyk."

"I didn't know that," Muffy said. "I'm not surprised you're here, though, because that's the way my day's been going. First I overslept, then my car wouldn't start, then I snagged a nail and that hurt like hell, and now you. One shitty development after another. You must have phoned when I wasn't here and talked directly to Mr. Marlyk."

"I did. You were probably in the powder room troweling on more makeup."

The door from Marlyk's office opened and a beautiful blonde swayed out. At first Nudger thought it was Helen; same size and build, similar complexion and hair coloring. But though they were the same age and type, this woman was a few inches shorter and had thicker, broader features than Helen's. Ten more years, twenty more pounds, and she'd lose her good looks. But she had them now. Did she ever. She noticed Nudger and smiled—smashing smile; got him in the knees. Then she said, "See ya, Muffy," and walked out the door.

Nudger watched her sashay across the sunny lot to a Dodge

convertible and drive away. His heart ran behind the car a few
hundred feet, then turned back.

"Pleasant-looking girl," he said.

Muffy B. Blue smiled. It was nothing like the blonde's smile; it
was as if suddenly Muffy knew where he was vulnerable and had
gained some advantage on him. "Her name's Melissa. She's a
talented one. Very talented, in fact. You interested? Bet you are,
you macho devil."

"It's only you I'm interested in," Nudger told her. "I find myself thinking about you at odd times, like when I'm cabling out the
drain."

"Piss on you," Muffy said.

"What would that cost?"

"For you, free."

The office door opened and Brad Marlyk stepped halfway out.
He was wearing a not so muted green plaid sport coat today with a
pastel green shirt and brown and green striped tie. In that outfit he
could take Muffy anywhere. He looked at Muffy, then at Nudger,
as if he might be interrupting something and wondered what it
was. Then he shrugged and said, "Nudger, c'mon into the office."

Nudger found himself again seated and looking across the wide
desk at the pony-faced little guy with the stallion ego. The sport
coat had plenty of shoulder pad, making Marlyk almost appear to
be wearing a forties-style zoot suit. Proud of his broad shoulders,
was Marlyk. Little dude but tough. Thought so, anyway.

"Muffy still giving you a bad way to go?" he asked. He seemed
to admire the hard-nosed woman in the outer office. Nudger wondered if she might be more than an employee and maybe owned
part of the operation. A place like Partners Unlimited couldn't hire
just anyone to meet and greet potential clients.

"I think she secretly likes me," Nudger said.

Marlyk grinned, oversized teeth ridged and yellow in the late-
afternoon sunlight wedging through the slanted blinds. "Naw, believe me, she doesn't. The people she likes, she acts just like a

model receptionist when they come in. She's polite and picks up on their needs, if you know what I mean. Really, Muff's a very sensitive person."

"Think she'd say yes if I asked her for a date?" Nudger asked.

"I think she'd boot you in the balls. Zap! Before you could think about it. Seen her do that to people who irritate her. I mean that." Marlyk tilted far back in his chair and crossed his arms. His getting-down-to-business pose. "What is it you want, Nudger, other than to give my secretary a kiss and a bounce?"

"I found out you lent Jake Dancer some money. I'd like to know how much and what for."

"Sorta private information, wouldn't you say?"

"It won't be if I can't find Dancer and the police get in on the hunt. I'd have to steer Missing Persons this way for sure. It'd be my professional obligation as well as my duty as an upstanding citizen."

"Persuasive argument," Marlyk said. "Maybe could even get you elected to something someplace, you work it into a speech. You know, you're just the type to give a guy a kick in the teeth for doing a friend of a friend a favor."

"How much of a favor?"

"A thousand bucks' worth. Dancer said he needed it to pay off a gambling debt or the people he owed might hurt him. That was such an honest approach I gave him the money."

"At a high interest rate, I'm sure."

"The prime rate," Marlyk said. "Whatever it happened to be at the time. We didn't even put anything down on paper. That's the way I work, I decide to lend an acquaintance money. I'm just like a bank, only more trusting."

Marlyk was some pumpkin, and sort of fun to talk with; he fooled with his own mind while he tried to play with yours. "But with a different sort of collection department," Nudger said.

"Not me. Not for a thousand measly dollars out to a guy like Dancer. I figured when I gave him the money I'd probably have to eat the loss. I mean that. I did it mainly for Helen Crane."

"She knew about the loan?"

"No. Dancer didn't want me to tell her. But I knew he'd be hitting her up for the money next. And Helen's a sweet kind of girl; she'd have lent it to him. This Dancer's a likable kid, Nudger, but a class operation like Helen could do miles better if she tried."

"She loves him," Nudger said.

"Yeah. Odd, ain't it?"

"Did Dancer ever pay you back any part of the money?" Nudger asked.

"Naw, never mentioned it again, once he had it in his hand. He was supposed to repay me in three installments, one each month. The second payment's due in two weeks and I never saw the first." Marlyk gave an exaggerated shrug with his wide, wide shoulders, a slow lifting and falling of expensive plaid material. "My loss is some bookmaker's gain. Way life goes."

"Helen didn't think Dancer knew you well enough to borrow money from you."

"Hah! Guy like Jake Dancer meets somebody once, he knows them well enough to put the touch on them. He saw right away I had a very generous nature and he took advantage of it. I'm tough and sophisticated, Nudger, but I got a soft heart."

Nudger looked closely to see if Marlyk was kidding. He saw no sign of it. Marlyk meant it.

"It fits with this business you have," Nudger said, "serving mankind."

"You think you're kidding, but it's the truth. I provide companionship, fight the thing people fear the most: loneliness."

There was enough truth to what Marlyk said that it shut up Nudger.

"Sometimes," Marlyk went on, "it's more than just an escort, a woman to look glamorous on the arm of some out-of-town bigshot on an expense account."

"I'm sure it is more," Nudger said.

Marlyk tossed his head in that curious horsy manner, as if he'd been stung by a pesky insect and was trying to get it into side vision. "I don't like what I think you mean, Nudger. Also, I got no more time for your wise-guy bullshit. There's some important appointments on my calendar yet today."

Marlyk stood up, which brought him a few inches above eye level with Nudger.

"Got any idea where I might find Jake Dancer?" Nudger asked, not standing.

"You kidding? I've got more pressing matters to think about than the goofball boyfriend of one of my employees." Marlyk looked disgusted enough to spit. "Jesus, you do somebody a favor and it comes down to this! Some private cop doing his lame act in my office. Now get out or I'll have Muff call the police."

"Call them what?"

"Whatever it takes to get your investigator's license pulled."

Probably not an idle threat, Nudger thought. There might indeed be some very influential names on the Partners Unlimited list of clients.

"I mean that," Marlyk assured him.

Nudger had stood about enough of this anyway. He'd learned all he was going to here, and he was tired of listening to Marlyk. A guy like Marlyk was amusing, but only for a while.

Nudger got up, nodded, and walked from the office. Slowly, to let Marlyk know he hadn't been chased. All very deliberate.

In the anteroom Muffy was busy showing a well-groomed executive type how to fill out a form. ". . . really with-it personality," she was saying. The customer saw Nudger and was silent. He seemed a little embarrassed, as if he'd been surprised with his third-quarter earnings down. Muffy glared at Nudger.

"Mr. Marlyk gave me your home phone number," he told her. "I hope you don't mind."

"Not at all," she said. "There's some people I'd just love for you to meet."

*　　*　　*

After leaving Partners Unlimited, Nudger stopped at the Hilton Hotel bar near the airport and killed some time, making two beers last as long as possible. It was dim and cool in there, and he didn't want to leave until it was time to pick up Claudia at Incarnate Word. A couple of traveling men were at the far end of the bar arguing politics, and two rather prim-looking elderly women sat at a table and sipped fancy green drinks of a sort he had never seen. Nobody paid any attention to Nudger, which was fine with him. He didn't want to talk politics. He didn't want a fancy green drink. He wanted privacy and anonymity right now. Everyone needed a hideaway once in a while. A time-out from a rough game.

When he didn't feel he could get down another beer, and the bartender began staring at him expectantly, as if it was time again for Nudger to earn his place at the bar, Nudger went into the lobby and sat on a plush sofa and read a crinkled *Post-Dispatch* someone had left behind.

The heat wave was expected to continue. The President was talking about arms control and threatening a Middle East leader. There was rape, murder, mayhem, and political corruption. Everywhere, it seemed. The Cardinals were on the verge of a major trade for a pitcher after losing three straight games to the Cubs. The *Cubs*!

Considerably cheered by the knowledge that there were people worse off than he was, Nudger put down the paper, glanced at his watch, and left the hotel to drive to the hospital.

Claudia was already dressed when he got there, sitting on the edge of the bed waiting for him. The bed was a high one, and even with her long legs, her toes didn't quite touch the floor. She looked better tonight, as if nothing out of the ordinary had happened to her.

When she noticed Nudger had walked into the room she stood up, rushed over to him, and kissed him. "I can always depend on you," she said. She was holding the small bouquet of flowers

Hammersmith had sent but that Nudger, embroiled in his problems
with Dancer, had forgotten. They looked like peonies, but Nudger
knew little about flowers.

"They told me you had to keep those in water," he said. "A
vase or glass."

"They'll be okay; I've got wet tissue around the stems. They'll
keep for days without wilting."

He almost slipped an arm around her and pulled her close, then
he remembered her bruised torso. She was wearing a loose-fitting
gray blouse that concealed the taped ribs. He didn't think she was
wearing a bra, and he wondered if that was because of the cigarette
burn. He felt enraged all over again when he thought about the
business with the cigarette, and he had to compose himself.

She'd noticed his tenseness. "I feel fine now," she told him.
"Really, I'm all right."

"Have you had supper?"

"Here? Are you kidding? I thought we might go someplace together and have something tastier than cherry Jell-O."

As they walked from the room, Nudger poked his head around
the folding screen to say good-bye to Rose, but the other bed was
unoccupied.

"Rose's husband took her home this afternoon," Claudia said.
"The nurse told me she might as well be there; she's got incurable
cancer of the pancreas and doesn't have much longer to live."

Muffy had been right, Nudger thought glumly: it was that kind
of day. Maybe even that kind of world. He'd only met Rose once,
and he wondered why he felt so depressed at the prospect of her
imminent death. But whatever the reason, Claudia's news about
Rose seemed intimate and crushing.

He tried to shake that feeling as he rode the elevator down with
Claudia to sign out of the hospital, but he wasn't quite successful.

They went to Del Pietro's on Hampton and had toasted ravioli
appetizers, salads with the house dressing, pasta, and hot bread.
Claudia was glad to be liberated from hospital food. She seemed to
regard every bite of pasta as something precious, chewing slowly
for a long time before swallowing.

After spumoni and coffee, Nudger drove her downtown to the
Third District station house. There was a hole in his financial sta-
tus and his stomach was roiling, but it had been worth it, watching
Claudia relish a good meal.

When they were in Hammersmith's office, Nudger said, "Rose
is dying."

"Who?" Hammersmith asked.

"Rose. The woman who was in the hospital room with Claudia.
She's got terminal cancer and doesn't have long to live."

"Hmm, too bad," Hammersmith said, but Nudger wasn't sure
if he meant it. He'd probably forgotten Rose. He met a lot of
people. Hammersmith put him and Claudia in one of the tiny interrogation rooms with a set of mug books. The room had one window, covered on the outside with thick steel mesh. The glass was
almost too dirty to see through, but Nudger knew there wasn't
much of a view out there anyway. A wooden table and two chairs
were the only furniture. All that was necessary, for what usually
went on in the room. There was a faint, stale ammonia scent, like
that of urine, and of fear. It was quiet in there.

The books were well worn loose-leaf binders stuffed with
plastic-covered official photos of known offenders. Many of the
photographs were prison shots, full-face and profile. There were
no names beneath the photos, so that witnesses' identifications
couldn't be colored by having heard about any of the subjects.

"This might take time," Hammersmith told Claudia.

She told him she didn't mind taking the time. Then she sat down
in one of the chairs and dragged the first book across the table to
her.

Hammersmith excused himself and returned to his office.

After almost two hours, Claudia stopped leafing through one of
the books and said, "Him."

Nudger peered over her shoulder.

Her right forefinger rested on the black-and-white photo of a
man with a long face and a lantern jaw. He was staring at the
camera in a dispassionate yet subtly challenging manner, as if

barely concealing his disdain for the photographer. In the profile shot he was looking straight ahead, unconcerned, chin raised high as if to show off his good side. As if he had a good side.

"Any doubt?" Nudger asked.

"None," Claudia said.

Nudger told her to wait and then went and got Hammersmith.

"You sure about this?" Hammersmith asked, looking at the photo where Claudia was pointing. Something in his voice.

That's when Nudger realized he might have seen the man somewhere before, too. He'd been thrown because it was impossible to judge someone's size in a stark photograph. And this wasn't a prison shot, with the height chart marked clearly behind the subject. It was the absence of scale that deceived. But this might be the big man who'd punched him around in the K-mart garage, the man who'd cut Jake Dancer's face with a knife.

"He's the one who burned me with the cigarette," Claudia said in a voice like taut wire.

"How come I'm not surprised?" Hammersmith said. "That's Lars Kovar."

19

"We'll put out a warrant for Kovar," Hammersmith said, leaning over Claudia's shoulder and closing the mug book. The heavy cover smacked down flat and made a slight breeze in the quiet room. "Last I heard, he was doing some collection work for a bookie name of Sammy Weld."

Nudger knew a few bookies, but he'd never heard of Weld. He wanted to meet him. If Kovar was one of the men who'd beaten up Jake Dancer outside the Marriott, Sammy Weld might be one of the bookies heavily into Dancer, though it was possible that Kovar hired out his bone-crusher talents to a number of clients. People like Kovar tended to go wherever their dark ideas of fun and profit led them.

A police siren yodeled shrilly outside on Chouteau, a sudden reminder of a universe beyond the tiny interrogation room.

"Where can I find Weld?" Nudger asked.

Hammersmith tilted his head, smooth jowls spilling over his collar. "You aren't planning to track down Kovar and go traipsing off on some kind of vengeance trip, are you, Nudge?"

"Hadn't considered it," Nudger said honestly. Kovar scared the hell out of him; he was content to let the police run the ungentle giant to ground and deal with him. "You and Fred Flintstone can hunt dinosaurs. I only want to talk to Weld. I think maybe somebody I'm investigating placed bets with him."

"This Jake Dancer?"

Nudger nodded.

"I told you I'd do some checking around, Nudge. Or have somebody check. Guy in Vice already talked to Weld, and Weld says he never met Dancer."

Nudger wasn't convinced. "Could be Weld has something to hide. What if he's the one who sent Kovar to see Claudia?"

Hammersmith arched his graying eyebrows and pursed his lips. It made him look like a cherub under stress. "Reason being?" he said.

"To impress me in a once-removed way that I should stop looking for Jake Dancer."

"Trying to scare you through Claudia, eh? Trouble for you or yours if you keep plugging away on the same track?"

"Well, I *am* scared," Nudger said. "And I and mine have already had trouble."

Hammersmith gazed at the floor for a moment, then he shook his head. "I don't buy it, Nudge. Weld has this thing about women, sees himself as an old-fashioned gentleman; he might hire

Kovar to pull your teeth out with pliers, but he'd never sic him on
Claudia.''

"What about Weld's backers?'' Nudger asked. "Does he have
any partners? Bigger operators who supply him with cash when he
needs it, or carry bets he wants to lay off?''

"Naw, he's an independent bastard. Kind of a character. He's
in his line of business mostly because he needs money to bolster
his image and ego. Not that he's above doing what's necessary in
order to collect a bad debt. That's gospel for people like Weld;
part of the package.''

"Sounds like some package.''

Claudia got up from the table and started to stretch, but her
bruised ribs caused her to drop her arms abruptly. Her face was
white.

"Maybe a vendetta wouldn't be such a bad idea,'' Nudger said,
noticing the twin vertical pain lines above the bridge of her nose.

"I'm more interested in prevention than revenge,'' Claudia said.
"What happened today is a piece of history I don't want repeated.''

Nudger wondered what Biff Archway would do if Claudia told
him about this. Probably go charging after Lars Kovar like a mati-
nee-idol commando and use his martial arts on the big man. Catch
some bullets in his teeth, flip the giant Kovar around, get even but
with fair play. Possibly smile through it all, enjoying this opportunity to work out by smiting one of the world's bad guys. Better
than jogging, or building up a sweat on Nautilus equipment. And
with a clear and noble purpose. And maybe a reward. Definitely a
reward from Claudia.

"Nudge?'' Hammersmith said.

"Yeah?''

"Sammy Weld spends a lot of his time at a bar called the Paddlewheel down in Laclede's Landing on the riverfront. Does a lot
of his business there, taking bets on everything from ballgames to
hopscotch. He scores well with the ladies and dresses like he in-

herited all of Errol Flynn's wardrobe, fancies himself a sort of
riverboat gambler.''

"The river again," Nudger said.

"So?"

"Parallel lines."

"Huh?"

"Never mind."

After Claudia had signed a complaint against Lars Kovar,
Nudger helped her out to the car, though she didn't need help. The
outside air smelled fresh and there was a southeast breeze, but it
was still hot and the humidity seemed to have risen even higher.

He got her settled on the passenger side of the Granada, then
walked around to get behind the wheel. He was glad again he
wasn't driving the Volkswagen. It wasn't the sort of car good for
transporting people with injured ribs. Its suspension had been shot
for years; it was the sort of car good for mixing paint while you
drove.

"This is a nice car," Claudia said, running a hand over the
Granada's vinyl front seat.

"An elderly widow named Mrs. Fudge owns it. I'm thinking
about buying it."

"You should. You should treat yourself better."

That night Nudger slept with Claudia, holding her until she
dozed off in the cold flow of air from the window unit.

They lay on top of the sheets to stay cool, but Nudger's back
was damp where it trapped his body heat against the mattress, and
Claudia's cheek was wet against his bare chest. Her dark hair was
lank and plastered to her forehead. St. Louis in the summertime.

Thunder awoke Nudger at five A.M. Lightning flashbulbed the
room seconds before each crash.

The intermittent jolts of pale light revealed Claudia's smooth
curve of hip and sweep of thigh where she lay curled next to him.
She whimpered but didn't wake up. Nudger reached over and
lightly rested the back of his hand on her forehead—cool now, not

perspiring—and she stopped making sounds in her sleep and her breathing evened out.

The rain fell in a steady torrent, overflowing the gutter and trickling noisily on the brickwork and gangway below. A brief break from the heat. A cool glass of lemonade made in heaven for a city that could use it.

When the storm was over, Nudger slept.

At seven-thirty the next morning he and Claudia showered together, standing shivering in the cold spray in the big, claw-footed tub in the old tiled bathroom. Then they dried with oversized rough terrycloth towels. Beach towels, actually, that she'd gotten with coupons from the back of a detergent box. His towel had a palm tree emblazoned on it; hers featured a V formation of pelicans winging picturesquely against an orange sun. Nudger was sure pelicans didn't fly in formation.

He thought about trying to coax Claudia back into the bedroom and causing her to be late for work, but he decided this might not be the time for that. Instead he helped her to retape her ribs with a ten-foot-long elastic Ace bandage. Then they got dressed and he brewed the coffee while she scrambled some eggs.

After breakfast he walked Claudia to where her car was parked on Wilmington a few buildings down the block. He watched her drive away, heading for her day of teaching summer school at Stowe High School out in the county. A few of her neighbors were at their windows, or already ensconced in the shade on their concrete porches, keeping a wary and critical eye on the neighborhood. Nudger had given them reason to wonder several times, but then he knew they liked to write their own soap operas. Well, no harm in that. Usually.

He got in the Granada and drove to his office, as aware as he'd ever been that his occupation and Claudia's didn't mix well. Grammar and guns; gamblers and grades; teachers and terror. Nope, not good. Not much in common to talk about over dinner, though their dinner conversation was occasionally lively.

At Nudger's office there was a message to call Helen Crane.

He did that first thing after switching on the air conditioner, hoping she had something new to tell him about Dancer's disappearance.

She wondered if he had anything new to tell her about Dancer. Fair enough. *She'd* hired *him*.

"Jake ever mention the name Sammy Weld?" Nudger asked.

"Not that I can remember. Why?"

"Weld's a gambler and bookmaker. He might be one of the people Dancer owes."

"He might be," Helen said, "but I don't think I ever heard his name from Jake or anybody else."

"What about a guy named Lars Kovar? Not a handsome man, and just a tad smaller than a California redwood."

"I'm sure I never heard that name," Helen said. "I'd have remembered it, and I'd recall meeting this Kovar if he's as big as you say."

"He's snow-peaked," Nudger said. "I'm going to try to find Weld this morning and see if Dancer's been in touch with him. There could be some connection by way of Lars Kovar."

"Who *is* Kovar?"

"He's a mean-tempered ex-cop, and he might be one of the men who beat up Jake downtown. He also likes to use women for ashtrays."

"What do you mean? He's into S and M? He burns them with cigarettes or cigars?" Helen, in her line of work, had heard of such things.

"That's what he does."

"Sick," Helen said.

"I understand he works for Sammy Weld in the collection department."

Helen was silent for a while. Then she said, "This is getting kind of hairy, isn't it, Nudger?"

"Downright furry."

"I don't like Jake being mixed up with those kinds of people."

"We don't know that he *is* mixed up with them." But Nudger was pretty sure of Dancer's involvement with Kovar at least. And Kovar and his equally mean sidekick were exactly the people a strung-out, vulnerable veteran with a drinking problem should avoid. War was hell, all right, but it wasn't the only hell.

Helen asked Nudger to call her if he learned anything about Dancer. She gave him a phone number and an extension where she could be reached most of the day and possibly that evening.

After she hung up, Nudger used his illegally obtained phone company cross-directory to find the address that went with the number.

It was the phone number of the Radisson Hotel. The extension number was one of the rooms—judging by the first two digits, a top-floor suite. Probably the chemical convention was ended, but VIP Morrison might have stayed over to further enjoy his perks. Maybe fighting for all those promotions had been worthwhile.

Nudger dropped the directory back into a bottom desk drawer with a thunk, then kicked the drawer shut. The things money could buy. He felt a little nauseated. He told himself it was the heat.

He stopped in the doughnut shop for a glass of ice water and some baseball talk with Danny, then he drove the Granada downtown to the riverfront to see if Sammy Weld was counting money and stuffing aces up his sleeve at the Paddlewheel.

Nudger was looking forward to this conversation. He hadn't met a riverboat gambler since . . . well, it must have been Howard Keel in *Showboat*.

20

Laclede's Landing is an area of antiquated brick buildings, many of which have been restored or are in the process of restoration, snuggled close to the west bank of the Mississippi in the great curved shadow of the Arch. Most of the streets are paved with brick that will ruin a car's shock absorbers in no time. The Landing is more a place for shoe leather than tires; in good weather its walks are teeming with tourists, locals, and strolling musicians. There are restaurants, bars, and specialty shops along the rough streets. A night out for some St. Louisans or visitors is a good dinner at a downtown or riverfront restaurant, then a stroll through the Landing with stops at jazz clubs or sidewalk cafes.

Most of the Landing's business is done on weekends and in the evenings. There were only a few people on the quaint narrow streets when Nudger parked the Granada behind a liquor truck. A truck driver with a huge stomach paunch straining his sweat-mottled T-shirt was off-loading cases from the back of the truck and dollying them across the bricks into the Paddlewheel. The dolly clattered loudly and the cases were dancing up and down almost violently enough to break bottles.

Nudger followed the bouncing bourbon. He glanced up before he pushed open the front door, a stained oak survivor from a long-gone antebellum mansion, and saw that the top three floors of the four-story brick building seemed to list toward the street and looked capable of tumbling down at any moment. Instant brick-pile. The first floor had been rehabbed and fitted with dark blue canvas awnings and tinted glass. A large riverboat was stenciled on the big front window, and the oak door was set next to what

121

looked like half of an authentic paddlewheel affixed to the front of the building and anchored to the sidewalk.

When he entered, Nudger wouldn't have been surprised to see old Mark Twain slumped over a stein of beer at a wooden table, wearing the ever-present wrinkled white suit and snarling ironies. Maybe there'd be a card game in a corner, sweaty guys relaxing after a hard day lifting that bale and toting that barge, or vice versa. Instead the place was empty except for the bartender signing for the liquor delivery.

Nudger sat at the end of the bar and waited while the truck driver knocked down a free can of Pepsi and chatted with the bartender, a youngish guy with a ragged mustache and a head of wavy dark hair. The Paddlewheel occupied the entire first floor of the building; dividing walls had been taken down and the original wood flooring had been sanded and refinished. Behind the bar was a large ornate model of a side-wheeler riverboat, churning away in artificial water made from cotton tinted brown like the nearby river, except for where it was supposed to represent white foam boiled up by the paddlewheels. Somebody had gone to a lot of trouble over that boat. Similar riverboats still traveled the waters only a few blocks away, tour boats like the *Huck Finn*. Or the *President,* up from New Orleans for the summer. Or cruise boats like the luxurious *Delta Queen,* floating hotels and entertainment centers that wandered up and down the length of the river, catering to wealthy guests who wanted an easygoing sampling of what was almost gone with the wind.

On the walls of the Paddlewheel were drawings and old photographs of riverboats. A huge overhead chandelier was made from a spoked wheel that had been used to negotiate tricky currents and shallows a hundred years ago. There were high-backed wooden booths along the Paddlewheel's wainscoted walls, Tables, with red cloths on them and a hurricane lamp in the center of each, were clustered in the middle of the room. Though the Paddlewheel was air-conditioned, and cool despite the increasing morning heat, there were half a dozen ceiling fans lazily rotating their broad wooden blades and casting soothing, flitting soft shadows over the walls and tables.

The bartender had a radio on low, tuned to a rock station playing music that didn't go with the decor. Vintage Beatles numbers. He appeared young only because of all the hair and the dark mustache, Nudger noticed, but he was actually in his early forties. Which explained why the music wasn't blaring through the place loud enough to make the riverboat behind the bar pitch and yaw on its cotton current.

After the delivery driver had left, rolling the clattering steel dolly ahead of him, the bartender ambled down behind the bar and nodded to Nudger, waiting for his order.

"One of those," Nudger said, pointing to the empty Pepsi can the driver had left on the bar. "Only make mine a Diet."

The bartender got him a Diet Pepsi, poured half of it in a glass, and set the can and glass on the bar in front of Nudger. Nudger laid a dollar on the bar. The bartender said the soda was a dollar ninety. Nudger wasn't surprised. He placed a second dollar bill on top of the first. The Beatles sang "Penny Lane." Nudger said, "Seen Sammy Weld yet today?"

He expected some diversion, a shifting of the bartender's dark eyes, a play for a ten-dollar bribe. Like in the movies or detective novels.

Instead the bartender, no romantic, said, "He'll be here about ten o'clock like he usually is. Sammy don't get up early enough to make it in any sooner."

"Guess there's nobody here that early for him to do business with anyway," Nudger said.

Again, no evasion. "Oh, he does some figuring over in that corner booth while he's eating breakfast. His bookwork, you might say. Or course, whatever business Sammy's in, that's got nothing to do with this place. Though he does make it kind of his office."

"Maybe he likes the food," Nudger said.

The bartender shrugged. He was wearing a blue apron with—what else?—a riverboat emblazoned on the chest. The boat looked

just like the model behind the bar, which, come to think of it,
looked exactly like the boat stenciled on the front window.
"Wouldn't blame him," he said. "We got the best waffles anywhere. Wanna try some?"

"Thanks," Nudger said, "but I've had breakfast." He looked
at his watch. Weld should be here in less than an hour. There was
a folded morning newspaper on one of the bar stools; he sometimes wondered why he bothered with a subscription. "How about
if I finish my soda over there in a booth and read the paper while I
wait for Sammy? I need to talk to him about a bet."

"Bet?" The bartender grinned. "I don't know from bet. What
you wanna to talk to Sammy Weld about is your business."

"And his," Nudger added.

"And none of mine."

Nudger knew that wasn't quite true. The Paddlewheel probably
appreciated the customers drawn in by Weld's action and gambler
persona. A little local color, some of it green. But if the bartender
wanted to play the innocent, that was okay with Nudger. What was
guilt but a matter of degree?

"Sure you don't want no waffles?" the bartender asked. "You
don't know what you're missing."

"Yep, I'm sure." This guy with his waffles was worse than
Danny with his doughnuts.

After settling into the booth, Nudger leafed through the paper,
taking in snatches of news as he turned pages: "The President
today . . . found in woods . . . Supreme Court ruled . . . Nica-
ragua . . . discrimination against . . . God in the third grade . . .
moderates in Iran . . . not really censorship . . . ruining our chil-
dren . . ." He didn't want to read anything in depth until he
reached the sports page, where saner minds like Sparky Ander-
son's and Yogi Berra's prevailed. Wow! The Cards had done it,
traded a good young outfielder for a one-time great pitcher coming
back from a rotator cuff injury.

Nudger didn't like the trade. How many pitchers actually recovered fully from rotator cuff injuries? What the hell was a rotator cuff?

At exactly ten o'clock, Sammy Weld shoved open the old oak door and bustled in like a busy man with a brisk schedule. He gave a jaunty little half-salute to the bartender, whose eyes darted to Nudger, then back, as if he were looking at something crossing the room at high speed.

Weld was medium height, a slender man, and what women called darkly handsome. He wore an ordinary cream-colored suit, a white shirt, but he had on a royal blue kerchief rather than a tie, neatly encircling his neck and joined by a large, jeweled, silver slide. He also wore a white, wide-brimmed hat, which he removed in gentlemanly fashion three steps inside the door to reveal a head of straight, black, precisely combed hair. Nudger remembered Hammersmith's remark about Weld and Errol Flynn's wardrobe. Weld was in his mid-thirties, and he moved with grace and decisiveness. But he was a bit too well turned out, too smug and prim. He would have appeared Hollywood-virile, as he no doubt thought he looked, only he was a shade too swishy to play the lead.

He ignored Nudger and walked to a corner booth and sat down. He really did have about him the air of a man arriving for work at his office. The bartender immediately brought him coffee and a little silver pitcher of cream.

Nudger got up and crossed the plank floor to the booth. "Sammy Weld?"

Weld looked up and smiled. He even had a little pencil-line mustache like Errol Flynn's. "You'd be Nudger," he said.

"How'd you know?"

"A Lieutenant Hammersmith of the Third District sent a message you might be looking me up. He advised me to cooperate with you, tell you no lies. Said to treat you like you was the pope." More of the handsome smile. "He don't know I'm not Catholic."

Nudger sat down across from Weld. He'd expected a southern-
gentleman drawl from the man; instead Weld spoke with a trace of
flat Ozark twang. Nudger had another, sudden perspective on him:
country boy trying hard to project a sophisticated image. "Is that
the only reason you'll cooperate?" Nudger asked. "Hammersmith's advice?"

"Nope. Got nothing to hide. Not from you, anyways." He
poured cream into his coffee and sipped, holding the cup delicately. Even extended his little finger slightly. Miss Manners
would love this guy, see him as an eager student and a challenge.
Half diamond, half lump of coal. "So what is it you wanna talk
about?"

"Jake Dancer."

Weld put down his cup and said nothing. And there was nothing
in his gambler's narrowed eyes other than anticipation as he saw
the bartender bringing over a plate of waffles and a small glass
container of syrup. The waffles did smell good, sweet and with a
hint of cinnamon. For a moment Nudger was tempted to order
some and eat two breakfasts. He was only about ten pounds overweight, so why not twelve pounds?

"What about Jake Dancer?" Weld asked as he forked in his first
bite of waffle. Here he would have shocked Miss Manners, chewing with his mouth open.

"Does he owe you money?"

"Surely does. Seven hundred and thirty dollars."

"Bad bets?"

Weld swallowed, took another bite of waffle, and shook his
head. Seemed he couldn't talk without a mouthful of food. "He
doesn't make nothing but bad bets, that Dancer. Horses, baseball,
golf, cards, you name it and he's lost his ass at it."

"Have you recently seen the part of him he hasn't lost?"

"Uh-uh, I ain't seen him for months."

"How about Lars Kovar?"

Weld stopped chewing. He swallowed again, hard. Took a sip
of coffee. "I ain't seen Lars for a few months, either."

"I thought he worked for you, in the collection department."

The conversation was getting serious, possibly even incriminating. Weld worked his eyebrows at Nudger. "Lars does jobs of one kind or another for me, from time to time. He works for lots of people."

"Who's he been working for lately?"

Slowly, Weld poured more syrup on his waffles, enough so that it almost ran over the rim of the plate. Gee, those waffles smelled delicious! "That I surely wouldn't know."

Nudger watched Sammy Weld enjoy his food. The gambler gave the impression that he was a man telling the truth. But then he probably ran a good bluff with bad cards. One thing he wasn't faking was his affection for Paddlewheel waffles.

"Claudia Bettencourt," Nudger said.

No reaction on Weld's controlled features. "This Claudia somebody I ought know?"

"Definitely not."

"Went to school with a Claudia in Poplar Bluff, but I don't remember her last name. This be the same Claudia?"

"No, she's someone Kovar burned a hole in with a cigarette," Nudger said. He felt himself getting angry and pushed the unproductive, sometimes dangerous emotion to the back of his mind.

Weld seemed deeply offended. He dabbed at his lips with a napkin and sat back from the table. "You don't think I paid Lars Kovar to do something like that, do you?"

"I don't know," Nudger said.

"Listen, here, Nudger, you ask around, you'll find I don't do that sorta thing to women. Either personally or hire somebody. I happen to respect women, and they respect me."

"That's your reputation," Nudger admitted.

That seemed to placate Weld. He scooted back close to the table and picked up his fork. "I'm a man whose word's good," he said. "You check and you'll find that's true about me, too. Fella in my business, his word's all he got. You steal my purse, I get another, but you steal my reputation and I'm in deep shit."

"Shakespeare?"

"You betcha. Point is, Nudger, I'm swearing to you I ain't seen
Lars Kovar or Dancer in at least a month. Hell, maybe even two
months. I'd appreciate it if you'd believe me and tell that Lieutenant Hammersmith I gave you what I could and he can loosen the
screws. It'd be the pure truth."

"I'll let him know," Nudger said. He stood up.

Weld smiled at him again. Handsome smile, all right, even if it
was a bit self-conscious. Capped teeth. Dashing. Nudger could see
why women liked Weld. He'd know how to weave illusions just
for them.

"I'll tell you this," Weld said, "take my advice and don't mess
with Lars Kovar unless you use surface-to-monster missiles. He
was a mean cop, but he's an even meaner civilian. He likes to hurt
people, Nudger. I mean, Lordy, he *likes* it! Your girl he burn with
the cigarette?"

"My girl," Nudger said.

"Kovar. The slimeball bastard!"

Nudger didn't want to talk with Weld about Claudia. "Your
waffles are getting cold," he said, and moved to leave.

"Nudger?"

"Yeah?"

"You seem like a sure-enough nice guy, but one not savvy
enough to avoid playing with explosives. You don't recognize the
odds. Gotta ask yourself, what are the odds?"

"You might be right."

"Well, I like you. My instinct tells me you're solid. You trust
me and I'll trust you. I sense you're a gentleman, and far as I'm
concerned gambling should be a business run for and by gen-
tlemen. If you wanna place a bet on whatever's going on, most
anytime, come talk to me here, at this table."

Nudger laughed and said he would.

"And a free tip," Weld said. "Don't bet on the Cardinals to
move up in the standings."

"What about the new pitcher?" Nudger asked.

Weld shook his head and said knowingly, "Torn rotator cuff."

"What's a torn rotator cuff?" Nudger asked.

"Something like a torn French cuff," Weld said, "in that I never seen a pitcher with one on his arm win a game."

Nudger decided that if he bet regularly with Sammy Weld, Weld would come out ahead.

Outside, the sudden intense heat seemed to bring Nudger's frustration to a boil. There was something vaguely pathetic about Sammy Weld that made life seem a hopeless game. One Nudger was losing.

No one knew where he might find Dancer. People had seen Dancer, talked to him, pitied him, liked him, lent him money, bought him drinks, said what a fine sort he was and how they didn't mind doing him favors. But always Dancer was somewhere else. If Nudger hadn't talked to him himself, he'd have difficulty believing Dancer actually existed except in the imaginations of gamblers, drunks, and bartenders. And in the misguided mind and heart of Helen Crane.

The one real possibility Nudger had left was the knowledge that Dancer would at some point contact Helen. Probably for a loan. Then he'd doubtless fade away again, not revealing his destination.

The quickest and surest way to pin down Dancer, Nudger decided, was to follow Helen Crane.

It was easy to find reasons to follow Helen.

He crossed the street and licked syrup from his fingers, wondering how it had gotten there.

Much about the world was puzzling.

21

Helen Crane's old blue Datsun was in the pay lot on the north side of the Radisson Hotel. Nudger found a spot to park out on the street, where he could watch the Datsun without being conspicuous. The lot was exposed except for a roof, providing good visibility of the rows of cars. He fed some coins into the meter, got back in the Granada, and waited.

Within half an hour the car's interior was too hot to endure. He'd started the engine a few times and sat with it and the air conditioner running, but he knew the motor would soon overheat that way in the ninety-plus heat of July in St. Louis.

Finally he got out, found some shade across the street, and stood with his back against a building, imagining that the gentle warm breeze was actually providing relief instead of making him hotter. But he felt as if he were melting like wax into his shoes. The sun seemed not to have moved; it hung like a glaring orange eye that, instead of setting, would observe the agony below it for another twelve hours before starting the torture all over again.

Nudger tried this way and that to keep cool, or at least *think* cool, and keep the Datsun in view simultaneously. At the moment, watching Helen Crane didn't seem like such a sound idea, but he knew the heat might be keeping him from being objective. A fried brain wasn't to be trusted.

At last he saw a car two rows behind the Datsun pull out of the lot. Its vacated parking space was in the shade of the concrete roof.

Nudger immediately got back in the Granada, drove into the lot, and occupied that space.

Into his damp shirt pocket went the ticket the lot's time-clock had stuck out at him like a greedy tongue as he'd entered. Parking here was figured by the hour; Nudger knew it would cost him a fortune if he had to wait much longer for Helen to emerge from the hotel. And on the phone she'd told him he might be able to reach her at the suite number that evening.

Now that he was out of the sun, he had to consider that this really was a dumb game he was playing, risking wasting his time while he acquired a wallet-busting parking fee. But it was the most sensible of his dwindling options if he wanted to find Jake Dancer. There were other people looking for Dancer, and he had to find him first.

He cranked down all the car windows, caught a hint of cross-ventilation, and settled back in the upholstery. He waited. Thinking cool thoughts.

At three-fifteen, like all things that come to those who wait, Helen Crane came out of the Radisson. She waited for the traffic to thin, then crossed the intersection and walked toward the lot where the Datsun was parked.

She was alone and wearing a pensive expression. Also a silky flower-print dress that swayed elegantly with each exaggerated extension of her thighs as she strode in her black high heels. She seemed to be in a hurry, and she had about her the lightened attitude of one whose business was finished and who was now on free time. Nudger was glad to receive the distinct impression that whatever had gone on in the top-floor suite of the Radisson, she was relieved that it was over. Working woman, leaving after a day at the office. Only a job.

But Nudger reminded himself that most of Helen's business was conducted in the evening. He heard the tap, tap, tap of her heels on concrete as she got nearer and walked to her car. The slam of the Datsun's door sounded hollow and hesitant. It wasn't a Cadillac or Porsche, it was saying.

Instead of heading toward her apartment on Osage, she cut east to Broadway and turned south, then made an abrupt right on Washington. Nudger knew where she was going.

She parked the Datsun on Washington, then crossed the street and entered the building that contained the downtown offices of Partners Unlimited.

Turning in the day's receipts?

That wasn't a fair speculation, Nudger decided. He didn't *know* what had happened in the Radisson Hotel.

He parked several car lengths back, still smarting from paying the extortion money to get out of the lot across from the Radisson. He was by a meter gaudy with the red flag of violation, but he stubbornly refused to stuff coins into it. There was a limit to how much a person should have to pay for the mere privilege of ceasing motion.

Ten minutes later a voice near his left elbow said, "You want me to hand you this ticket or stick it on your windshield?"

Nudger looked over to see a uniformed cop standing by the Granada's left front window. He was a stocky man with perspiration stains on his blue uniform shirt, and with a thumb hooked into his belt near his holstered revolver. All business, with hostility lurking an inch below the surface. So intently had Nudger been watching the building across the street that he hadn't glanced in his rearview mirror and noticed the cop writing the parking ticket.

"Whoa," Nudger said. "I was just about to drive away."

"Don't matter, sir."

"I only parked here to try to get my bearings. Hey, I wouldn't even call it parking. More like pausing."

"I would say parking. You been here at least ten minutes."

Nudger was getting mad. He didn't want this, not on top of the money he'd already spent parking, the grinding heat, and his thinning patience with Helen. He cautioned himself that his judgment might be affected by all of that, but he spoke anyway, adding to the sum of human folly. "Listen, I got some friends on the force."

"I bet I got more," the cop said, not liking Nudger's approach, but at the same time pleased to have found some focus for his irritation.

"Hell, I used to be a member of the department myself."

"Then you know that once a ticket's written, there's nothin' can be done about it," the cop said. Sweat trickled down the side of his nose and disappeared into the wilds of his brush mustache. He tore the parking ticket from his pad and stuffed it beneath the driver's side windshield wiper. He let the wiper snap back against the glass unnecessarily hard. Tempers sure were short under the press of a heat wave.

Nudger started to invoke the name of Hammersmith, but he saw that Helen had left the building and was walking west on Washington, away from him and away from where her car was parked. He noticed then that a large gray car was double-parked near the corner.

"Sorry, buddy," the cop was saying, softening a little. He'd realized the heat was affecting both of them. "How long ago was you on the department?" *Now* the guy wanted to be reasonable.

Helen was climbing into the back of the gray car; it had been waiting for her. "Over ten years ago," Nudger said, staring straight ahead. He started the Granada. The cop took a step back and glared at him suspiciously; heat from the engine and scorched exhaust system rose in odorous vapor around him, not doing much for his temper. He didn't like Nudger's brusque manner, didn't like being rebuked now that he was friendly. Hell, he had a job to do, like everybody else in this on-fire, fucked-up world.

"So now you're in a hurry, huh?"

"Big hurry," Nudger said, feeling no sympathy. The car was pulling out into traffic. It was a fifties vintage Cadillac, with long, sweeping lines and upswept tail fins. It glided majestically through the flow of newer, smaller domestic and foreign cars like a shark parting the waters of a teeming reef. Nudger put the Granada in gear. "See you in court. I intend to fight that ticket."

"You and F. Lee Bailey!" the cop said. He spat on the sidewalk.

Nudger thought briefly about pointing out that public expectoration was illegal, but he had a car to follow.

He drove away from the irate cop and fell in behind the Cadillac in the next block. He relaxed somewhat; the Caddie's size and unique appearance made it easy to tail from a prudent distance. Though the windows were tinted, Helen's blond head was plainly visible. She was alone in the backseat. The Cadillac was apparently chauffeur-driven.

At Tenth Street the finned behemoth coasted into a right turn and drove north for a while. Then it picked up Interstate 70 west. Nudger goosed the Granada to keep pace as the big gray car accelerated with deceptive speed down the access ramp. They settled into the outside lane and did precisely fifty-seven miles per hour all the way to 170, the Inner Belt highway, where they turned north.

Half an hour later they were well out of the city and driving on narrow back roads lined with trees. At the end of a dropping, winding ribbon of blacktop, the Cadillac braked to a stop before tall, black, wrought-iron gates.

Through the tinted back window Nudger saw the chauffeur's pale hand float up to the sun visor, where the electronic sender must have been clipped. The black iron gates twitched to life and swung open, the Cadillac glided smoothly through them, and the gates swept closed.

Only fleeting glimpses of the Cadillac's gray form then, as it passed along wooded slopes away from the road. It was traveling fast; Nudger rolled down the window and heard the rushing growl of its engine. It sounded as well as looked like a spanking-new car that had rolled off a Detroit assembly line into the wrong era. Some quality control.

Nudger pulled the Granada off the road and parked in the mottled shadows of a stand of tall trees that looked like spruce. But what did he know about trees? He got out and walked through the woods, along the fence line, making no noise on a carpet of pine needles and last year's soft dead leaves.

Black wrought iron quickly gave way to eight-foot-tall chainlink fence topped with three strands of barbed wire. Wicked hardware that meant business—the business of keeping out trespassers. But in the deeper woods, where few people ventured, the barbed wire was reduced to a single strand. Here was something Nudger could handle.

He removed his shirt and wrapped his right hand in it. Then he climbed the fence, gingerly used the wadded shirt to hold down the strand of barbed wire, and threw his leg over the fence top. The other leg followed, then the rest of Nudger. He dropped to the ground with only a scratch on his left wrist, and he hurriedly slipped his shirt back on.

He could hear the car again now, moving slower. The road must wind; large piece of property with hills. Praying there were no guard dogs on the estate—or wherever he was—Nudger jogged up a steep grade toward the sound of the engine.

As he neared the crest of the rise, the motor stopped.

A car door slammed. Whomp! Not like Helen's Datsun.

Nudger dropped to his knees, then his elbows, and carefully scooted forward to peer through the foliage.

The Cadillac was parked so near it frightened him—no more than three hundred feet away. And now he saw the vast rust tile roof he hadn't noticed through the trees.

The roof belonged to a rambling stone house trimmed in black and surrounded by perfectly groomed hedges. Thick ivy had grasped its way up one wall, even over some of the windows, and several brick chimneys jutted from the gently sloping roof. Beyond the house, Nudger saw the smaller, steeper roof of another building. Possibly a garage, or a guest house. And far beyond that, through the trees, glinted the silvery curve of the river. Prime real estate. Whoever lived here wasn't likely to be someone Nudger would recognize from K-mart.

The chauffeur, a very thin man in a black uniform complete with visored cap, was holding the Cadillac's right rear door open for Helen. Two shapely, nyloned calves, pressed close together, swung from the shadows of the car. Red high heels were planted firmly on the gravel driveway. Smooth muscles flexed and neatly turned ankles tensed to bear body weight.

Red? Had Helen been wearing red shoes? Nudger pictured her elegant, flowing walk from the Radisson to her car. He saw black shoes.

It wasn't Helen who climbed out of the spacious back of the car. It was Melissa. The woman Nudger had seen coming out of Brad Marlyk's office at Partners Unlimited. The one he'd at first thought was Helen.

Somewhere behind the house a dog began barking. It sounded like a large dog. Nudger didn't want to be bitten even by a small dog; he remembered the pain a tiny Schnauzer had inflicted on him when he'd solved that dognapping case.

He let himself slide backward out of sight, then he ran hunched over through the trees to where he'd scaled the fence.

He kept imagining the rustle of something following him through the high brush. Sometimes the rustling seemed to be alongside him, as if whatever was there might be running parallel with him, out of sight but very close.

Finally he was at the fence.

With a glance behind him, he scampered upward, digging the toes of his shoes in between the chainlinks. The effort hurt his feet, and the fence made a metallic rattling noise that seemed startlingly loud.

He didn't do as good a job of holding down the strand of barbed wire this time; he avoided being injured, but a six-inch flap was torn out of his pants leg as he dropped to the other side of the fence. He landed awkwardly, and for a moment thought he'd sprained his right ankle.

But after a few panicky, experimental steps on the hard earth, the ankle felt okay.

Nudger was outside the grounds, and none the worse for his adventure.

None the better, either.

It took him another ten minutes to follow the road to where the Granada was parked.

The car seemed to welcome him like home. Inside it, with the key in the ignition and the engine throbbing, he felt sheltered and safe. Still nervous, though.

He'd have chewed antacid tablets all the way back to the highway, but when he probed his shirt pocket he found he was out of them. Or maybe he'd lost them scrambling over the fence. It wouldn't have taken much jostling for them to have worked out of the shallow pocket. He should have put a spare roll in the glove compartment.

It had been a day for poor planning.

22

Nudger drove toward the city. He looped over I-70 through downtown and stopped at Hodge's Chili Parlor in Union Station for a late supper. He ordered a Super Slinger, a concoction of beef patties, eggs, and potatoes, covered with chili and topped with a tamale. Slingers were a weakness of Nudger's; his intestinal tract despised them but his taste buds loved them dearly.

After sating himself with culinary sin, he lingered over coffee. Then he decided to go by the office and check for messages before driving to his apartment, downing a cold beer, and trying to sleep after an unproductive day's work.

Only an occasional car swished past on Manchester as he left the Granada parked facing west and crossed the street toward his of-

fice. The triangle of cloth where the barbed wire had ripped his
pants flopped against his thigh as he walked. Though it was past
ten o'clock and had been dark more than an hour, heat from the
pavement radiated through his soles.

He glanced into the closed Danny's Donuts, then used his key to
unlock and open the door next to the doughnut shop. The stairwell
air was hot and stale and came out at him like bad breath. He left
the door unlocked and climbed the steep wooden steps to his
office.

It was still warm in there, too. Though he only intended staying
a few minutes, he switched on the air conditioner before rewinding
the tape on his answering machine and punching the Play button.
He told himself again he should buy one of those machines that
would enable him to phone in some sort of signal no matter where
he was and have his messages relayed to him. Or might that only
be complicating his life?

As he listened to various messages urging him to buy magazine
subscriptions, get free estimates on waterproofing, and call Eileen's lawyer immediately, he stood in the cool breeze of the air
conditioner and stared out the window. Manchester lay in dim,
diffused illumination from the streetlights. There were no cars
parked below other than the Granada and, half a block up, a black
Chrysler LeBaron convertible. The kind Lee Iacocca claimed was
born in America, but that had Japanese engines. Nudger didn't
remember the Chrysler being there when he'd crossed the street.

". . . I'll leave you with nothing but your bare ass, Nudger!"
Eileen was suddenly saying from the answering machine. She
sounded more calmly vindictive than angry. That scared Nudger.

He turned quickly and pushed Fast Forward. Eileen's voice took
on a zany chipmunk quality, then abruptly deepened.

Realizing he'd forwarded the tape too far, into the next message, Nudger backed it up to the end of Eileen's call and played it
at normal speed.

"This is Sammy Weld, Nudger old buddy. I'm phoning you
right at . . . quarter past ten. You said you was looking for Jake

Dancer, so I thought I'd let you know he's right here in the Pad-dlewheel, drinking only beer and looking more or less sober. Also looking kinda nervous. If you get this message soon enough to get to Dancer, figure you owe me a favor. Maybe have your friend Hammersmith talk to them Vice guys about hanging around here and scaring away my customers. Ain't those people heard there's a state lottery now and gambling's moral?''

End of message.

Beep. "This is Union Electric calling. Your June utility bill—''

Nudger switched off the answering machine. Then the air condi-tioner. He did a quick patch job on his pants with cellophane tape, applying it on the inside of the torn leg. A seamstress couldn't have done it better; no threads showed. Then he draped his sport jacket over his arm, turned off the desk lamp, and hurried from the office.

This time of night, with little traffic, it would take him no more than twenty minutes to drive to the Paddlewheel.

The place was crowded, mostly with people about ten years younger than Nudger. Men in lightweight sport coats or in shirt-sleeves milled around carrying drinks. The ceiling fans churned away at the cigarette smoke, moving it around but not doing much to dissipate it. An old Credence Clearwater Revival song, "Proud Mary,'' was blasting from speakers mounted over the bar. River music. Somebody shouted "Yeee-ipe!'' A woman who'd had too much to drink laughed too long and too loud. Why weren't these people home in bed?

Through the crowd Nudger got a glimpse of Sammy Weld, sit-ting in his booth and talking animatedly with a chubby black man who wore a single dangling gold earring. The black guy was grin-ning and shaking his head, causing the earring to glint on and off like a signal light. Nudger was about to make his way over to the booth and ask Weld if Dancer had left when a huge bald man in a tropical-print shirt shifted position to reveal the scene behind him, and there was Dancer seated alone at the end of the bar.

When Nudger scooted onto the stool next to him, Dancer glanced over, did a slow double take, then said, "Nudger, my good pal. You looking out for me like some kinda guardian angel?"

"Why'd you leave the cabin?" Nudger asked.

Dancer gazed into the empty beer stein in front of him on the bar. "Place was getting littler and littler, walls inching in on me. Felt like that, anyway. I mean, nothing happens out there in the quiet. You're just alone. All by yourself. With yourself. No people. That's not good, Nudger. I gotta be with people now and then."

The bartender, a different one from the mustached man who'd been there that morning, sauntered over, smiled, and raised his eyebrows inquisitively. Nudger pointed to Dancer's empty stein and held up two fingers.

When the drinks came, he paid for them and then swiveled slightly on his stool to face Dancer. "How come you're not comfortable alone with yourself, Jake?"

"Ha! Lotta reasons."

Nudger realized Dancer was more affected by alcohol than he'd thought when he'd sat down next to him. Career drinkers could be like that. He held it well, gave little outside sign of inebriation while he downed one drink after another and got fused to his stool. But the dark eyes had a watery, remote quality, and the pale, ravaged-choirboy features seemed more gaunt and haggard than when Nudger had last seen Dancer.

"Vietnam giving you dreams?" Nudger asked.

"No. Well, maybe. Sometimes. Killing can haunt a man."

"Been a long time, though."

"Well, that's what haunting's all about, isn't it? Look how long those ghosts of murdered Englishmen haunt those castles in Europe. Give the descendants of their killers fits."

Nudger had to concede that Dancer had a point; sometimes, instead of fading, guilt could ripen with time.

"Something in me doesn't abide killing anything, Mr. Nudger. American or Vietnamese, large or small."

"That's one of the good things about you, Jake."

He smiled his ruined poet's smile; almost angelic. But in another couple of years his teeth would be bad, his sallow flesh would sag. Nudger could see age and alcohol and guilt creeping up on him outside as well as in. "Helen tell you that, Mr. Nudger?"

"Not in so many words," Nudger said. "Helen loves you. A woman like her, do you know what that's worth?"

"Whaddya mean?" Dancer asked. There was a sudden undercurrent of tension in his voice.

Nudger wondered if he knew about Helen's extracurricular activities for Partners Unlimited, Helen at the Radisson Hotel. "I mean the fact that she cares deeply for you."

"That's just the problem," Dancer said. "I know she doesn't deserve all the trouble I'm bound to bring down on her."

"What kind of trouble?"

Dancer took a long sip of beer, his Adam's apple working rapidly as he swallowed. "Worst kinda trouble," he said, setting down the stein so it rested crookedly, half off its coaster.

"Maybe not the worst, Jake. Maybe for her the worst is worrying about you, not knowing where you are. Thinking there's something you won't share with her."

"Some things shouldn't be shared," Dancer said. He bowed his head. Nudger saw he was biting his lower lip and thought Dancer might begin to cry. Dancer's shoulders began to tremble. Dumb, sad, victim who couldn't help himself, on a dark carnival ride all alone to the end.

Nudger slid down off his stool and put his hand on Dancer's thin upper arm, picking up some of the trembling. "Come on, Jake."

"Don't wanna go. Tried to place a bet here, but the man says I got no more credit. Cards' new pitcher's gonna win twenty games, pitch 'em to the pennant. All I wanna do is bet on tomorrow's game."

"You've got no more business here, then. Let's go."

"Back to the cabin?"

"Not now. Back to my place, get some sleep. You'll feel better. Like before."

"Yeah, I remember what you did for me, Nudger." Dancer tried to focus his gaze on Nudger. "Was that because Helen hired you to look after me?"

"Not entirely. It was because two guys had been punching you around and you needed help. You ever heard of Lars Kovar?"

Dancer didn't answer. Instead he reached for his beer stein and knocked it over, said, "Shit!"

"Time to get outta here," Nudger said.

The bartender came over and began wiping up the spilled beer with a folded white towel. "Getcha another?"

"We're done," Nudger told him, and laid money on the bar.

Dancer got down off the stool, leaned for a second on Nudger, then began a winding, unsteady course toward the door. Nudger walked behind him and a little to the side, ready to brace him if he began to fall. Sammy Weld caught Nudger's eye and nodded; the black guy with the earring was gone now, and a beautiful dark-haired woman in a green dress sat across from Weld in the booth. She looked about twenty-five. As Weld turned back to her she reached across the table and clasped his hand with both of hers and smiled. Nudger wondered about the odds.

Dancer made it outside without help, though he was listing a few degrees to the right. The noise from inside was surprisingly faint in the hot night air. Thick old walls and door.

Nudger pointed to the Granada, and they made their way toward it over the rough paving stones. Dancer did need Nudger to keep him from falling a couple of times before they reached the car. Once, as Dancer lurched against him, Nudger almost twisted a knee and would himself have needed help walking.

Slouched in the passenger's seat, Dancer was silent as Nudger maneuvered the Granada slowly onto smoother pavement and drove uphill away from the river. In the confined space of the car, he could smell the alcohol on Dancer's breath. Guy might be flammable.

On the highway, Dancer turned to look at Nudger and said, "I wanna hire you."

Nudger laughed. "Helen's already hired me. So in a sense I'm already working for you."

"If you look at it that way," Dancer said, "I'd like for you to keep an eye on Helen. You know, watch after her."

"Why?"

"Whoever's after me, they might try to get to me through Helen. I'm scared for her."

Nudger thought about Claudia. "You know who's after you, Jake. I want you to tell me."

"Will you keep an eye on Helen?"

"Sure." Easy.

Dancer closed his eyes.

"Jake?"

No answer.

"Jake? What about Lars Kovar? You know who he is, don't you?"

But Dancer was asleep. Or pretending to sleep.

Nudger left the Granada's air conditioner on high, but he cranked down his window a few inches to get some fresh air as he drove.

It might be toxic just being near Dancer in a closed car.

23

The next morning Nudger sat at the counter of Danny's Donuts, watched a bluebottle fly buzzing around the display case, and waited for a secretary from across the street to finish buying a dozen glazed to go.

The secretary, a tiny dark-haired woman in her fifties whose name Nudger thought was Judy, laid a ten-dollar bill on the counter and said, "You'd think the bastard'd walk across the street and buy doughnuts himself maybe one day outta the year."

"You'd think so," Danny agreed solemnly. Holding waxed paper between thumb and forefinger, he fished into the display case repeatedly for doughtnuts and nimbly plopped them into a white, grease-stained box.

"I hired on to type and file and answer the phone," Judy said, "not to run errands for the boss's wife or buy breakfast outta petty cash for the sales staff. Lazy sons of bitches! I oughta quit."

"Oughta," Danny said.

"And today!"

"No sense puttin' things off."

"If I didn't have a daughter in college I'd tell 'em what to do with their job and their errands and doughnuts."

"Maybe after graduation."

"Tell 'em to hire some other gofer," Judy said.

"That's exactly what to tell 'em." Danny carried agreeing with his customers to an extreme that often amazed Nudger. But then he had to be polite; there wasn't a lot of profit margin in a shop that didn't sell many doughnuts even on a fast day.

"I got the same rights as any goddamn man," Judy said. She was hyped up this morning, all right. On fire.

"Just exactly the same."

Judy collected her change and the greasy white box, then stalked from the doughnut shop and back across the street to her unhappy and demeaning employment. One riled feminist. She was sure she'd found an ally in Danny, someone who understood and stoked her fury.

"Ain't she cute when she gets mad?" Danny said, looking after her and smiling. "She's a widow, you know."

"Didn't know," Nudger said.

"I thought about asking her out."

"Well, why not?" Nudger wondered how long it would take Judy to see through Danny and kill him. Or at least start buying doughnuts someplace else. He didn't feel qualified to advise Danny, or anyone else, in affairs of the heart or groin.

Danny set a foam cup of coffee and a Dunker Delite on a napkin in front of Nudger. Gift for the day: abdominal cramps.

"Something I need you to do for me," Nudger said.

"Just ask it, Nudge."

"There's a guy named Jake Dancer asleep on the couch in my apartment. He'll be sleeping awhile longer. Could you arrange for Ray to watch the shop now and then while you drive over there and checked on him? I left a note explaining who you are."

Nudger's apartment was only six blocks from the doughnut shop, and Danny had done this sort of thing for him in the past.

"No trouble, Nudge. Breakfast rush is over, so it'll be slow here for a while."

Nudger knew the breakfast rush today probably had been Judy, and things would be slow at the doughnut shop for the next several years and then some. "Dancer's having problems with the bottle," he said. "He might run to thirst even in the morning."

"I understand, Nudge."

And Nudger knew Danny did understand. Danny had worked through his own problems with booze. He was an alcoholic who stayed dry mainly through Alcoholics Anonymous, an organization he was sure had saved his life.

"I'll phone Ray and make sure he's free," Danny said.

Ray was Danny's cousin who lived down the street at the St. James Apartments. Ray survived on a deftly juggled income of Social Security disability pay, a small pension, and Unemployment Compensation. Nudger had never known him not to be free.

Danny went over to the phone, dialed his cousin's number, and talked to him for a while in a low voice. Nudger couldn't understand what he said. Probably Ray was trying to borrow money again.

After a few minutes Danny returned to the counter. He wiped his fingers on his gray towel, as if talking to Ray had somehow contaminated them. "Ray says he'll be glad to spell me. Says it'll cost me some free doughnuts."

"I'll pay for those," Nudger said.

"You kidding, Nudge? I got some old doughnuts I keep around just for Ray when he tries to hold me up for doing me a favor. All I do is heat 'em in the microwave before I take 'em over, and the dumb yuk thinks they're fresh-baked."

Nudger thought about donating his Dunker Delite to the cause, but he knew that would hurt Danny badly. Besides, it would be better if Ray got some really stale doughnuts. Healthier for him. Some of the grease would probably have drained out or evaporated.

Nudger thanked Danny, then dutifully ate the Dunker Delite and forced down most of the acidic coffee.

"I'll phone in now and then to make sure everything's okay," Nudger said. "When Dancer wakes up, tell him there's a fresh carton of orange juice in the refrigerator. I appreciate this, Danny. I'll make it up to you."

"No need, Nudge. This is what friends are for. Good friends, anyway."

Nudger got down off the red vinyl stool and left the shop. Had he actually, even for an instant, considered spurning a Dunker Delite and wounding this man? Talking to Danny could be a humbling experience.

Nudger sat parked outside Helen's Osage apartment until almost ten o'clock. Then he followed her through dappled sunlight as she drove away in the blue Datsun. She'd closed the car door on the hem of her dress, and a patch of red material fluttered like a proud pennant in the wind.

She drove downtown again and parked on Washington. When she got out of the car she noticed her dress had been caught in the door and bent gracefully to smooth the material. As she walked away she glanced down a few times to check the wrinkled hem.

Nudger parked again and waited.

He was careful this time to be sure it was Helen when she emerged from the office building. No doubt about identity today; she climbed back in her Datsun and confidently pulled out into the stream of traffic. She cut off a bus at the corner, ignored in queenly fashion the angry but futile blast of its horn, and wove through downtown traffic onto Highway 70 going west.

She got off on Lindbergh and drove to a string of motels near the airport. The sun glared through the Granada's windows and Nudger had to squint to keep the Datsun in sight.

He followed the little blue car into the parking lot of the Merrivale, a smaller motel on the west side of Lindbergh, and drove to the end of the blacktop lot, near a huge dumpster that had jagged pieces of cardboard jutting from its skewed steel lid. He sat there with the engine idling and watched Helen enter the motel lounge.

Thunder rolled over the lot, making the car vibrate, and an airliner flying startlingly low tilted into a roaring climb over the motel. The Merrivale was below one of the flight patterns at Lambert International Airport. It might be tough to sleep here when the wind was wrong.

The sound of the aircraft made Nudger remember that the county office of Partners Unlimited was nearby; he wondered if Helen would go there when she left the motel. Probably a lot of Partners Unlimited's business was conducted in this area, layovers between flights. Love on the go, and then departure at gate such and such, then nothing but a recollection somewhere over Philadelphia or Denver. Fuck-'n'-Fly. Only a matter of time before franchises sprang up.

Nudger waited fifteen minutes, and four more takeoffs. Then he left the Granada and walked into the motel lobby, which consisted of a registration counter, several padded chairs, a long table full of travel brochures, and a rental car desk where a man in a white shirt and blue tie sat talking to a young couple about rates and conditions for a subcompact. "Does the radio work okay?" the young guy asked.

Nudger settled into one of the padded chairs near the desk. The

woman behind the reservation counter would assume he was waiting to rent a car, as would the rental agent.

From where he sat, Nudger could see into the lounge. Helen
was at the bar talking to a tall man with rimless glasses and graying hair. He wore a blue business suit and had the glossiest black
shoes Nudger had ever seen. They reminded him of a kid he'd
known in high school who'd buff his shoes to mirror finish so he
could sneak glimpses up his dates' dresses.

Helen smiled at the man. She rested a hand on his wrist. He
rested a hand on her thigh. Nudger thought it was kind of early for
that, but business was business.

"Help you, sir?" the man behind the car rental desk asked
Nudger. The young couple had gone; Nudger saw them outside,
walking across the glaring lot toward a plain white car the size of a
toy wagon.

"I'm waiting for someone," Nudger said.

The woman behind the reservation desk overheard and gave him
a dubious and rather unfriendly look. This was no place for
loiterers to come in out of the heat.

Nudger glanced back into the lounge and saw that Helen and the
man in the blue suit were standing now and the man was leafing
some bills onto the bar. Helen leaned against him, as if to prompt
him playfully toward where she wanted him to go. It was an un-
characteristically coy gesture for her.

They began walking toward the lobby. Nudger stood up and got
out of there.

Back in the Granada, he peered around the dumpster and saw
Helen and the man emerge from the motel office. At first he
thought they might get in one of the parked cars, but they strolled
past the line of vehicles and climbed the steps to a concrete and
steel catwalk that ran in front of the second-floor rooms.

The man used a key to open the door to the end room, then
stepped back to let Helen go in first. He glanced around, as if
afraid somebody he knew might be watching. Then he tossed the

key a few feet into the air, caught it neatly, and made a fist around it. He followed Helen in and closed the door.

Nudger popped an antacid tablet onto his tongue and chewed. "Damn!" he said. But he'd known what Helen did for a living before he'd followed her here. What did he expect, that she was lying to him about being a prostitute and actually sold flowers on a busy corner? She was doing this for Dancer. The one good thing in his life, and she was doing this. Why didn't the bastard level with her, go out and steal some money if he had to pay off a debt to stay alive?

Nudger felt like storming into the motel room and snatching Helen away from there. But he knew that was the adolescent in him that sometimes got him, and other people, in trouble. Helen was a grownup with free will; how she chose to earn her money was none of his concern. Or shouldn't be. He had his own debts to pay and wished there was a better way than the stomach-churning occupation that had led him here.

He felt small and dirty sneaking around behind Helen, but Dancer was right about her possibly being in danger. He hoped Helen was right about Partners Unlimited screening their clients before sending women out on assignment.

Nudger found himself wishing the man and Helen would emerge from the room after a few minutes and drive away, that she'd merely followed him up there to get something he'd forgotten, or for some other innocent reason. Nothing sordid. Why, this could be a relative visiting between flights, maybe her brother from Albuquerque.

But the brother appeared at the room's single window and yanked the drapes closed. He was wearing only white jockey shorts. Nudger wondered how a man that age kept his stomach so flat. Guy who didn't work out five times a day like Biff Archway.

Hell with this, Nudger thought. He was getting depressed.

Since he knew where Helen would be for a while, he decided to

call in and check with Danny about Dancer. There was a phone
booth on the corner of the lot, near the street.

Ray answered at the doughnut shop and told Nudger that Danny
had left about twenty minutes ago to drive over to look in on
Dancer. Nudger punched in the number of his apartment phone
and waited five rings before the receiver was picked up.

He heard only breathing.

"Danny?"

"That you, Nudge?"

Nudger knew immediately that something was very wrong.
Danny sounded short of breath, angry. "It's me, Danny. What's
going on?"

"Couple of fellas came in here and tried to grab your friend
Dancer. Forced their way in by breaking the chain lock outta the
door. Me and Dancer fought them, and Dancer got away. The two
goons finally shoved me off them and took out after him."

"Was he on foot?"

"He was, but they wasn't. They drove off looking for him in a
black convertible. I think it was one of them little Chryslers."

"Were the two men big?"

"One was. The other was gigantic."

Kovar and friend. "You okay, Danny?"

"Yeah, they didn't hurt me. They were interested in Dancer. I
was just sorta an obstacle they had trouble moving outta their way.
I think I bought him enough time, Nudge. He had a good head
start on them and probably cut back through the gangway. Plenty
of places to hide, this part of Maplewood."

Whew! "Thanks, Danny. I really do owe you."

"You don't, Nudge. You want me to phone the police?"

"No. I think you should get out of there, in case the two men
after Dancer come back. You don't want to fool with those guys."

"Okay."

Nudger started to hang up, but Danny's voice stopped him.

"Listen, Nudge, while I got you on the phone, I been talking to
that elderly lady out in Kirkwood about the car. Mrs. Fudge. She
wants to know if you like it."

Nudger was astounded. Danny's mind would gravitate toward the trivial even in the middle of an earthquake.

"Tell her I want to buy the car, Danny."

"That's great, Nudge!" He sounded happy. For Nudger. For the lady selling the car. It was as if he were making a fortune on some complex deal he'd engineered. But Danny was simply being Danny. Naive, purely practical, gullible Danny. Small mind, giant heart.

From the stifling phone booth, Nudger saw the drapes swing open again in the second-floor end room.

A 747 took off and climbed steeply above the motel. Its shadow flitted hugely over the phone booth. All those different lives up there together, roaring toward the same place at the same time.

Jet thunder shook the ground, like a stern warning before a storm.

24

Nudger expected to find his apartment a mess, but there was little sign of the struggle Danny had put up against the men who'd tried to get at Dancer. The chair by the couch was turned over, a lampshade was tilted crazily, and one of the sofa cushions lay on the floor. Looked like the scene of a well-behaved teenagers' party. Dancer must have gotten out of there fast; he'd have had to, considering that Danny couldn't hold back two oversized thugs very long.

After straightening up the apartmennt, Nudger got a cold can of Busch from the refrigerator and sat on the sofa in the cool draft from the air conditioner. He wondered how to go about picking up Helen's trail again. He was sure that by this time she'd have left the Merrivale Motel. Her business there was no doubt consummated, unless the guy with the glossy shoes and white jockey shorts was more than he appeared and normally wore a red and blue caped costume. Her apartment might be the logical place to wait for her now, and to wait for Dancer to try to contact her.

But Dancer was smart enough to know that whoever was after him might be watching Helen, waiting for him to show up near her. He was also devoted enough in his haphazard fashion to want to be around her and protect her. On the other hand, that was what he'd asked Nudger to do, keep an eye on Helen and make sure she came to no harm.

Nudger pressed the cold, curved surface of the beer can against his forehead. Some occupation. Some life. It was all getting confusing, out of hand. Doubly dangerous. He wished there were someone keeping an eye on *him* so *he'd* come to no harm. Like his favorite teacher had in the third grade.

He lowered the can and dabbed moisture from his forehead with his sleeve. Third grade. Mrs. Hughes had been her name.

The phone jangled, making him start and slosh a little of his beer out of the can and onto his hand. The mess he was in, and had helped to make, was getting to his nerves. His stomach stirred, growled loudly, might have called him a fooool.

He got to the phone in time to answer it on the third ring.

"This Nudger?" A man's voice. Unfamiliar.

"It is," Nudger said.

"Don'cha recognize my voice? This is Lem Akers, Claudia's neighbor. You and me talked a few times in the hall over on Wilmington."

Now Nudger knew the voice. Or rather the speech pattern. It was the voice itself that had thrown him; seventy-nine-year-old Lem Akers sounded forty years younger on the phone.

"I think you might wanna drive over and hear me out," Lem said from his long-ago youth. "'Bout your Claudia."

Nudger's stomach tightened painfully. "What about her?"

"Well, you know how sound sometimes carries through the

vents in these old apartments. Way they laid out the furnaces, one for each unit, so they had to run miles of ductwork—"

"What is it, Lem?" Nudger said, trying to keep Akers on the subject. He knew Akers's favorite pastime was keeping an ear to the ductwork to eavesdrop on his neighbors. Nudger and Claudia sometimes propped a pillow against her bedroom heating vent when they wanted to be sure they weren't overheard. He occasionally wondered how effective that was, how much of what was personal between them was actually between them and old Lem Akers.

"There's times you can't help but overhear, Nudger. Whole building's like a damned intercom, what it is."

"What did you overhear this time, Lem?"

"I think you oughta know, a man came to Claudia's apartment a while ago. Not that Biff fella, either; ain't no big deal when he comes and goes. Happens all the time."

Nudger clenched and unclenched his jaws. "One man?"

"That's what I said, ain't it?"

"Big man?"

"Naw, I'd say average size, on the thin side. Dark hair and mustache. Good-looking guy, but kinda beat down, like his dog just died and he was trying to keep up a plucky front."

Dancer! What was Jake Dancer doing at Claudia's? Nudger's gaze flicked to his desk drawer where he kept his address book. The drawer was half an inch from being closed. A corner of white paper stuck out of one side. He reached over and opened the drawer, saw the mess inside. His address book, personal papers, letters from Claudia, in crumpled disorder. Dancer must have wanted to find Nudger and had rummaged through the drawer and seen Claudia's name and address. Learned of his relationship with her and thought that might be where he could be found. Dancer hadn't been thinking clearly, but had he ever? Nudger's eye caught something else, an empty bottle of his favorite scotch in the wastebasket by the desk.

"Had a name like Prancer," Lem was saying. "Or maybe one of them other reindeer."

"Dancer?"

"Yep, that's it. Anyway, I thought nothing of it till I heard what they was saying. She hadn't invited him in. Didn't know who he was at first. He used your name to get inside. He was drunk, and looking for more to drink. Had himself a thirst, all right."

"He still there, Lem?"

"Nope. That's why I think you better come on over. Claudia left with this Dancer fella, but I don't think she wanted to go."

"What makes you think that?"

"Why, I heard her tell him so. He paid her no never mind, though, and off they went."

"He kidnapped her?"

"Uuh, nope, wouldn't exactly say that. Though the law might. Who knows what the law means these days, what with half the punks in the country walking around free an hour after each arrest. That's why it ain't safe on the streets, sometimes not even in your own house or apartment. No place in the city's safe. Like goddamn Sodom and Gonorrhea, Nudger. In the Bible."

"Maybe in there somewhere," Nudger said. "Don't stray, Lem; I'm driving right over to talk with you."

The young voice was disdainful. "I was the one called and said you better come on over. Why the hell should I stray afore you even get here?"

Nudger had no answer for that. He hung up the phone and got moving.

"Never been in here," Lem Akers said, "though I knew, from what I couldn't help overhearing, what the place looked like. Neat little housekeeper, your Claudia. Good woman in a lotta ways." He leaned on his cane and peered around Claudia's apartment, nodding slightly now and then, as if fact matched imagination. From what he'd listened in on, he had the place pegged, down to the worn spots on the carpet. He was a tall but stooped gray man with long, skinny arms, and grasping hands sprinkled with liver spots. His eyes were blue and watery and sad and seeking, and sometimes bewildered. Old eyes that peered at everything too closely, as if they might finally see something they'd missed all these years, some acceptable way out.

Nudger stood with his fists on his hips. Claudia's apartment seemed normal enough. He walked to the kitchen and saw an empty bourbon bottle and an empty gin bottle in the wastebasket. Other than that, nothing that told him anything. He wandered around the place briefly but found nothing that might help reveal what had happened or where Claudia had gone, no carefully disguised message, no trail of bread crumbs.

"What exactly did you hear?" he asked Lem Akers.

Lem brightened, sucking on his dentures. He liked having something to say to someone who wanted to hear it. It was a change for him. "I happened to be looking out the front window when I seen this Dancer fella walk into the building."

"Did you see him get out of a car?" Nudger asked.

"Nope, he was on foot. Then I heard him tromp up the stairs and knock on Claudia's door. Said he was trying to get in touch with you and you'd given him her name and address. I could tell right off he'd been drinking, but I don't think Claudia realized it. She invited him right in soon as she heard your name. Well, I still didn't think much of it. I mean, Claudia's a fine-looking woman, with male friends, and that's the way it should be. Got a nice figure, your Claudia. Hell, my late wife Maureen, she had no tits and her neck got all leathery in back in her later years, like she was some Marine been out in the sun. Used to call her that, Marine instead of Maureen. Leathernecks, Marines was sometimes known as back then. She never caught on; musta had a brain smaller'n a pea—"

"What did Dancer say after he got inside?" Nudger interrupted. He'd talked to Lem before and knew the old guy was logical enough if he could only be kept on track.

"Said he wanted a drink. And Claudia got him one and then tried to phone you, but you wasn't home."

Dancer must have come straight here after fleeing from the apartment. Claudia had called after Danny had talked to Nudger on the phone, but Danny had already left to return to the doughnut shop.

"She tried your office and the doughnut shop, then, but couldn't get ahold of nobody except some guy named Ray who didn't seem to know asshole from elbow."

So she'd called the doughnut shop before Danny arrived there after leaving Nudger's apartment. That put Dancer here with Claudia at about—Nudger looked at his watch.

"It was ten-forty on the button when Dancer knocked on Claudia's door," Lem said. He'd been watching Nudger, thinking along with him, seen him glance at the wristwatch. Wily old bastard.

"What happened when she told Dancer she couldn't get in touch with me?" Nudger asked.

"Well, he had himself a real snootful by that time. Got kinda rowdy and demanded more to drink. Claudia was scared and fetched it for him, and that only made him worse. What caught my interest is he started talking about Vietnam like it was worse than France in forty-four where I was, then yapping about remorse and murder. Goddamned Vietnam wasn't the only war ever fought. Then, after a while, he said he didn't have a car and wanted Claudia to drive him someplace."

"He say where?"

Lem lowered gray eyebrows and looked irritated at being interrupted. "Said 'someplace,' is all. Claudia said she didn't want to, and he got insistent. Didn't outright threaten her or anything. But he knew what he was doing and scared her just enough so she'd drive him. I'd of been scared too; the guy was stretched tight and seemed near some kinda breaking point. They left in Claudia's car. I thought about calling the police, but I knew you was a private cop so I thought I'd call you first, let you decide if you wanted the police in on it. Tell you, Nudger, I don't trust the regular police. They ain't the sort of cop you are; you break rules and they break ribs. I know. Once this guy I worked with in the foundry punched out Maureen and she came to all groggy and said I did it. Hell, by the time she remembered what had really happened, I was in the jug getting rough-handled by some of them boys in blue. It wasn't no hands-off, Miranda bullshit like there is now. Called me a wife-beater, shoved me around, busted some small bones. I got nothing but contempt for the police, Nudger; wouldn't give 'em snow in the wintertime. Wasn't till Maureen sent her worthless sister Flora around—"

"Here," Nudger said. He pressed a folded ten-dollar bill into Lem's lean hand and felt clawlike fingers explore, recognize the special feel of folding money, and grasp. "This, too," Nudger said, holding out his last business card. "Phone me if anything else happens here, Lem. Will you do that?"

"No need for the card," Lem said, "I know both your home and office numbers. Hell, yes, I'll call you if I think there's something you oughta know. Called you the first time, didn't I?"

"Sure did," Nudger said. "You handled it right. Thanks, Lem. Thanks a lot."

Lem actually looked a little embarrassed as he hobbled out with his cane, the green of his money peeking from between his fingers.

Nudger walked outside to his car, wishing he'd never gotten Claudia involved in his work. But he thought she might be safe with Dancer. When he sobered up he'd probably apologize to her and send her home. But Claudia didn't know that and was already in a state of perpetual fear after her bout with Lars Kovar. That was probably why she'd gone so willingly, without a struggle, when Dancer had demanded she drive him.

But would Dancer remain his kindly self while drunk? He'd been that way when Nudger had seen him under the influence, but the effects of liquor could be unpredictable and weren't necessarily consistent.

Stretched tight and near some kinda breaking point.

Nudger tried not to imagine the terror Claudia might be experiencing now with a drunken Dancer. This was all a mistake, he told himself. Something that would work itself out. The temporary delusion of the bottle was to blame. Not Nudger. Booze and circumstance.

He knew better.

Nudger wristed perspiration from his forehead and climbed into the Granada. He hoped Dancer was the sweetheart everyone said he was. Drunk as well as sober. Reputations could be deceptive. And how much agony could Dancer stand before he broke?

Stretched tight . . .

Nudger drove to a phone booth to call Hammersmith and tell him what had happened. Where Lem Akers wouldn't overhear. Lem remembered that fracas with his wife Marine and might not cooperate if he knew the regular police were involved.

25

Nudger sat at his desk and watched the heat rise in wavering vapor from the tar roof across the street. The way it distorted things and made them shimmer played with distance and perspective and lent the world outside the window an unreal quality. On both sides of the window, there were certain pertinent realities Nudger was having a tough time catching and pinning down.

Hammersmith had put out a pickup order on Dancer, along with the description and license number of Claudia's car. It was time to try not to worry about Claudia, and to help her in the best way possible by watching Helen Crane in case Dancer tried to contact her. Helen, meanwhile, should be told about Dancer's abduction of Claudia.

But Nudger had phoned Helen's apartment and gotten no answer. Brad Marlyk, at Partners Unlimited, also claimed not to know Helen's whereabouts. Helen had had an appointment this morning, he'd said, and wasn't due to work again until tomorrow night. Nudger asked where and with whom. Marlyk said that was confidential. Nudger persisted until finally Marlyk said Nudger should go fuck himself and then hung up. Nudger called back and tried to pry the information out of Muffy B. Blue, but she told him exactly what Marlyk had suggested, in precisely those words. Great minds, same channels.

Nudger leaned back and felt his damp shirt adhere to the spindles of his swivel chair. He reached into his pocket for his antacid tablets and broke one loose from the roll. Then he thought about Dancer scaring Claudia into providing his transportation. Anguished, lovable Dancer. Dangerous Dancer? It was difficult to know, talking to Lem Akers, just how much pressure Dancer had applied to Claudia to get her to go with him. Why hadn't he simply demanded her car keys? Maybe, even in his drunken state, he'd realized he shouldn't drive. Possibly he even thought she'd gone with him willingly.

Danny knocked on the office door, stuck his basset-hound features inside, then smiled slowly and entered all the way. He had his customary gray towel tucked in his belt, greasy from wiping down the stainless steel counter in the doughnut shop downstairs.

"Mrs. Fudge wants her money," he said.

Nudger tilted forward in his chair. "Huh?"

"For the car. You said you wanted to buy it. She said she wants eight hundred for it."

"Seems a lot, considering it's rustier than Stan Musial."

"Not too much for a car these days, Nudge. Besides, she's an old lady; it's hard to bargain with her."

"You mean she doesn't hear too good?"

"I dunno. I guess she hears okay."

"Tell her six hundred," Nudger said.

"Nudge!"

"I talked to a guy about the Volkswagen, Danny. I can only get four hundred for it. Two hundred more's about all I can scrape together. I'm not being cheap; it's the mathematics of the thing. Tell the old lady that; she's short on money, she'll empathize."

Danny sighed and shook his head. "I'll try, Nudge."

He left the office looking despondent. Nudger heard his slow and heavy descending tread on the stairs. The street door clattered open and closed. Air stirred briefly over the office floor, not doing a thing to cool the place.

Five minutes later the phone rang. Danny calling from the doughnut shop.

"She says six hundred's okay, Nudge. The car's yours. Congratulations."

Seemed an odd thing to warrant congratulations, but Nudger thanked Danny.

"I'll drive out there later with the money," Danny said, "and take care of the title, even get it notarized for you by a pharmacist friend of mine. I know you're busy right now, what with Claudia and all. Any word yet?"

Nudger told Danny there was nothing new.

"Sure this guy won't hurt her?" Danny asked.

"I'm not sure of anything," Nudger said, too snappishly.

Silence. Danny's delicate psyche was injured.

"Sorry," Nudger said, immediately feeling low enough to slither under his desk blotter.

"Hey, I understand, Nudge. It's just that, you know, I like Claudia."

"Yeah. Listen, I can give you the money for the Granada soon as I sell the Volkswagen."

Danny's voice regained the old enthusiasm. "If you already got a deal on the Volkswagen, I can follow you over to where you're gonna leave it and drive you back in my car."

Nudger agreed to that.

Feeling uncomfortable in the cramped little Beetle, he drove to Sands Auto Body over on Watson Road, followed by Danny in his old blue Plymouth. Will Sands owned half a dozen used Volkswagens at any given time, customizing them into all-terrain vehicles and selling them for large profits.

All the way to Sands's, the VW ran beautifully. It hadn't driven this smoothly or had this much pep in years.

It knows, Nudger thought. It knows.

Sands was a huge, ruddy man with red hair and gigantic yet gentle hands that manipulated things mechanical with the precision of a surgeon. Something about the gleam in his eye when he eagerly handed Nudger the promised four hundred dollars made Nudger think he might be selling the Volkswagen too cheap. But that was usually the way he felt when he sold anything. Wanted to snatch it back immediately and ask ten percent more.

He wasn't one to get sentimental about inanimate iron, but as he walked away from the dented old Volkswagen he couldn't help glancing back at it. It seemed to glare soulfully at him as if he were betraying it. Didn't it know it would soon sport fresh paint, brand new oversized tires, a roll bar, and a snazzy half-canvas top? New automotive life. A new identity and a new owner who wouldn't get it shot at or rammed.

"Ready to go, Nudge?" Danny asked.

Nudger took one more backward look at the Volkswagen, angry with himself for feeling sentimental about a car that had been such a curse all the time he'd owned it. He hardened his heart to match German steel. "Serves you right, you little Nazi bastard."

"Say what, Nudge?"

"Nothing, Danny. Let's get outta here."

As they neared the office, Nudger saw a police cruiser parked at the curb in front of the doughnut shop. It had been washed recently and it gleamed in the sun. A blue uniform was leaning with his buttocks against the front fender. His arms were crossed. He had his cap off and was holding it, so he wouldn't be so hot. There were dark perspiration stains on his shirt beneath the arms, extending in curved patterns almost all the way down to his belt.

"Wish he'd go someplace else," Danny said. "He's scaring away customers."

Nudger didn't think that was much cause for worry at this time of day. Not many people ate doughnuts in the afternoon or evening, and it took a night's sleep before Danny's regular customers forgot the weight and grease content of a Dunker Delite and returned for more. Pastry masochists seeking their daily fixes.

Danny parked his old Plymouth a few feet behind the patrol car. The police car's whip antenna was gently vibrating. Its engine and air conditioner were running and its windows were rolled up. There was another blue uniform inside, in the passenger seat, with his head sharply bowed as if he might be reading something.

Nudger's stomach took a dive as he straightened up out of the Plymouth. He had some idea of why the police were here: Claudia. But he didn't know what kind of news they'd be bringing.

He thought about praying, but that would be hypocritical and might bring worse results than if he rode this out on his own. God was no fool and was aware Nudger would backslide later.

Not this time, Lord. This is different. Not this time!

The blue uniform was a blond kid with tiny pink-rimmed gray eyes and an underslung chin. He was slim everywhere but around the waist, where franchise food and hours of sitting in a patrol car had hung a generous spare tire of flesh on him.

He stood up straight from where he was leaning on the cruiser, uncrossed his arms, and said, "You Nudger?"

Nudger said he was.

"I'm patrolman Wallace Stivers. Lieutenant Hammersmith sent us to get you. Wants us to drive you to meet him."

"Where?"

"The morgue. Lieutenant wants you to look at a floater."

Christ, no! Claudia! Nudger's breath left him and he bent forward, his hands on his knees. He tensed his stomach and tried to regulate his breathing, tried getting blood back to the brain.

Danny grabbed his arm and helped him to stand upright. The pavement was undulating and tilting like a funhouse sidewalk at an

amusement park. But Nudger wasn't having fun. He swallowed,
then fixed his eyes straight ahead to orient himself and lessen his
dizziness. His stomach was spinning now, plunging.

"You okay, pal?" Stivers asked, putting on his cap and stepping forward, as if to be in position to help if Nudger weakened
again and went down. "Jesus, you look pale as beer foam."

"I'll be okay."

"What's a floater?" Danny asked.

"This one's a dead woman we just pulled from the river,"
Stivers said. "She was some fine piece before she died. You can
still tell, despite what the fishies did. Say, she ain't somebody
either of you guys was close to, was she?"

Nudger and Stivers barely caught Danny in time as Danny's
knees buckled.

26

Nudger listened to the rumble of the steel gurney's spoked
wheels, watched in frozen fascination as the attendant's pale, with-
ered hand—not unlike that of a corpse—reached for the linen-
contoured face. The white sheet rustled crisply as it was drawn
back, not just from the face but from the entire body. Nudger
heard himself gasp, then his breath hissed into the quiet, echoing
morgue. Usually breathing wasn't permitted here.

Hammersmith gazed at him over the dead woman. "Lord,
Nudge, you didn't think . . . damn, I'm sorry. I shoulda told you
it wasn't Claudia. I mean, it never occurred to me."

"It's all right," Nudger said. He felt warm with relief even in
the coolness of the morgue. Claudia was alive! Claudia was, in
fact, in the hands of someone everyone regarded as a sympathetic,

gentle wanderer through life, even when he was drunk. Nudger
kept his mind away from the violent people of his past who'd
fooled him with similar reputations.

"This one was fished out near where we found the other two,"
Hammersmith said. "Hard to say how long she's been dead, but I
wouldn't guess more than a day. Maybe not even that long. So
what do you think?"

Nudger couldn't make himself look directly again at the
blanched form before him. "I think this is getting old."

"Me, too. I wish we could stop it. One thing, this one hasn't
been in the water long enough to look like something not human.
Know her?"

Why should Hammersmith think he'd know the dead woman?
Did the corpulent lieutenant actually think Nudger got around town
so often and thoroughly that he was bound to have knowledge
of murder victims? Or did Hammersmith simply enjoy sending
Nudger's queasy stomach into acrobatic maneuvers?

Nudger tucked up his courage and stared down at the corpse
without blinking, pretending toothpicks were propping his eyelids
open.

He stiffened with shock. *Helen!* He thought immediately of
Helen. Same size and general build, same hair coloring, and probably the same complexion—allowing for all that time submerged.

But there was something, thank God, that was different.

The river had worked on her, so he didn't recognize her right
away. Even when her features struck a chord of memory, he
wasn't sure. But Hammersmith was probably right; Nudger might
know the victim's identity.

"Melissa."

"What?" Hammersmith asked. "Talk louder, Nudge. She
won't mind."

"I'm not sure, but I think her name's Melissa."

"Last name?"

"I don't know it. I only saw her up close once, when I was in the west-county office of Partners Unlimited. I remember her because she resembles my client.''

Hammersmith looked interested. "She one of the employees out there? One of the girls that go out on jobs?''

"Yeah. If this is her. I can't be positive it is. I only saw her briefly one time, and then mostly from the back.''

"Speaking of her back," Hammersmith said, and nodded to the attendant.

Deftly but not without effort, the attendant turned over the body. The limbs were stiff; rigor mortis hadn't been broken.

Nudger was sickened as he looked down at the lacerations on the woman's back and buttocks.

"Lash marks," Hammersmith said. "She's been beaten with a whip. There's marks on her wrists and ankles where she was tied. Look at the bottoms of her feet, Nudge.''

Nudger walked around to the end of the gurney and stooped down. This was unreal, wasn't happening. The pale feminine feet were marked on the soles with a series of blackened round spots. The flesh there and on the bottoms of her toes was torn and discolored. Nudger knew what the circular marks were before Hammersmith told him.

"Cigarette burns, Nudge.''

Nudger stood up, feeling queasy.

Hammersmith was surveying the murder victim with seeming dispassion. "Way the bottoms of her feet are messed up, and her backside, what we think is that somebody burned her soles, then whipped her to make her walk barefoot over rough ground. Maybe worse. There's some ground glass in her feet.''

"Sweet Jesus," Nudger said. "Mutilated breasts, maimed feet . . .'' He was having a difficult time believing what he'd seen. Didn't want to believe it. He was a member of the same species as whoever had done these things.

"There's monsters among us in human skin, Nudge.''

Nudger's abdomen twitched beneath his belt, which was suddenly much too tight.

"Let's get outside," Hammersmith said. He must have figured Nudger had suffered enough. Or was that it? What was next? A cigar? Please no, not a cigar!

Nudger was ready to leave.

The blue uniforms were still at the curb in the patrol car. Stivers was behind the wheel. The air conditioner was whining and straining away beneath the tick, tick, tick of the idling motor. Heat rolled out from beneath the car.

Hammersmith held the rear door open and Nudger lowered himself into the backseat. He watched Hammersmith walk around the front of the car.

The lieutenant ambled back and opened the streetside rear door and sat down beside Nudger. The seat cushion sighed and shifted toward his bulk. Stivers and his partner stared straight ahead in front of the wire mesh separating the front and back of the cruiser's interior; they didn't in any manner want to nose into Hammersmith's business. Stivers seemed to be studying a moth that was flitting desperately against the windshield. Nudger had the feeling Hammersmith could have shot him in the head and tossed the body out without attracting the attention of the two loyal patrolmen. Cops were a clannish bunch and sometimes carried it to extremes.

"What are the odds on the body being this Melissa?" Hammersmith asked. He wasn't smoking but he must have been most of the day; in close quarters he smelled like one of his loathsome greenish cigars. If the car's interior hadn't been cool the odor might have overcome Nudger.

"A little better than fifty-fifty," Nudger said. He swallowed the sour taste at the back of his tongue.

"Hmph. You're not much help."

Nudger was getting irritated; he hadn't asked to be brought to this horror show. He'd rather have sat it out. "I didn't tell you I could solve this with my crime kit."

"You like Ike?" Hammersmith asked.

Nudger stared at him. Such an erratic bastard was Hammersmith. Unpredictable. But usually with a purpose. "Ike who?"

"Eisenhower. The general and president. You know the one—bald head, big grin, like he could eat Democrats alive and not even get indigestion."

"Sure," Nudger said wearily. "I liked Ike. Helluva golfer."

"The woman in the morgue must have liked him, too. She had one of his campaign buttons gripped in her hand when we fished her from the river."

Nudger looked to see if Hammersmith was kidding. "A campaign button from the fifties?"

"I think this one was from fifty-two," Hammersmith said. "That's what a professor in the political science department at St. Louis University says, anyway."

"So what's it mean?"

"That she was a loyal Republican, maybe. Though I don't think Ike would approve of some of the bullshit going on now. No, I'm sure he wouldn't."

"I don't follow politics," Nudger said.

Hammersmith leaned forward so Stivers could hear him distinctly. "Drive Mr. Nudger back to where you picked him up."

Stivers said, "Yes, sir."

Hammersmith patted Nudger's knee. "You watch out for yourself, Nudge. I'll get in touch if we find anything on Claudia or Dancer."

"But there's nothing yet?"

"Not yet," Hammersmith confirmed. "Sorry. Give us time."

"I don't have much choice."

"Don't at that, I'm afraid." Hammersmith unwrapped one of his cigars and stuck it in his mouth. Sighting over it slightly cross-eyed, as if it were a gun barrel aimed at Nudger, he said, "Shee you, Nudge." He opened the door and worked his body out of the car, then slammed the door.

As the patrol car pulled away, Nudger watched Hammersmith

light the cigar and trudge back toward the morgue entrance, trailing green smoke. He probably enjoyed smoking in the morgue, where most of his company wouldn't dream of objecting.

"I'm glad he waited till he got outa the car before he lit that thing," Stivers's partner growled. "He'd lit it in here, I'd have told him about it, made him put it out."

It was the only thing Nudger had heard him say, but he felt a strong kinship with the man.

Stivers laughed at his partner. He had a reedy, nasty laugh to go along with his mean eyes and chin. "You wouldn't have told him shit and you know it." He turned his head a few inches, not looking back, but as a signal that he was talking to Nudger. "Ain't that right, Nudger?"

"Wouldn't know," Nudger said, discouraging conversation.

They drove along the hot, bright streets in silence. Nudger wondered what Claudia was doing, what she was thinking, beneath that same heartless sun.

27

Nudger's apartment phone rang at eleven o'clock that evening. In no mood to talk to anyone, he reluctantly left the sofa and his cold Busch and crossed the room toward the jangling pest. He'd been unable to locate Helen Crane, and there'd been no word on the whereabouts of Dancer and Claudia. Brad Marlyk had checked and said that Melissa was alive and well and that none of his employees was missing. He'd already told the police that and was tired of repeating it, he'd snapped at Nudger, and then abruptly hung up. Nudger hated it when people cut him off in the middle of a phone conversation. Though it had occurred hours ago, he was still mad.

He snatched up the receiver and barked a hoarse, unfriendly hello.

"Gee, Nudge, you sound like you got a sore throat."

Danny.

Nudger took a deep breath and wished he'd brought his beer to the phone with him. "It's okay, Danny, I dozed off, is all, and my throat got dry."

"I just called to tell you not to worry, I took the money out to Mrs. Fudge in Kirkwood and I got your title all signed, sealed, and notarized. The Granada's yours."

"Fine," Nudger said. "And thanks." He hadn't even thought about the car since his last conversation with Danny. There was a season for all things. Danny didn't know summer from winter.

"Any news yet on Claudia?" Danny asked, getting around to matters of secondary importance.

Nudger told himself not to be so rough on Danny, whose priorities were straight in his heart if not in his head. "Nothing," Nudger said. "Nothing on Dancer, either. I hope he's hunkered down peacefully somewhere asleep with his bottle of Born Again, and Claudia's on her way home."

"Born Again? You mean that cut-rate bourbon?"

"The same."

"I drank that brand a couple of times, Nudge. Harsh stuff."

"Dancer likes it."

"Well, tells you something about the guy."

"Maybe."

"Mrs. Fudge wanted me to tell you there's a screwdriver in the Granada's glove compartment," Danny said.

Nudger wiped his palm over his forehead. Sweaty. Greasy. "Screwdriver? What for?"

"She didn't say, Nudge. In case something goes wrong, I

guess. She was just being considerate. You know how old ladies are; she might think you need a screwdriver to change a tire.''

Nudge knew how some old ladies were. He remembered one named Agnes Boyington who'd casually killed people.

. ''Be sure to let me know when you hear anything on Claudia,'' Danny said.

''Okay, Danny.''

'' 'Night, Nudge.''

'' 'Night.''

Nudger replaced the receiver and staggered back to the sofa. He suddenly felt exhausted. Or had he finally admitted to himself there was nothing more he could do tonight except escape into sleep? One way or the other, he wanted desperately to lie down on the sofa.

He drained the can of beer in a long series of gulps, as if it were something he was obligated to do once he'd started. Then he took off his shoes and set them to the side so he wouldn't trip over them when he woke up, and stretched out on his back on the cushions.

He closed his eyes and within seconds Helen Crane strolled into the room. She was wearing a flowing blue oversized blouse that came down to her knees. Nudger was sure that was all she was wearing. Muffy B. Blue was behind her, face made up like a clown's but with sensuous red lips, glaring around as if basking in the knowledge that Nudger lived in what, in her estimation, was a dump. ''Fuckin' small-timer,'' she said to Nudger. ''He's not,'' Claudia said. Danny said, ''I have a pharmacist friend who will notarize that fact.'' Dancer said, ''Ain't you gonna offer your friends a drink?'' ''Tell me what everybody wants'' Nudger said, ''and we'll drink toasts and exchange secrets.'' ''Screwdrivers,'' the guests said in unison. ''We all want screwdrivers.'' Brad Marlyk said, ''We all mean that.'' Hammersmith glided in with a huge cigar jutting from his mouth. There was a dead girl on his arm; her blond hair was wet and she was staring at everyone through black holes where her eyes should have been. ''Ladeesh and gen'lemen,'' Hammersmith said around his cigar, ''the nesht

presheden of the Unided Shtates!'' "Then she can stay," Nudger
said, "but that cigar's gotta go." "Trade it for a shcrewdriver,"
Hammersmith said. "Lesh drink up!"

The softly rumbling, ticking sound of gurney wheels rolling
over the smooth morgue floor. The rotted, fishy smell of the river
down by the levee. Water lapping, lapping.

"Oh, Jesus!" Nudger moaned. "All I got is this Born Again
bourbon. That and water. I'm so sorry!"

"What are the odds?" Sammy Weld was saying. "What are the
odds?"

Muffy B. Blue said, "Fuck you, Nudger."

Nudger didn't care. Sticks and stones and bones. What bothered
him was the feeling that there was something obvious he ought to
know but didn't. Something vitally important. He rolled over and
began snoring lightly, his body twitching once, violently, as he
dropped into deeper, dreamless sleep.

Nudger awoke in total darkness and sat straight up on the sofa.
He looked at his watch's luminous hands: 2:45. The air conditioner
was still humming away, but he was sweating where his body had
been wedged against the foam rubber cushions.

He sat there for a few minutes with his elbows on his knees,
staring into blackness. His mind had finally made the tenuous but
worrisome connection, and he knew what he had to do.

What are the odds?

He groped with his left hand, switched on a lamp, and made his
way to the phone. The carpet was rough beneath his soles and he
realized he was in his stockinged feet.

There was only one person he knew who could give him the
information he wanted at this lean hour. Jeff Levine, a police reporter for the *Post-Dispatch,* who worked the night beat at police
headquarters on Tucker and Clark.

A tolerant desk sergeant told Nudger to wait and he'd see if
Levine was around, and a cacophony of muted, yelling voices
came over the line. Nudger heard the sergeant shout, "Guy name

of Nudger." A minute of total silence, as if the connection had been broken. Then Levine was there.

"Nudge?"

"Yeah."

"You're up late. Or are you up early?"

"Little of each, Jeff. I need some information. Who better to call than my old buddy who owes me forty-eleven favors and has an encyclopedic mind?"

"So let's see if we can make it forty-ten. What do you need to know, Nudge?"

"There's a big, big estate up in north county, off Lost Woods Road. It's fenced in. The entrance is blocked by a fancy iron gate that opens electronically."

"No problem, Nudge. That's where Otis Heineker lives."

Nudger waited about half a minute, then said, "I'm supposed to know who this Heineker is?"

"Well, maybe not. He retired about ten years ago. I know the place you're talking about because I was out there for an interview after the sale of the department stores. You remember Heineker's Department Stores."

Nudger did. They'd been St. Louis's largest, and among its most expensive, department stores, and had been sold to a nationwide chain. For a couple of years the stores had continued to carry Heineker's name, with a hyphen. It was supposed to make for a smooth transition and retain customers. Then the "Heineker" was quietly dropped.

"*That* Otis Heineker," Nudger said.

"Right. Big money, Nudge. Major wealth. I was toiling for the financial page when the deal went through. I don't recall the exact amount Heineker got out of the stores, but then, it was enough so that an exact amount doesn't matter. A complicated deal, too; deferred payments, stock options, low-interest loans . . ."

"What kind of guy is Heineker?"

Levine laughed. "Who knows? He doesn't mix much with people anymore. He'd have to be in his early seventies, and he was a kind of recluse even before he retired after the sale of his business.''

"I thought you interviewed him, Jeff.''

"I did. But only about the 'merger,' as he insisted on calling it, even though he'd relinquished all control of the stores. We didn't speak about his personal life. That was one of the conditions for the interview.''

"He got any family?''

"I'm not sure. He had a wife, as I recall. I also recall that she died not long after he retired. A shame, all that money. But then she was rich enough even before the old man struck the mother lode.''

"Anything else you can think of about Heineker?''

"Nothing definite. I've heard rumors he's in ill health. The kind of rumors you can believe or not. Guy in his seventies, so he's in ill health. Something we can all look forward to. Those of us who are careful, Nudge.''

"You can include me among the careful.''

"But not among the lucky.''

Nudger was in no frame of mind to argue.

"Forty-ten now, Nudge,'' Levine said.

"I'm keeping count,'' Nudger assured him. He thanked Jeff Levine for his help and hung up.

It was three A.M. Someone had once told Nudger that three in the morning was the hour of deepest sleep or deepest depression. The emotional balance point between dawn and darkness, hope and despair.

He opted for hope, splashed cold water on his face, and wrestled his shoes on.

There was little traffic at this precarious hour. He could be at the Heineker estate in about forty-five minutes, well before dawn.

He didn't really want to go there, but he forced his body through the motions as if it were a numb automaton: leave the apartment, lock the door, clump! clump! clump! down the stairs and outside to his car.

Drive.

Sometimes, when you were scared, the best thing was to try to ignore it and get on with what you had to do. Other times it was better to stay scared and safe.

The trick was knowing one time from the other.

28

There were no other cars in sight in the northbound lanes of Highway 170. Nudger seemed to be driving into endless darkness. Occasionally, brilliant southbound headlights would emerge from the black void, like the eyes of things pursued, flash past him going in the opposite direction, then fade away as red pinpoints of light in the Granada's rearview mirror.

Nudger kept his eyes fixed forward on the rushing, rough-textured pavement in the car's yellowish high beams. He thought about the fifties campaign button found in a dead woman's hand. The rakish fins of a chauffeur-driven Cadillac that had taken Melissa to the Heineker estate. Fins popular on cars of the fifties. It all might mean nothing, but Nudger was curious about the Heineker estate, and despite his twitching stomach he was deter-mined to satisfy that curiosity.

He had no legal right to sneak around the grounds. Probably even the police would have a difficult time entering, considering Otis Heineker's clout and his penchant for reclusiveness. And there was really nothing to present to a judge and obtain a warrant. Most likely there was no reason for either Nudger or the police to be mucking around on Heineker's property. The dead woman

wasn't Melissa; Brad Marlyk had confirmed that she was alive.
That is, if Marlyk wasn't lying, or tricked into thinking Melissa
hadn't died. If he hadn't simply been careless in his confirmation,
maybe relying on someone else's word that Melissa had recently
been seen alive.

The tarred expansion joints in the concrete highway were still
sticky from the cruel heat of day. Nudger listened to the steady,
repetitive kisses of the Granada's tires passing over the tar strips at
even intervals, marking time and distance and apprehension.

He was eager to get to the Heineker estate, eager to end the
tension of not knowing. Though even if Heineker was somehow
connected with the Ike button and the dead girl who looked like
Helen and Melissa, Nudger's snooping around might not reveal
anything. What are the odds? he asked himself. The words seemed
somehow familiar.

He chewed antacid tablets and drove.

When he reached the turnoff on Lost Woods Road, he slowed
the Granada to below ten miles an hour and studied the foliage in
an effort to get his bearings. He was reasonably sure he was near
where he'd parked the last time he was here. The tall iron gates
should be about half a mile ahead.

The leafy woods on each side of the road seemed to lean in
toward the wavering wash of the headlights, forming a tunnel that
narrowed ahead of Nudger, then widened and opened to black sky
as he passed.

He drove a little farther, until he saw a space between two huge
trees where he could pull off the road and at least partially conceal
the Granada. He stopped the car and switched off the headlights,
leaving the engine idling. A sense of isolation and fear pressed in
on him with the night. Fear and doubt.

When his eyes had adjusted to the darkness, he let the Granada
roll forward and parked it in the black shadows exactly between
the two big tree trunks. There was barely enough room to get his
door open and squeeze out. But he might, he noticed, be able to

steer the car in a tight U-turn here and head back the way he'd
come, in a hurry if it became necessary.

Carrying a flashlight, and one of the car's rubber floor mats, he
walked along the road toward the iron gates. He had the eerie
feeling that dozens of eyes were watching him from the dark
woods. Off to his left, in the distance, he saw the smilelike curve
of the moonlit river gleaming through the trees, and he knew his
location exactly.

He left the road and cut through the woods toward the section of
fence he'd scaled yesterday to get onto Heineker's property.
Around him, small things stirred in the darkness. Night creatures.
Vines and low branches clutched at his ankles, entwining him in
snares too weak to hold fast.

The fence was easy to find in the moonlight. Nudger tucked his
flashlight into his belt and approached the heavy chainlink topped
with the single strand of barbed wire. His stomach was quivering
and his heart was slam-dancing against his ribs. *What am I doing
here? Really? I should be clerking in a paint store or selling insurance to veterans. Not this. I don't want to do this.*

His stomach growled. Sweat rolled down his face. He tasted
coppery fear.

Do it!

He tossed the heavy but flexible rubber floor mat up so it was
draped over the barbed wire. Then he stuck his fingers through the
fence and began climbing.

With unexpected ease, he scaled the chainlink and dropped to
the other side of the fence. The Heineker side. The barbed wire
hadn't touched him. Commando Nudger! He'd have congratulated
himself if he weren't so scared.

For a while he stood motionless and listened. The only sounds
were the ratchety screams of locusts in the surrounding woods, and
Nudger's pulsing heart. There was no motion. Not even a breeze
to stir the high leaves and alter the shadows. It seemed much
warmer on this side of the fence.

Nudger untucked his shirt. He held the flashlight low and

wrapped in his shirttail to mute the beam as he walked. It cast just enough faint illumination on the ground to allow him to make his way without tripping over anything.

Ahead, the random pattern of stars was blocked out by something massive and dark. The roof of the main house.

A scuffing sound made Nudger gasp and back into the shadows. He slid his thumb off the flashlight button and the beam died.

Peering through the leafy branches, he saw that he was much nearer to the driveway or a walk than he'd imagined. The sound he'd heard was the scraping of a dog's paws on concrete.

A man in a dark uniform was swaggering along walking a large German shepherd on a leash, moving away from the house. He was shorter and much heavier than the Cadillac's chauffeur. Hefty but not fat. The dark bulk on his hip might be a holstered gun. The dog had tall, pointed ears that seemed held erect by invisible wires. Ears like that could hear for miles; the rest of the dog was big enough to do something about whatever was heard and not liked. The animal seemed well aware of its prowess and strutted beside the stocky man like an eager, combative shadow.

Private security guard, Nudger thought. For a man of Otis Heineker's means, that wasn't unusual. But it made tonight all the more dangerous.

Nudger considered creeping back the way he'd come. Considered it seriously.

But he was here now, more than halfway to where he wanted to get. It would be frustrating to give up. Cowardly.

Nudger thought about that "cowardly." Should it be "sensible"?

Tonight the two words seemed interchangeable. But Nudger absently thumbed an antacid tablet off the roll in his breast pocket and flipped it into his mouth, then continued moving toward the house. A job was a job was a job. Or maybe the crux of his existence. What was he if he didn't do his job? Not for his client—for himself. He'd lost almost everything else; what would he have left?

He knew the answer.

He didn't dare risk using the flashlight again as he edged forward.

The huge house was brick beneath the ivy smothering the front walls. It was dark except for a dim light in an upstairs window, possibly a nightlight. There were shutters on the top windows, and large, striped canvas awnings on those on the ground floor. Some of the windows had decorative iron grillwork over them. An outside central air-conditioning unit was humming away somewhere nearby, causing metal on metal to vibrate softly and almost musically.

Nudger skirted the house, as well as a circle of garish light cast on the smooth lawn by an outdoor fixture in back, and made his way to the smaller, similar building behind the main house.

The scaled-down house was completely dark. It was the size of a small, two-bedroom starter home, also brick. It, too, had iron grillwork over some of the windows, but no awnings. No ivy, either. What looked like a multicar garage was attached to it in back.

Concealed behind a row of hedges that scratched his face and arms, Nudger crept along the side of the house to a window unprotected by iron. He inserted his fingers against the edge of the upper wooden cross-frame and pushed up on the window until his fingertips tingled with pain.

Locked.

He could see the latch clearly on the other side of the glass; he should have looked before expending all that effort. When would he learn these things? Should he have taken that mail order course in detection? Gone for that diploma with the fancy border design of little guns and badges?

He forged through the bushes to the next window, then on to the last one on that side of the house. They were both locked; probably all the windows were carefully latched, if there was a security force mentality operating here. On the other hand, there was no sign that the window was wired to an alarm system.

Nudger remembered the patrolling guard. The jaguar-sized dog with the radar ears. He gulped. He raised the butt of the flashlight and, with minimal force, shattered the pane near the window lock.

Before trying to open the window, he stood fearfully, listening to the night, imagining his ears were at that moment as pointed and sensitive as the German shepherd's.

But the breaking glass hadn't made much more noise than a loud cough, so after a few uneasy minutes he felt safe enough to proceed.

He removed a jagged piece of glass, then reached in and worked the brass latch.

He raised the window and climbed inside, gingerly holding the closed drapes out of his way so he wouldn't get snagged on them.

He was on plush carpet. He risked the flashlight beam and saw that all the drapes in the room were closed. It was a small den or living room furnished with a sofa, basket chairs, and a big-screen, blond console TV with a video recorder hooked up to it. There were a couple of blond wood tables, a pole lamp with three bullet shades. On the TV, by the recorder, was a ceramic panther with plastic flowers sprouting from the planter in its lean back. On the wall behind the sofa was a painting of a weeping clown on black velvet. Next to that, a poster of James Dean with his thumbs hitched in his jeans, looking as sullen and unhappy as the clown. At each end of the sofa, on the low, blond tables, were matching ceramic lamps with roses painted beneath their glaze. Place looked as if it had been decorated by Frankie Avalon on a budget.

And yet there was the suggestion that it was *supposed* to look that way, that it was all done for effect: a 1955 living room plucked whole and authentic from a time capsule.

Or almost authentic; there was the video recorder on top of the blond television.

Nudger crossed the room and made his way down a short hall. He was sure the house was empty, but he walked as quietly as possible. He considered removing his shoes, but he didn't like the idea of having to run in his stockinged feet if he was discovered.

Besides, the spongy carpet was doing a good job of muting his footfalls.

He tried the door at the end of the hall and found it locked.

Interior locks were usually little problem. Nudger got his Visa card from his wallet and inserted its honed edge between the door and frame. He stooped low and concentrated, working the plastic card carefully against the angled steel latch. Bending it not quite far enough to snap it in half and end his charge account woes.

It took him only a few seconds to slip the lock and swing the door open.

This was a different kind of room altogether. The walls were covered with framed photographs, many of them black and white. The flashlight beam played over a bare leg, bare breasts, a plastic smile.

Pinups. Otis Heineker had a room full of pinups.

Well, there was still fire in the old guy.

But there was something about these pinups. Nudger entered the room all the way and stepped closer to the display of photographs.

The top row consisted of older shots, obviously professionally done. Several of them were of an attractive blond woman in her thirties. They weren't pinups, but looked like studio portraits. The woman was fully dressed, in the style of the fifties. In several poses she was wearing a sweater, with a bra that made her large breasts remind Nudger of the bullet-shaped lampshades on the pole lamp in the living room. She wore her hair in bangs and a page-boy in some of the photographs. In others she had her long hair pulled back to reveal her full facial beauty. Nudger held the beam on one of the hair-back photographs and studied the woman closely.

Something with a thousand tiny cold legs crept across the back of his neck.

It was undeniable. She resembled Helen Crane.

The women in the other photographs also resembled Helen Crane, the woman in the top row of photographs, and each other. They were in various standard cheesecake poses in some of the photos. In others they were bound with what looked like miles of skillfully knotted rope. Ugly welts, lash marks, were evident on their nude bodies. Despite the dated hairstyles, the photographs gave the impression they'd been taken fairly recently.

Nudger swung the flashlight beam across the room like a scythe, to the opposite wall.

The photographs here were even more explicit. In some of them the women were badly maimed, untied, and gazing at the camera as if pleading for mercy. There was a ring piercing a breast of one of the women. A dog leash was clipped to the ring and held up by someone not in the picture so that it trailed out of the frame. Another woman had a bruised and swollen face and held her arms out hopelessly, as if reaching for something she knew she'd never touch. Another sat with her legs extended straight out in front of her; the soles of her feet were lacerated, and dotted with what Nudger knew were burns. Her head and upper body were slightly blurred; the photographer had deliberately focused the lens on her injured feet.

Nudger held the flashlight close to that photo. The woman's hair was plastered with perspiration over her forehead and across one eye. Though the visible eye was resigned and half closed, her mouth hadn't given up yet on life and was distorted in agony. Nudger recognized her, though he'd seen her only twice when she was alive.

Melissa.

He slid her photograph out from beneath the glass of the frame, folded it once, and slipped it into his pocket. Then he did the same with a photo of the fully clothed blond woman on the opposite wall. He felt soiled and vaguely guilty about the hint of desire the photographs had raised in him, along with his revulsion.

There was another door in the room.

This one was unlocked. Nudger eased it open and found that it led to the garage. Moving forward, and abruptly down a step, he smelled the faint odors of oil and gasoline.

He shot the flashlight beam around and saw that there were no windows in the garage. Groping with his free hand, he felt a wall switch and turned on the lights.

The garage was spacious; room for four cars easily. There were only two parked in it: a brown Studebaker convertible similar to one Nudger had owned as a kid in 1956, and the stately, finned gray Cadillac. Both cars looked as if they'd been manufactured an hour ago.

There was a long wooden workbench along one of the walls, and a pegboard on which tools hung from steel hooks. Nudger expected to see screwdrivers, wrenches, a rubber mallet—tools for working on cars. Or maybe some lawn equipment.

Some of those tools were on the board, but others looked less familiar.

Nudger walked to the workbench and saw a set of heavy-duty punches and awls, various oversized needles, half a dozen cigar boxes full of steel snaps, studs, and turnbuckles. Tools for working leather. For creating the constraints on the women in the photographs.

Nudger looked around the garage and recognized some of the photos' backgrounds. The crude paneling with the kidney-shaped water stain. The brick wall with the thick iron brackets set firmly in mortar, for manacles and chains. He realized then that most of the photographs had been taken either here or in the first room he'd been in. The Frankie Avalon room.

There was a tall cabinet up on legs against one of the garage walls. Its thick steel doors were secured by a heavy padlock. Probably that was where the implements of torture were stored. Here in the garage, along with automotive smells, was the same faint scent of ultimate desperation that Nudger had been aware of in the interrogation room in the Third District station house. Human beings exuded something in their mortal terror, something that lingered and haunted.

He remembered the women in the morgue. What had been left of them after the river, and what they'd endured before death. Then he recalled some of the more graphic photographs, and the

video recorder and large-screen TV. He clenched his teeth and
held in check his rage and the nausea that gripped him. In this
place snuff videotapes had been made either for sale and distribu-
tion or for private, twisted amusement. Death, recorded visually
for the sadistic pleasure of others, must have finally been wel-
comed, and embraced like a lover, by the women from the river.

No more, Nudger thought. *No more!*

He switched off the garage lights and made his way through the
fifties-decorated guest house and back outside. Creepy. "American
Bandstand" gone mad. He was glad to be out of there.

As he emerged from the shelter of the bushes, he saw that there
was still only one dim light in the main house. The darkness
around him was quiet.

Quiet! Where were the cicadas? What had happened to their
raucous, ratchety mating signals?

Possibly something had alerted them. And brought about the
sudden silence Nudger remembered from the woods of his boy-
hood. In a primal vestige of the mind, silence was a warning.
When something dangerous was on the prowl, stillness meant survival.

But *he* couldn't be still; he had to get off the Heineker estate.

He crossed the bare stretch of lawn, feeling terribly exposed, as
naked and vulnerable as the women in the perverted display of
photographs. He ran hunched over and could hear his heels strik-
ing the drought-hardened earth. Sweat caught the corners of his
eyes, causing them to burn. He hoped he wasn't perspiring all over
the photographs in his pockets, obscuring them.

He had to make himself move slowly through the woods. If he
ran he'd make too much noise. He remembered the German shepherd, and what might have been the bulk of a pistol on the stocky
guard's hip.

Metal glinted ahead in the moonlight. He was almost to the
fence. He'd almost brought it off! Made it home!

"You!"

The loud voice behind him froze Nudger.

"You! Halt!"

Nudger's signal to run. He burst forward with more speed than he thought he could accomplish through the thick woods. Leaves brushed his arms. Small branches whipped across his face, stinging him more painfully than the salt of his sweat in his eyes. Underbrush dragged at his ankles.

He didn't know if he was being pursued and didn't want to look back to find out.

"Sic!" the voice commanded behind Nudger.

Oh, Christ! The dog was after him!

Nudger gasped for air and stretched his legs for longer strides, feeling sharp pain in the backs of his thighs. He was sure he could hear the rustle, the panting, of the German shepherd pursuing him through the brush. A game to the dog: chase, catch, chew, tear. Kill?

There! Ahead was the dark shape of the rubber mat draped over the barbed wire. Nudger hurdled a fallen limb and sprinted for it. Like the goddamn Olympics!

Deep growling now behind him; he couldn't tell how near.

He flung himself against the chainlink fence, scrambling up, up, up!

But he was scaling the fence in painfully slow motion. Time was dragging for him; was it for the dog?

When his hand touched the rubber mat he seemed to receive a jolt of fresh energy. And as he glanced behind him and saw the dark, bounding form of the dog not a hundred feet away, he got another spurt of adrenaline.

He gripped the mat and pressed it against the barbed wire, pulled his aching body higher, higher . . .

Over!

The dog slammed into the other side of the fence like the Nudger-seeking missile it was. It didn't bark, but it snarled softly. That was infinitely more frightening. This dog knew its business and would be merciless and workmanlike in disassembling Nudger—if the lovely fence weren't separating them.

"Bart!" A man's voice was shouting now. "Where you at, Bart?"

Nudger didn't know if Bart was the dog or its handler. Or possibly the slender chauffeur. He wasn't so curious he wanted to stay and find out.

He ran along the road toward where the Granada was parked, fast but not flat out, trying to regain some breath and composure. For a moment he had to stop, turn in a circle to make sure of where he was, terrified he might have taken the wrong direction on the road. *Was it even the same road?*

But there was the squarish form of the car hunched between the two trees. He reached it, gripped a door handle.

Inside. Safe.

He'd left the key in the ignition switch. He pressed it between his sweat-damp thumb and forefinger, twisted it.

The engine ground but didn't start.

He tried again.

It didn't start the second time.

Or the third.

Nudger began to tremble. He felt an overpowering rage. The car had run beautifully when he was considering buying it. Now, after the deal was closed, it was revealing its true despicable self!

The people chasing Nudger would kill him, maybe in the worst possible way. He could hear them shouting in the distance. If he got out of the car and ran, the dog—or dogs—would surely pick up his scent and catch him. If he stayed here he'd be discovered momentarily. If he kept trying to start the car, the grinding sound would immediately draw his pursuers.

Nudger squeezed the steering wheel. If only he could kill Danny and the old lady who'd sold the Granada! If only he could do that before he died himself!

Then he remembered the screwdriver Mrs. Fudge had wanted Danny to mention.

He popped open the glove compartment door and there it was,

all alone except for a wadded Kleenex. He'd owned plenty of old cars and he had a good idea of why the screwdriver was important.

Not yet! Nudger told himself. Death could wait for some other night.

Maybe.

He yanked the hood latch and got out of the car, carrying the screwdriver and flashlight. Quickly he raised the hood and unscrewed the wingbolt holding the air cleaner to the carburetor. He shone the flashlight down the carburetor's throat.

As he suspected, the butterfly valve that controlled the mixture of air and gas was stuck closed. The automatic choke wasn't working. It was a common and chronic ailment of older cars.

Nudger inserted the screwdriver down the carburetor throat, wedging the valve open, and left it there. He saw scratches on the carburetor where this had been done many times before, and he suddenly felt confident that he'd indeed found the problem—why the car hadn't started.

The shouting was closer now. Whoever was searching for him was headed in this direction. When he tried to start the car again, they'd certainly hear.

He hurriedly got back in the car, squeezing through the narrow space between tree and door. Then he held his breath, placed his foot on the accelerator, and twisted the key.

The starter ground . . . wavered.

The battery was running down!

Nudger pumped the accelerator in panic. He twisted the ignition key again and held it, letting the starter grind and grind.

And grind.

Slower and slower.

The engine sputtered. Turned over. And roared.

Nudger whooped and pounded on the steering wheel. He loved the rusty old Granada again. Forever!

He climbed out of the car, removed the screwdriver, and slammed down the hood, leaving the air cleaner on the ground. He was back behind the steering wheel in two seconds.

He jammed the car into gear and guided it through a tire-spinning U-turn. It made it easily, clearing the trees on the other side of the road by at least an inch! What a vehicle!

No reason for silence now. Nudger gunned the motor and roared through the woods along the narrow road. On curves he could hear branches screech along the fenders. The Granada bucked and soared over ruts and bumps, but it never faltered.

He was moving so fast he needed to pick up only a few miles per hour when he reached the main road, then the highway. He knew he'd gotten clear and was safe.

Doing sixty on Interstate 170, he realized he'd forgotten to switch on the Granada's air conditioner and he was soaked with sweat.

Oddly, though, he wasn't uncomfortable. Not at all. Even if his chest was heaving and his arms and hands were quaking.

The hell with it. He left the air conditioner off and cranked down his window. A blast of air filled the car and swirled madly around him.

He was alive.

More than simply alive—he felt great!

29

As the tall iron gates sprang open, the German shepherd came bounding hard. It wasted no motion. Ears back and fangs bared in a warrior's grin, it made no sound other than the soft patter of its paws on the driveway.

"Great-looking dog," said one of the county cops who'd pried open the gates with the hydraulic jack usually used to remove accident victims. He was a blond man with sergeant's stripes on his brown uniform. Nudger could tell he loved dogs.

"Shoot it," his commanding officer said ruefully.

The cop raised his 12-gauge riot gun, held it steady, and waited while the dog closed to within a hundred feet. "Poor bastard's only doing his duty," he said.

"You, too," Nudger said. He was getting nervous.

The riot gun roared and bucked against the sergeant's shoulder. The dog dropped into a heap and didn't move, as if it had suddenly struck a glass wall and broken its neck.

"Okay," Hammersmith said. "Fine work."

The County Police major who'd given the order to shoot the dog glanced at him pointedly, not liking his authority usurped. This wasn't the city, wasn't Hammersmith's official jurisdiction.

But it was time to get down to why they'd come here. There were a dozen police cars angled on the road before the gates to the Heineker estate. The area was unincorporated, and the County Police were here in force. So was the Major Case Squad from St. Louis proper, whose job it was to investigate serious crimes throughout the area. So was the Mobile Reserve, which sometimes aided the Major Case Squad. Hammersmith had allowed Nudger to accompany him.

The news media people, who'd trailed the noisy caravan in large numbers, were kept at a distance. It was for their own protection, they were assured, and only temporary. They grumbled and broke out the long lenses and distance sound equipment.

Brown uniforms, blue uniforms, plainclothes officers, and lone civilian Nudger poured through the gates, past the mound of fur that had been the German shepherd. Nudger felt like a Roman centurion attacking an ancient city. Some of the Major Case Squad officers, wearing blue baseball caps with SLPD lettered above the bills, carried shotguns and fanned out to advance out of sight on each side of the driveway. Hammersmith and Nudger, and the commander of the Major Case Squad, walked up the center of the driveway. Nudger realized they didn't know how far it was to the house; the gates should have been forced wider so they could have driven.

Not that they expected Otis Heineker or whoever else was on the grounds to be surprised. Not after the sirens, and the bright flashing light display that had rivaled the brilliance of the early-morning sun. Then the blast of the riot gun. Once Hammersmith had heard Nudger's story and seen the photographs, it hadn't taken long to obtain a warrant and coordinate forces for the arrest of Otis Heineker. Things had to be done in a hurry; Heineker knew someone had been snooping around the grounds last night, though he might have assumed that Nudger was simply an ordinary prowler, or that some adventurous teenagers had climbed the fence seeking thrills.

This was a case that would hold media attention for months and could make careers. It had its PR aspects too, the law falling evenly on everyone, no matter how rich and important. Thus the light-and-siren show.

There was a shot off to the left, from the woods. Another. Someone shouted.

"Jesus!" Nudger said.

"Get to cover, Nudge," Hammersmith told him, gripping his elbow and yanking him toward the shelter of the trees.

More shots. Flat, slapping sounds that didn't echo.

"The security guard I told you about," Nudger said, when they were well within the woods. He looked around. The Major Case Squad commander had gone in some other direction.

"Security guard shit," Hammersmith said. "Ordinary security guards don't shoot at cops. Guy's gotta have a good reason to shoot at this task force. Looks like D day here."

"I showed you some good reasons," Nudger said, remembering the photographs.

"Stay here, Nudge. You really got no cause to be along. This is police business."

"C'mon, Jack—"

"I mean it," Hammersmith said. "Could be your license, Nudge, if you fuck up things here. Don't move from this spot."

"But Jack—"

With a look that suggested he had no more time to argue, Hammersmith drew his revolver and moved off in the direction of the gunfire. Fat as he was, he glided through the woods like a wily Indian.

Nudger waited a few seconds. Then, staying in the shelter of the trees, he made his way toward the house.

What gun battle? A man Nudger took to be Otis Heineker, and the skinny uniformed chauffeur, were standing beneath the portico of the main entrance. Neither was armed. Neither seemed to notice there was shooting on the property. They were gazing in the direction of the road, looking glum and not talking. Probably, Nudger thought, it was the guard dog's hefty handler waging war with the police.

They saw Nudger immediately when he stepped from behind the trees, and watched him walk up the driveway. There was another flurry of shots from the woods.

These two were some pair. Otis Heineker was stooped and frail and gray and almost as skinny as the chauffeur, who looked like a cadaver who'd been jolted to life with electricity. Heineker was wearing lightweight tan slacks, a white shirt, and a gold ring and watch he must have paid for with one of his department stores. Despair tugged at the chauffeur's gaunt features. But not at Heineker's craggy face. Beneath his bushy gray brows, eyes of blue and glittering intensity glared haughtily at Nudger with the stubborn, nothing-to-lose defiance of the very old. There was a wild, undiminished hunger in those eyes. His thin lips writhed but he made no sound.

When Nudger was within twenty feet of the two men, the chauffeur said in a high, squirrely voice, "You a policeman?"

Nudger watched both men carefully, ready to bolt if either reached for a weapon. "Nope."

The chauffeur sneered. When he did that he resembled Claudia's ex-husband Ralph Ferris, who looked like a skinny, ornery young Frank Sinatra. "A reporter, I'll bet. Got here ahead of the troops so's to get a story."

"Private investigator," Nudger said.

The chauffeur said, "Sheeit!" Drawing out the word as if he could taste it and didn't like it. Didn't like Nudger. Well, it was mutual.

Otis Heineker spoke then, in a firm, reasonable voice that belied his appearance of egocentric madness. "Ronnie, do these people think they're here to party?"

"No, sir," Ronnie the chauffeur said. "What I been warning you about all these months is finally happening."

Heineker's cold blue eyes focused like laser beams on Nudger, as if Nudger were to blame for all of his troubles. And in a sense maybe he was. But Heineker's mind seemed too loosely hinged for him to realize that.

He startled Nudger by saying, "Ah, this is Nudger."

"Yes, sir," Ronnie said glumly. "Him, all right."

"Ronnie's mentioned you, Mr. Nudger."

"Been mentioned to me," Ronnie said. "More'n I liked to hear."

Heineker stared out over his wooded kingdom. The shooting had stopped. Nudger wondered if it had all been between the assorted law enforcement agencies, firing at each other. Someone in the woods shouted something indiscernible. There was an answering shout.

With a sigh, Heineker said, "I'll go inside now, Ronnie. See that I'm not bothered." Despite his frail, hunched frame, he moved with spring and strength as he turned and strode toward the door.

Nudger wasn't sure where Heineker was going. To destroy evidence? *The photographs?*

"Wait a minute!" Nudger yelled, and ran forward.

"Hold on, bub," skinny Ronnie said, acting as if he weighed

two hundred pounds and could toss Nudger aside like a wadded napkin.

Heineker had disappeared inside the front door.

Nudger started to follow and Ronnie grabbed his shoulder. Then Ronnie screamed shrilly. Nudger jumped. What the hell was this? Martial arts?

No. Nudger easily shoved Ronnie aside.

But as he moved toward the door, the fallen Ronnie was clutching his leg. "I'm tellin' you, Nudger, don't go in there! You can't!"

Nudger dragged Ronnie a few steps, then tried to push him away. Ronnie was a game one; he sank his teeth into Nudger's thigh. He knew how to bite to the bone.

The pain leaped like a searing, paralyzing current to Nudger's brain and almost dropped him. It also enraged him. He clubbed the back of Ronnie's scrawny neck with his fist. Then with both fists.

Ronnie let go.

Whimpering, he crawled a few feet away and curled into a ball, playing turtle like a kid.

His leg still pulsing with pain, Nudger shoved his way in through the front door.

He was in a spacious, high-ceilinged hall. There was an oriental rug on a polished hardwood floor, a brass plant stand with a fern on it, oil paintings and a gold-framed mirror on the walls. In the mirror Nudger saw the door to another room. Heineker was inside that room, reaching into a desk drawer.

Nudger whirled, fixed the direction of the doorway, and ran toward Heineker.

The old man glared at him, surprised, and raised a revolver from the drawer.

Hammersmith was behind Nudger, shouting, "Nudge!"

Heineker's seamed, gray face twisted in panic and he extended an elbow. Nudger knew why and threw himself across the desk.

The wasted body crumpled light as paper against his hurtling bulk. Heineker flew to the side as if struck by a vehicle, barely diverting the direction of Nudger's charge. There was an explosion and something ruffled Nudger's hair. He was down on the floor with Heineker.

"Criminal!" Heineker screamed at him. He tried to lift the gun but Nudger grabbed his wrist. "Criminal!"

The frail arm strained upward, inward; Heineker was still trying to follow his violent exit plan. His breath in Nudger's face was sour, corrupt as the man himself. He was wheezing and spraying spittle.

"Wants to kill himself!" Nudger gasped. The stench of cordite from the fired pistol was suddenly thick enough to taste, overpowering even Heineker's breath. Nudger held on tight to the scrawny arm.

Clatter and voices. Shadows in turmoil. Hands and feet and uniforms closed in. A glossy black shoe mashed Nudger's fingers into the carpet.

The fingers of his other hand were pried one by one from around Heineker's bony wrist. He saw that the revolver was gone from Heineker's freckled hand.

Nudger was yanked to his feet, not gently.

"Goddamn, Nudge!" Hammersmith's voice. *"Damn!"*

Heavy breathing, more muttered curses. The room was filling up with people.

Then, "Let him loose."

Bruising fingers were removed from Nudger's upper arms. A tightly clenched fist relaxed its grip on his wadded shirt front.

"He would have shot himself if I hadn't stopped him," Nudger said, already defending his license. He realized then that no one other than Hammersmith was aware of Hammersmith's instructions to him to stay in place in the woods.

The Major Case Squad commander looked mad enough to order Nudger destroyed in the manner of the German shepherd.

Otis Heineker was held by two burly county officers, his jaw trembling but jutting arrogantly, his blue eyes suddenly sane. "I'm

saying nothing," he stated in his firm voice. "I wish to consult
with my attorney."

"Yes, sir," the county major said, sounding a lot like Ronnie.

"You *do* know who I am?"

"Yes, sir," the major said again.

And he read the old man his rights.

On the ride back to the city, in Hammersmith's unmarked Pontiac, Nudger said, "The little chauffeur, Ronnie, bit me in the
leg."

Hammersmith said, "We're still going to be hard on him," and
touched flame to cigar.

He was, among other things, slow to forgive.

30

She came to Nudger. He trudged upstairs to his office without
checking with Danny to see if he had visitors, and there she was,
seated in the chair before his desk. Even from the back, even before he smelled her cloying sweet perfume, her overblown bulk
and the explosion of white ruffles around her neck told him it was
Muffy B. Blue.

Nudger walked around her, sat down hard in his swivel chair to
make it squeal, and served her a smile. "So, you couldn't stay
away from me. Passion's a compelling force."

Muffy observed him with the disdain most people reserved for
child-murderers. Her dark mascara had run, and despite five layers
of pale makeup her nose was red from crying. She looked more
than ever like a clown who'd sprouted mammary development and

discovered sex and liked it. Didn't sound like a clown, though. "I won't bullshit around. I want something."

Nudger stared past her, out the window, wondering what kind of game she was here to play. Though it was only nine A.M., she'd probably heard the news of this morning's arrest of Otis Heineker. Who hadn't heard? The media hadn't had so much to talk, write, and lie about in years. They were going at it with all engines.

"Why aren't you at work?" Nudger asked.

"Called in sick. Aren't you curious about what I want and what I got to offer?"

"I'm not sure. Does Brad Marlyk know you're here?"

She squirmed uncomfortably on oversized buttocks, making the wooden chair groan. "Nobody knows I'm here but you, Nudger. We can work a trade, I figured. You're stupid, you're ugly, but you can help me."

"And I can hardly refuse when you ask so nice."

"I want you to be my intermediary with the police."

"Sounds like a job for your lawyer."

"It was my lawyer advised me to come here, dumbfuck. He said it'd look better for me if I cooperated with you in your investigation. You're big in the news, boy. He also told me there was no good way outta what happened. It's not so hard to understand; this way it'll be you and me that set the record straight."

"That makes some sense," Nudger said. "If this is about Partners Unlimited in regard to Otis Heineker."

"It is. And I'll tell you the facts, if you promise to go to your friend Hammersmith and put in a good word for me. Let the law know I was the one helped you out. If you break your promise, I'll deny this conversation happened. See, I've got nothing to lose."

"Unless Otis Heineker or his chauffeur talk first," Nudger said, "or already have talked."

"I've got no way of knowing what anybody else is saying," Muffy said. She glanced at her jumbo digital watch. The pattern

on its face altered; numbers changed, time pressed. "That's why
I'm here so early talking to you."

Nudger picked up a pencil and rolled it between his thumb and
forefinger, feeling its hard, hexagonal regularity. He didn't want to
help Muffy B. Blue, but he *did* want to hear what she had to say.
One of life's compromises. "I'll talk to Hammersmith," he said.
"But only if you deal straight with me."

She snorted. "Nothing to deal. The cards have already been
dealt, and I got a shitty hand."

Nudger tapped the pencil point on his desk, making a series of
black dots. He noticed the entire front of the desk top was marred
by tiny, dark indentations; this was a habit he'd have to break. He
put the pencil down and said, "Tell me about Otis Heineker."

Muffy licked her red, red lips, as if lubricating them to make
what she had to say slide out easier. "He has this fixation about
his dead wife, and the early years of their marriage in the fifties.
He's hung up on the fifties in a big way. Old guy's a head case
with a thing about the past. And I mean a *thing*! His obsession,
you might say. Anyway, he hired girls from Partners Unlimited
who resembled his dead wife Helen."

Nudger couldn't help interrupting her. "Helen?" He sat forward.

"Yeah, that was the wife's name. Anyway, Marlyk and
Heineker had this business agreement, where Heineker would send
plenty of money and Brad would send a woman to him who looked
like his precious Helen. This went on a few years. Heineker's
chauffeur, Ronnie, was the one made the actual arrangements and
drove the women out to the estate. Some of the girls wouldn't go
back there because Heineker was into very rough stuff. He liked to
tie them up and flog them while Ronnie taped or photographed
them, that kinda thing. Not so unusual; more than a few of our
customers get their rocks off that way. But not so extreme. Then,
last year, one of the girls died up at Heineker's place, in his house.
An accident. Trouble all around. Marlyk helped the old bastard
cover it up, got rid of the body for him with creepy Ronnie. That's

when Lars Kovar and Buddy got in on the deal, to protect Marlyk's interests."

"Buddy?"

"Buddy Drake. He's the security guard that got killed by the
cops in the shootout this morning."

"He was actually Marlyk's man?"

"Yeah. Buddy and Kovar did whatever muscle work needed
doing. Like a couple of times when girls objected to Heineker's
rough treatment and ran away from the job, developed loose
tongues. The ladies had to be taught to follow instructions and
keep quiet about what happened."

"Was it Buddy and Kovar who worked over Claudia Bettencourt?"

"You got it. That was Marlyk's idea. To make you think about
backing away from snooping around about Jake Dancer."

Nudger swallowed his anger. For now. He wanted to keep
Muffy talking. "I don't get the connection."

"You will. What happened is that old Heineker got worse and
didn't know when to stop with the girls we sent him. One night
one of them tried to run and he got carried away and deliberately
killed her, strangled her. Marlyk covered up for him again, and
then . . . well, it got to be expected the girls wouldn't come back.
Marlyk would recruit them if they looked vaguely like Helen
Heineker, sometimes even talk them into dyeing their hair. He'd
make sure they were the type whose disappearance wouldn't make
much of a stir, then, when Ronnie delivered the money, he'd send
them up to see Heineker as if it was a regular job." She shook her
head. "But it wasn't a regular job at all. After that first death,
Heineker went more and more kinky and violent, and got into
snuffing the girls as part of his sick routine."

"How many girls?" Nudger asked. His stomach was tossing
around and he felt sick. Muffy had been drawn into this an inch at
a time, perhaps like Brad Marlyk, too greedy to give up the fortune Heineker must have been paying Partners Unlimited. She
talked about it calmly, the horror escaping her. Business was busi-

ness; the slaughtering of cattle, sheep, and prostitutes was all the same in her jaded mind. He thought about the dead women from the river. Not cattle. Not sheep. People. The loathing he felt for Muffy B. Blue almost compelled him to stand up and wrestle her out the door, get the sight and perfumed scent of her away from him.

"You gotta understand there was a ton of money in this, Nudger, or it would never have happened."

"I can imagine how much money," Nudger said, remembering what Jeff Levine had told him on the phone about the sale of Heineker's Department Stores.

Muffy adjusted her collar where a ruffle was tickling the folds of her pale neck. "Heineker killed half a dozen of the girls over the past year or so. Ronnie would clean up the mess, take them to a place on the river, and dump the bodies. Old Heineker got so crazy and divorced from reality he wouldn't even remember the next morning what had happened; he had to look at the pictures and videotapes Ronnie took. Brad wanted those photos and tapes destroyed, but Heineker refused; they were his collection and he valued them, watched them regularly. That's why Buddy was at the estate as a guard, to make sure nothing happened to all that snuff porn. Sometimes he and Kovar would join the fun with Heineker. They were in some of the tapes and photos, too. That was okay with Marlyk; it kept them tied to the job. Made it less likely any of the incriminating porn would stray to the wrong hands."

Nudger didn't tell her that Ronnie had destroyed all of the tapes and photographs before the police got to the main house that morning. That fact hadn't been released to the media. And there was no way for Nudger to prove the origin of the two photos he'd stolen. The only hard evidence against Heineker and Ronnie was what Muffy was telling Nudger and would tell the law. Heineker and his chauffeur were already protected by a phalanx of high-powered lawyers with the connections and ability to cloud the issue, perhaps even to create enough smoke for Heineker and Ronnie to walk through to freedom.

"When Heineker saw a photograph of Helen Crane," Muffy said, "he went totally ape-shit. Even had Ronnie drive him into the city and then park someplace where he could look at her in person. He had to have her, he said. Christ, she was even named Helen, same as the original. Marlyk said no, she wasn't like the other girls, and she had a boyfriend who'd raise the alarm if she disappeared. Heineker doubled the price on her. Then doubled it again. You'd of thought he believed in reincarnation and figured the two Helens were one and the same. Makes you wonder what really happened to his wife. Anyway, that's when Marlyk agreed to give him Helen Crane, but first Dancer had to be gotten outta the picture."

Nudger felt the pieces drop coldly into place. So that was what it was about, not gambling debts. Not money Dancer owed. Dancer had simply been the man in the way.

"Dancer was half looped all the time anyway, so Marlyk had Kovar and Buddy lean on him for some money they said he owed. They beat him up, scared him, but not enough. They were a little surprised when they realized Dancer actually thought he owed the money. Poor fucker probably made bets all over town and forgot about them when he was sober. Anyway, that gave Marlyk an idea. He had Kovar and Buddy convince Dancer that when Dancer was drunk he'd murdered those women found in the river, the ones Heineker had killed. I don't know if Dancer believed it entirely, but he believed it enough it sent him off his rocker drinking and gave him the guilt shivers."

Guilt that he couldn't tell Helen about, Nudger thought. He imagined the agony that must have grabbed hold and thrived in the vulnerable Dancer. A debt he couldn't pay, then murder he might have committed. Some reward for the nonconquering hero. Make him a victim again.

"Heineker was so far gone on kinky sex and killing that Ronnie and Marlyk were scared he was going to go even further around the bend, get careless and blab, and incriminate everybody in murder. So they worked out this plan to get the big payday from

Heineker and cover themselves. Marlyk would send Helen
to Heineker. When he was done with her, Ronnie would put her in
the river but make sure she was found and could be identified.
Then they'd convince Dancer he'd killed Helen when he was
drunk, just like he'd murdered those others. They'd see he got
nailed for the killing, and Dancer would confess to the murders of
the other three women found in the river. The cops would buy into
it; they're always eager to clean up homicide cases. Everybody
would be off the hook, and Ronnie would talk sense to Heineker
and try to get him to seize the opportunity provided by Dancer's
arrest and find some other kinky form of amusement.''

"And if Heineker wouldn't—or couldn't—go along with that?''

"Then they'd have had no choice other than to kill him and
make his death look accidental. Or like suicide. Heineker has a
history of sometimes being depressed and suicidal. Ronnie was in
a good position to take care of whatever needed doing.''

Nudger leaned back in his squealing chair and marveled at the
neatness of it. The tragic symmetry. Perfect murder times seven.
The women's deaths would be officially solved, and Otiş Heineker
would be under control or dead. The only living loser would be
Dancer, the disturbed veteran who would either be on death row or
in a mental hospital.

"Know where Dancer is now?'' he asked.

Muffy shrugged. "Nobody does. Dancer took Claudia whatsher-
name on his own. Since yesterday afternoon, Marlyk's had Kovar
out looking for both of them.''

"What will he do if he finds them?'' Nudger asked. "Will
Claudia become another murder victim for Dancer to think he
killed?''

"That I honestly don't know, Nudger.''

Nudger didn't believe her. He wanted to grab her by her fat,
pasty neck, choke her, make her suffer the way the women in Otis
Heineker's snuff tapes had suffered. At least she really didn't
know if Kovar had found Claudia and Dancer. Nudger knew that if
they *had* been found, Muffy wouldn't have mentioned that the

search was still on. It was a matter she'd have denied any knowledge of, instead of establishing it as another danger she'd warned Nudger about.

One thing he had to give Muffy: She didn't pretend she enjoyed cooperating with the law. She didn't put on the sickening act Nudger had seen in other betrayers, as if they deserved a halo and a certificate of merit. She was blatantly looking out for herself and maneuvering for advantage.

"When are you going to tell this to the police?" Nudger asked.

"This morning. First I need to go by work and get some things from my desk. Stuff I don't want anybody to see; you know what I mean?"

"I've got some idea," Nudger said.

She stood up slowly and placed her fists on her fleshy hips. "Damned if I don't feel better after telling you this," she said. "Like when I was a good Catholic and went to confession and spilled my guts to the priest. You don't suppose I got a conscience, do you, Nudger?"

"No."

She smiled, nodded, and strutted out the door, suddenly buoyant. She had hope and, for her, a clean soul.

Nudger picked up the phone, called Hammersmith, and told him about the conversation with Muffy B. Blue. Hammersmith said they'd get somebody on her, to bring her in before anyone else could get to her.

But it was already too late.

They must have suspected when she didn't show up for work that morning. They must have followed her when she came to see Nudger.

After she walked out his office door, Muffy B. Blue disappeared.

"She never got to Partners Unlimited," Hammersmith said on the phone when he called back an hour after Nudger's call about Muffy. "Her car was found out on Dale Avenue, parked crooked against the curb with a door hanging open."

"What about Marlyk and Kovar?"

"We got Marlyk in custody, Nudge. He's playing dumb and knows we haven't got the juice to hold him. Kovar's probably the one got to this Muffy woman before we did. Rough on her."

Nudger almost said that Muffy deserved it, and maybe she did. Still, he found himself feeling sorry for her. He remembered the women in the photographs.

"I can give my version of my conversation with her," Nudger suggested.

"You know what that would be in court, Nudge."

Nudger did. Hearsay. Worthless.

Which left Brad Marlyk and Lars Kovar still officially clear of complicity and confident that Dancer eventually would be arrested for the murders. Which left Dancer still on the run with Claudia, actually thinking that while drunk he'd murdered three women.

Nudger was left with only a dark knowledge and an unfounded story about a bizarre conversation, which would be inadmissable in the trial of a monster who was also an influential citizen. A trial that would probably never take place.

Nudger's talk with Muffy B. Blue had instilled in him a frustrating sense of horrible injustice impending.

And increased fear for himself and for Claudia.

31

Nudger suspected Helen Crane would be home this morning, and she was. There'd be no business as usual today at Partners Unlimited. Brad Marlyk was in police custody, though he wouldn't be for long, and Muffy B. Blue was somewhere Nudger chose not to imagine. The Marlyk arrest and Muffy's disappearance were already in the news; if Helen listened to the radio or watched TV after getting out of bed this morning, she'd know things were in a whirl where she worked.

She hadn't been out of bed long. When she answered Nudger's knock she was wearing a light blue robe and was barefoot. Her blond hair was tousled, as if it had been disarranged for a wind-blown TV commercial. Her eyes were still swollen from sleep, the puffy lids lending them an angled, symmetrical directness that penetrated to something deep in Nudger. She hadn't been awake quite long enough for the worry of her life to have settled in and molded her features for the day. Nudger had never seen her looking better.

"You shoulda called," she said sleepily, "let me know you were coming." She raked her fingers through her hair and messed it up even more. There was no way she could make it unflattering.

"I was in the neighborhood . . ." Nudger lied.

She smiled, familiar with that one. "And you thought you'd drop by," she said. "C'mon in. I have some coffee on."

The apartment was cool. She'd apparently left the air conditioner in the front window running all night. Nudger could hear and smell the coffee perking in the kitchen. The living room was neat, as if it had been recently straightened, but there was a cobweb draped in the ceiling corner over the air conditioner, swaying gently in the cool breeze. Lately, Helen had carried too much on her mind to think about dusting.

He sat on the low sofa and watched her stride gracefully on bare feet into the kitchen. She was a study in synchronized motion, difficult to look away from.

A moment later her voice called, "Cream or sugar?"

"Neither," Nudger said.

She returned to the living room carrying a steaming mug of coffee in each hand. One of the mugs was plain brown ceramic. The other was white plastic, and on the side was written "I ♥ my coffee," with a red heart where the word "love" would have been.

Helen handed Nudger the brown mug, then sat down on the

opposite end of the sofa. She curled her toes under, as if embarrassed by them. Nudger didn't see why; she had great toes.

She said, "News?"

"Everything fit to print and some that's not," Nudger said, and he told her what there was to know. Told her about Melissa and the other dead women and the photographs, and Muffy B. Blue's story and subsequent disappearance under ominous circumstances.

Helen wasn't as interested in her uncanny resemblance to Helen Heineker, and her near miss with death, as she was in Dancer's continued flight from imagined horrors.

"We've got to find Jake, Nudger!" Her voice had picked up a beat and her gray eyes were brighter and more alert. Nudger's words, and the coffee she'd been sipping, had brought her awake all the way and heaped more concern on her. Love and caffeine were a potent combination. Nudger thought "Dancer" should be substituted for "coffee" on her plastic mug, after the sappy red heart.

"It'd be stupid for Kovar to harm him or Claudia now," Nudger said. "If Kovar's got an IQ that isn't in the minus range, he'll do nothing but make himself unfindable."

"But we can't be sure of that."

True enough. It was risky trying to predict how a twisted mind like Lars Kovar's would react. This was a goon who tortured people for kicks and was party to murder.

"I'll keep looking for Dancer," Nudger assured Helen. "I'll make the rounds again of places he frequents, talk to bartenders and bookies."

Helen set her coffee on the sofa arm and stood up. "I'll go with you." She flicked him a brief, sad smile. "Nowhere else to go. It looks like I'm unemployed."

Nudger thought about it and saw no reason why she shouldn't accompany him. "I'll wait while you get dressed," he said. "Can I use your phone?"

"Won't even charge you a dime," Helen said. She motioned with her head toward the white, push-button phone on the table near the door, then stood up and moved toward the bathroom. The hem of her blue robe swished artfully around her ankles, as if flaunting the fact that it was draped on her.

Nudger heard a shower hissing as he used his forefinger to peck out the number of Danny's Donuts. Lucky robe. Lucky shower.

"Anyone been by?" he asked, when Danny answered the phone.

"Jesus, Nudge! I been trying to reach you. Claudia called."

Nudger held the receiver away from his ear for a second, as if he'd misunderstood Danny and there was something wrong with the connection. "Claudia? Where from, Danny? She all right?"

Danny's voice took on a soothing quality. "She said to tell you she's fine, Nudge, though she's in a hospital or clinic out in Hawk Run." Nudger knew Hawk Run, a tiny country town about five miles from the cabin.

The cabin! The last place he expected Dancer would return to, and one of the few places Nudger or the police hadn't looked for Claudia.

"Dancer had her at some cabin. She slipped away from him and was wandering around lost in the woods for a while, Nudge. Highway patrol picked her up on the road and took her to this Hawk Run clinic, where the doctor sedated her and she was unconscious for a long time. They didn't know who she was, who to call. When she came around, about an hour ago, she told them and they called me trying to get in touch with you. I talked to Claudia, Nudge; believe me, she's okay. She left the number of the clinic so you could call her."

Nudger wedged the receiver between ear and shoulder to free his hands, then jotted the number on his wrist with a ballpoint pen that had been lying near the phone. He thanked Danny, pressed down the cradle button, and punched in the number of the clinic.

He stood motionless. Between rings of the phone in Hawk Run, he could still hear the shower running in the back of the apartment.

A Dr. Mathison assured Nudger that Claudia was fine and uninjured except for scratches and myriad insect bites that were under control. She'd been exhausted when the highway patrol brought her in after finding her slumped by the side of the road. She'd mumbled a few incoherent sentences but was unable to identify herself, so, after she was examined and her minor injuries were tended to, the doctor had prescribed rest. When she'd awakened an hour ago, she'd immediately demanded to use the phone.

Mathison gave Nudger back to the switchboard, and, after a series of clicks and a few seconds of Muzak, he was patched through to Claudia.

"I'm sorry I brought this down on you," he told her. "You know that, don't you?"

"I know it," she said. "It's over now." She sounded strong enough. "I'm okay."

"Lem Akers told me Dancer took you from your apartment," Nudger said. "What happened after that?"

"Dancer was drunk, and we left because there was no more liquor in the apartment. I knew I had to go with him, and he demanded that I drive. After winding around for a while going nowhere, he made me take us to an isolated cabin. I tried to remember how we got there, what the cabin looked like from the outside. It's a gray A-frame—"

"I know the place," Nudger interrupted gently.

"There was a bottle there. Dancer began drinking again. He didn't harm me; he even seemed at times to forget I was there. But he'd done something to my car under the hood so I couldn't drive away. He scared me when he started moaning about some murders he'd committed. Then he started crying. Sobbing."

"He hasn't killed anybody," Nudger said.

"That doesn't surprise me. I wasn't as afraid as I should have been. There was something about him; he was so full of remorse. So innately gentle. I really don't think he would have hurt me, but I wasn't sure enough to try to leave over his objections. Then he got on the subject of his deserving to die, of suicide. That's all he talked about the rest of the night and all the time we were in the cabin. I made myself stay awake, and when he finally fell asleep, I sneaked out into the woods. I don't know how long I wandered around until I reached a road and waited and the highway patrol found me.''

Helen was in the doorway, dressed now in white slacks and a peach-colored blouse, still barefoot, watching Nudger. She looked clean and fresh and damp. Her blond hair was dark with moisture, curled up tight at the ends, and glistening.

Nudger said, "You sure you're all right, Claudia?"

"I'm getting tired of people asking me that."

"I'm coming to get you," Nudger said, "but I've got one stop to make first."

"The cabin?" Bright woman, all the way back from sedation.

"He might still be there," Nudger said.

"I'm afraid he might be."

Nudger knew what she meant. Looking at Helen, he said, "I love you, Claudia."

The sound of sniffling came over the line, then the clattering of the phone in the Hawk Run Clinic. Muzak. Dial tone. She'd hung up.

Helen was regarding him with her calm gray eyes. "Did she say she loved you back?"

"Actually," Nudger said, "she cried."

Helen shrugged. "Better than if she'd laughed."

"Dancer might be at the cabin," Nudger said. "That's where he went with Claudia."

"Then that's where we're going," Helen said, and whirled and ran for the bedroom and her shoes. Glittering drops of water flew from her hair to pattern the white wall.

Nudger had the feeling events, as well as Helen, were outracing him as he followed her out to her car.

32

An hour later Helen parked her tiny blue Datsun next to Claudia's equally small white Chevette. The Chevette's hood was down, but it was unlatched and inclined an inch from closing. Dancer must have left it that way after sabotaging the car so it wouldn't start.

When the Datsun's clattering toy engine stopped, silence rolled in. The cabin's front door was closed, and the windows were down despite the heat. Nothing moved. Dancer didn't clomp out onto the plank porch to greet them.

Nudger stood up out of the Datsun and stretched his back and legs. He heard cartilage pop. Helen had walked around the car and was making for the cabin. Dry brush crackled beneath her feet, and her shoulders were squared and stiff with tension and resolve.

"Wait!" Nudger said. "Let me go in first."

She paused just long enough for him to step up onto the porch ahead of her, then she was pressing behind him as he held his breath and opened the door. Her fingertips touched lightly against the small of his back, tentatively urging him forward.

The air in the cabin was stale and unbearably hot. There was no sound other than the lazy, wavering drone of a wasp or horsefly.

One hurried glance told Nudger the cabin was empty.

He saw that the bottle of Born Again was missing from the mantel.

Backing onto the porch and closing the door, he bumped into the softness of Helen.

"Isn't in there," he told her.

"I saw." She glanced at the surrounding woods. "He didn't drive out of here. Maybe he's around someplace."

"Maybe," Nudger said, shivering in the hot sun like a burn victim. His stomach ached and growled, trying to tell him something. That's where Nudger's hunches began, in the pit of his stomach. Something was as wrong as could be here; he knew it. He glanced at Helen, who was hugging herself as if she'd felt the same dread breeze.

Nudger led the way. They hiked down the winding, narrow dirt path to the river, because that way offered least resistance. Possibly they'd find Dancer on the bank fishing for carp. Sober and hopeful and recovered from his fit of remorse. Possibly.

What they found were Dancer's black leather loafers, placed parallel to each other on the decrepit, weathered dock.

Tucked inside the left one was something white, a note to Helen confessing to the murders.

A suicide note.

33

Hammersmith phoned Nudger the next day to tell him Lars Kovar had been picked up in Illinois. A tracer had been placed on the phone of one of Kovar's friends, a junkie and an informer for the Vice Squad. When Kovar called him from a public booth in Fairview Heights, police pinpointed the source of the call and had the Illinois law surrounding Kovar before he'd hung up the phone.

"Guy was too big to hide," Hammersmith said. "And Kovar being an ex-cop, you might say we looked for him with particular enthusiasm."

"What about Heineker and Brad Marlyk? And our friend Ronnie?"

"None of them's stupid. They knew they were nailed, or we wouldn't have been able to get bond withdrawn and collar them again. Soon as they all found out Claudia was with Dancer at the time Melissa was killed, eliminating him as the murderer, they started falling over one another trying to cut a deal in exchange for spilling what they knew."

"How good a deal can they make?" Nudger asked. He could feel justice slipping away.

"Kovar knows how the game's played and he's already done his plea bargaining. He's given us all we need, Nudge, and the others are just flapping their gums and moving air around. My guess is Kovar will get life but might hit the streets again in about ten years. But the others'll see life terms without parole, or maybe the gas chamber."

"Not the gas chamber," Nudger said, "not with Heineker's money." He heard the gasping, slurping noises of Hammersmith laboring to get a cigar burning.

"Could be you're right, Nudge." Slurp! Wheeze! Like a locomotive chugging resolutely toward lung cancer.

"They find Dancer's body?" Nudger asked.

"Naw. They're still dragging the river around the cabin, searching downstream. You know how it is. The river sometimes don't give up its dead for months, and sometimes not at all. They might never find Dancer. All we know, he might float all the way to the Gulf. Make a meal for a shark."

Hammersmith's phone lit up then, he said, and he had to hang up to wage war on crime. Click! Buzz . . . before Nudger could reply.

Nudger sat for a moment in front of the phone and thought about Dancer's pale corpse suspended just beneath the surface of the sea as a shark closed in. The shark rolled onto its back, the way Nudger had read somewhere they had to in order to open their mouths wide and get at their prey. They were huge, some of those sharks. When fishermen cut them open, they sometimes found the damndest things in their stomachs.

He tried to think about something else. Anything else.

A week later somebody did find what was left of Dancer, not near the Gulf but ten miles downstream from the cabin. The river had done to him what it had done to the women he'd thought he killed. A sort of practical joke worked by fate.

Helen Crane identified the body. Afterward, she drove home and curled up in her bed and refused to speak or eat. She stayed that way until a friend found her days later.

At the time of the murder trial, six months after the arrests, she was interned in the state asylum on Arsenal Street, where Marlyk and Kovar had assumed Dancer might live out his days if he pleaded insanity. Fate at it again. Fate loved irony.

Helen's testimony wasn't necessary. Marlyk and Kovar got life sentences as accessories to the murder of Melissa Underwood. Ronnie the chauffeur was sentenced to die in the gas chamber. Otis Heineker pleaded mental incompetence and was confined indefinitely to an expensive sanitarium in the east.

The law grinding fine.

A few months after the trial, Nudger heard Helen had been released from state care, and with the sizable insurance settlement she'd received from Dancer's death, she'd moved to California to be with her family. She had a chance to achieve contentment. Nudger hoped it would work for her.

It was on one of the coldest days of the year that he found the brown package in his office mail.

He carried it upstairs and set it on his desk, tossing aside the various bills, threats, and ads that had been resting on top of it inside the street door. It was about the size of a shoebox, maybe a little longer, and wrapped in thick brown paper, padded, and taped. There was no return address on it.

The warmest place in town had to be Nudger's office. He'd

complained about the lack of heat, and the landlord had sent out someone to work on the pipes. Now the old steam radiator beneath the window wouldn't stop clanking and emitting enough heat to bake biscuits. Nudger had his sleeves rolled up, but his armpits were sweating profusely and staining his shirt as he used scissors to cut the tape and peel open the brown package.

He sat gnawing his lower lip, puzzled.

Inside the padded package was a bourbon bottle. Empty.

Well, not empty, exactly. There was a neatly folded, crisp thousand-dollar bill inside.

Nudger stared at the opened package and his heartbeat quickened and he began to sweat even more. He could hear his breath hissing in the quiet office.

The postmark read California.

The whiskey was Dancer's brand.

Born Again.